Verena drew

Denzell might hav█
have seen Verena█
outside the Ruishtons' front door. Dear
heaven, but what charm there was in his smile!
Had she not trained herself all these long
years to suppress even the slightest outward
display of emotion, she feared she must have
given him the satisfaction of knowing how
much he had moved her. Her control had
never been so severely tested. Eligible, indeed.
Heaven send Mama did not get wind of his
interest!

Elizabeth Bailey grew up in Malawi, returning to England to plunge into the theatre. After many happy years 'tatting around the reps', she finally turned from 'dabbling' to serious writing. She finds it more satisfying for she is in control of everything—scripts, design, direction, and the portrayal of every character! Elizabeth lives in Kent and, in time spared from writing, teaches GCSE and A-level drama at a local school.

A FRAGILE MASK

Elizabeth Bailey

MILLS & BOON

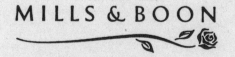

All the characters in this book have no existence outside the imagination of the author, and have no relation whatsoever to anyone bearing the same name or names. They are not even distantly inspired by any individual known or unknown to the author, and all the incidents are pure invention.

Harlequin Mills & Boon Limited,
Eton House, 18–24 Paradise Road, Richmond, Surrey TW9 1SR

© Elizabeth Bailey 1996

ISBN 0 263 79598 5

Set in 10 on 11½ pt Linotron Times
04-9606-85441

Typeset in Great Britain by CentraCet, Cambridge
Printed in Great Britain by
BPC Paperbacks Ltd

CHAPTER ONE

FINE flakes, still drifting through the air, sparkled in the early morning sun. The heavy fall in the night had shrouded the countryside in a winter blanket of white, but it would not last; for the air was warm, as the young gentleman visitor discovered immediately, upon flinging up the window of the bedchamber allotted to him by his hosts.

Mr Denzell Hawkeridge pulled the nightcap off his head, spilling a profusion of fairish locks over the neck of his nightshirt. He looked out upon a large patch of ground beyond the garden, in which a group of urchin children were engaged, he saw, blinking sleepily upon them, in building a snowman.

A very proper occupation, he conceded, under the circumstances, if a trifle energetic. For Denzell, lured by his friend Osmond Ruishton into spending some days at Tunbridge Wells before Christmas was well upon them, with the promise of 'absolutely nothing' to do, had every intention of doing precisely that.

Filling his lungs with a fresh country breath, he yawned contentedly. This was the life! Not that he had not enjoyed the Season. He had. So much so, in fact, that he was quite tired out from the hectic pace one was obliged to maintain in Town. Not to mention the exigencies to which he had been put, cudgelling his ingenuity to steer that fine line between flirtation—for with so many pretty girls about any man must be tempted to it—and the avoidance of matrimonial traps.

He had no desire to settle with just *one* female, not

yet awhile. All he wanted now was to lounge about, enjoy a little idle conversation with his hosts, and avoid women. Especially young women who might wish to marry him.

It was a fine thing to be heir to a worthy barony, but it could be a curst nuisance to be an eligible male. A nuisance, and extremely exhausting. Yes, this had been an excellent notion of Osmond's. The Wells was so dead at this season that the chance of any debutante coming within a hundred miles of the place was too remote to be worthy of consideration. He could be off guard and laze at his ease.

He was glad, for instance, to think that it was not he, but some benighted female who was obliged to cavort about in the snow in company with these busy youngsters. For there was a female with them, her back to him just now as she leaned to help infant fingers pack snow against the rapidly expanding waistline of the snowman. A nursemaid, perhaps. A shout floated up to him.

'Hoy, Charley! Gimme a. . .'

He could not hear the rest, but the voice told its own tale. And now he came to look at them, the children did not appear to be the offspring of the gentry, their frieze garments rather rougher than those in which Osmond's elder boy, only recently breeched, was likely to appear.

'Is we done 'ere, missie?'

The female straightened up, and shifted to the other side of the snowman, and Denzell, a budding connoisseur in the matter of female dress, at once recognised that the brown pelisse she wore was of too fine a cut and material for any servant, edged as it was with a fur trim.

There was a sudden disturbance to one side, a running boy bumping into another.

'Hoy, watch out!'

'Ow!' came clearly as the second boy slipped and went down.

'You donkey!' shouted another.

General laughter and a flurry of calling ensued, and Denzell caught a glimpse of the lady's face as she dashed to the rescue. Evidently her assistance was not needed, for the boy picked himself up unhurt amid the ribald catcalls and chanting of his companions.

'Lawks, Joey!'

'You look like the snowman.'

'Joey's covered in snow-oh.'

The shouts faded in Denzell's ears, for the lady lifted her head as she stood poised, still ready to help, and his gaze became riveted upon her face.

It was, even at this distance, one of the most beautiful countenances he had ever seen: a perfect oval, with eyes set wide apart, a nose classically straight, and a mouth shaped in so pleasing a bow that any artist seeing it must at once beg its owner to sit for him. A cluster of loose curls escaping from under a close-fitting bonnet, small-brimmed and ornamented with knots of ribbon, whispered a promise of golden treasures within.

Fascinated, Denzell stared. Chaste stars! Not one among the debutantes paraded for inspection in the Season just ended could have held a candle to this girl. She was young, too. Some few years his junior; eighteen or nineteen, he judged. But why in the world was a beautiful girl of marriageable age immured in this rural backwater, unless she was already wed? Was he mistaken in the status of the children? Might one of them even be her own?

Yet he had no eyes to search for this possibility

among the urchins. His attention was all for the lady as he watched the warmth of a smile enter her face while the children, finding Joey's trip into the snow an enticing lark, began to fake falls so that they might also receive a cargo of snow upon their small persons.

This sport led naturally into a snowball fight, which the lady made no attempt to discourage—definitely not a nursemaid!—but watched with laughing enjoyment, brushing an errant snowflake away from that heavenly face with the back of one glove-encased hand.

Denzell's breath caught. What animation! Such a glowing vivacity! She was utterly delightful.

All at once two small figures erupted from under Denzell's window, and he recognised young Felix Ruishton, his godson, all of four years old, running to join the fray; and tottering after in his infant dress, with their nurse Dinah in hot pursuit, little Miles, his brother.

Felix dashed across the garden and hurtled through the back gate, and Denzell saw the girl bend down to greet him with both hands held out, and a warm welcome on her lips, delivered, although he could not hear the words, in a pleasantly musical voice.

So she knew Felix and Miles? Capital! Denzell shut the window and crossed to the bellpull to summon his valet. His determination to abjure the society of young women was forgotten. There was no time to lose. He must dress at once. Undoubtedly Osmond and Unice could identify this dazzling beauty, and he must know who she was instantly.

Nevertheless, it was quite half an hour later before he made his belated appearance, suitably attired for the country in a frock-coat of dark blue tabinet for warmth, over a grey cassimere waistcoat and breeches of black corduroy.

He entered upon a scene of contented domesticity in

the Ruishtons' cosy breakfast parlour, a neat apartment with faded yellow paper to the walls and spreading warmth from glowing embers in the grate of a simple marble-framed fireplace.

'Who,' he demanded without preamble as his hosts looked up to welcome him, 'is the fairy princess even now blessing your back garden with her entrancing presence? And does she already have a prince on her leading string? If not, be warned that I intend to apply at once for the position.'

Osmond Ruishton, as casually clad as his guest but affecting stronger hues of plum and a salmon waistcoat, was seated to the window-side of the round mahogany table fashioned in the Hepplewhite style. He lowered the *Gazette* upon which, as befitted a family man at breakfast, his attention had been engaged, and gazed at his friend over the top of it. 'What the devil are you talking of, Hawk?'

'The girl, dear boy, the girl. And don't pretend you don't know her, because Felix and Miles have just been clasped to her bosom.'

Looking at his wife, Osmond shook his head. 'Mad. Stark mad!'

Unice Ruishton, in a plain round gown of cambric, long-sleeved and made high to the throat, had been busily engaged in plying her spouse with ham and eggs from a central dish, and keeping his coffee cup filled from the steaming pot by her elbow from which emanated a tempting aroma, but she paused in this work, a frown creasing her brow.

'What in the world is the matter with you, Denzell?'

'Unice,' he responded in the tone of one afflicted by anxiety, as he dragged a chair out and took his seat between them both, 'have pity on me. My head is reeling, my heart is bursting and I must know her name or I shall go mad!'

'Go mad?' interpolated Osmond. 'You are mad!'

'Whose name?' asked Unice, bewildered, her pansy eyes blinking at him out of a pleasant countenance surrounded by dusky locks worn fashionably long just now under a lacy wisp of a cap. 'Who is it you mean?'

'The ravishing female who has been building a snowman with a gang of urchins outside my window.'

The puzzlement vanished from Unice's face. 'Oh, I see.'

It was no mean part of Unice's attraction that she was apt to treat all her husband's bachelor friends as if they were an extension of her responsibilities to Osmond, and in need of such female care and guidance as she might be able to offer—a trait that rather amused the lighthearted Mr Ruishton than afforded him grounds for jealousy. Their mutual devotion was, besides, plain for all to see, particularly at a time when Unice's natural plumpness was exaggerated in the course of her third pregnancy—to which the coming fashion of high waists was admirably suited.

She gave Denzell her full attention. 'What does she look like?'

'Look like!' echoed Denzell. 'Deuce take it, Unice, there cannot be *two* such beauties in this town! Who is she?'

'Oh, Lord!' uttered Osmond disgustedly, at last grasping the purport of his friend's conversation. 'Don't tell me you're at it again.' He threw down the *Gazette* and addressed his wife. 'He hasn't been here five minutes and already he's setting up a flirt.'

'Flirt? Nothing of the sort,' objected Denzell instantly. 'I'm going to whisk her off to Gretna Green.'

'Ha! I wish I may see it!' snorted his friend.

Denzell merely grinned. He was perfectly aware that it could come as no surprise to his closest intimate since the days of their early youth that he should be eulogising over some female. But that would not prevent Osmond from indulging in a good deal of carping and criticism, a form of good-natured banter that was customary between them.

'I thought you told me you were finished with females,' Osmond accused.

'Finished? No, by George!' Osmond cast up his eyes, and Denzell grinned again, amending, 'Well, only temporarily.'

'Extremely temporarily.'

'But this is no ordinary female, dear boy. This is a clap of thunder.' Denzell turned back to his hostess, and noted that she was pursing dubious lips. 'Aha! So you do know her. What is it, Unice?' he asked coaxingly. 'Is she married, or do you fear my honourable intentions?'

'Your *what* intentions?'

'Osmond,' interrupted Unice, casting a glance at her husband that seemed to Denzell somewhat flurried, 'I fancy he is thinking of Verena.'

Denzell lost interest for the moment in the possible significance of her manner. 'Verena,' he murmured reverently. 'Verena, Verena, Verena.' He sighed deeply. 'My God, I'm in love!'

'Oh, Lord, here we go,' groaned Osmond. He watched his guest lift the cover off the silver dish and serve himself with a generous helping of ham and eggs, and observed drily, 'No loss of appetite accompanies this sudden flush of ardour, I see.'

Denzell twinkled, taking up his knife and fork as Unice bustled to supply him with bread and butter, and to fill his cup from the steaming coffee pot. 'I shall force it down, dear boy, for the sake of politeness, you know.'

A rude noise was Osmond's only answer. Then a thought struck him and he brightened, his gaze seeking out his wife again. 'Verena! Lord, Unice, you don't mean the Chaceley chit?'

Mrs Ruishton laid down the coffee pot. 'Of course I do, my love. She is forever playing with the traders' children. I dare swear it is Mr Burrow's and Mr Stapley's boys, and the children from the Friends Brewhouse.'

She sighed. Situated as their house was, just off the main London Road about halfway up the town, away from its main hub by the chalybeate spring, it was inevitable that her son should make friends of this somewhat undesirable sort.

'I do not altogether care that Felix should enjoy such company, though I dare say no real harm will come of it.'

'Never mind that,' said her husband carelessly. 'The boy must play with someone, after all. But only think, Unice,' he added on a gleeful note, 'Hawk must needs set his sights on the one female who will prove impervious.'

'What do you mean, impervious?' demanded Denzell, starting out of an agreeable reverie where he fitted the name to the vision of that enchanting face.

'It is quite immaterial,' cut in Unice before her spouse could respond. 'Osmond, you are not to let him trouble the poor girl. You must forbid him to do so.'

'Forbid Hawk! Are you out of your senses, Unice? You don't suppose I have any influence over the fellow, do you?'

'None whatsoever,' Denzell averred, and turned, his

fork poised in the air, to address Mrs Ruishton. 'But why do you speak of her as a poor girl?'

'In any event,' went on Osmond, without giving his wife an opportunity to answer, 'I'm dashed if I take responsibility for Hawk's actions. Bad enough having the fellow battening on us, never mind holding him when he's got the bit between his teeth like this.'

'You would invite me,' Denzell pointed out, digging into a thick portion of ham. 'On your own head be it. But do be quiet, dear boy. I am trying to have an intelligent conversation with your wife.'

'Trying to turn her up sweet is what you mean.'

'Unice, I know you care for this fellow, God knows why, but do, for pity's sake, ignore him and attend to me. Who—is—she? Is she married? Why "poor"?'

'Why ask?' countered Osmond irrepressibly. 'You'll catch cold at it, if you choose to try your tricks on that one, I can tell you now.'

'It is only jealousy that makes you say so. How you ever succeeded in attaching this charmer has always been beyond me.'

Osmond took this in good part. He was not as well endowed by nature as Denzell, who had a little the advantage in both height and looks, but good features and an amused eye rendered him not unattractive, despite the girlish brown mop of shorn hair that his friends were inclined to deprecate. What he lacked, which Denzell had in abundance, was that elusive quality, charm.

It was not precisely the smoky glow of Denzell's blue eyes, nor yet the shapely lips ever hovering on the beginnings of a smile. It had nothing to do with the manner of his dress, modish but inconspicuous, nor with his obstinate adherence to the custom of tying his own long hair loosely in a ribbon at the back, a fashion going as rapidly out of style as was the natural female waistline, which had recently risen to sit just below the bosom.

Not one of Denzell's numerous female admirers could have said just what it was that caused the heart to race faster in her breast, or her knees to weaken whenever he chanced to smile at her in a particular way. But every one of them would have agreed that, whatever it might be, it was irresistible. That he was also an accomplished flirt apparently only added—in the sapient opinion of his observant friend—to his attractions.

'Tell me, Unice,' he was continuing, turning to his hostess again, 'were you inebriated when this fellow offered for you?'

A crack of laughter from Osmond acknowledged a hit. But although Unice smiled, she dealt her visitor a smart slap on the arm. 'For shame, Denzell. You know perfectly well that it was love at first sight with us both.'

'Exactly. And now that I, in my turn, have fallen victim to the tender passion—'

'Ha!'

'—it would be cruel in you,' continued Denzell, ignoring his host, 'to withhold any little item concerning the lady who has dashed the heart from my chest in an instant. Tell me all!'

Unice grimaced. 'But, indeed, Denzell, I believe Osmond is in the right of it on this occasion.'

'What do you mean, on this occasion? I'm always in the right of it.'

'Do be quiet for a moment, dearest.'

'Yes, for pity's sake, "dearest", hold your tongue!'

Osmond rolled some crumbled bread and flicked it at his friend. Denzell, naturally enough, returned the compliment, and battle was fairly joined until both combatants were firmly called to order by the lady of the house.

'I declare, you are worse than Felix and Miles, the pair of you!' she complained.

'Well, Hawk shouldn't be so dashed insulting,' uttered her husband impenitently.

'I like that. You began it.'

'Enough, both of you!'

'Send him away, Unice,' begged Denzell, 'and then you and I may enjoy a comfortable cose about the beautiful Verena.'

But Osmond refused to go anywhere, repeating his conviction that Hawk would come to grief if he meant to attempt to storm the citadel that was Miss Verena Chaceley.

'Verena Chaceley,' repeated Denzell in a provocatively passionate tone. 'Even her name is music. And you give me hope, Ossie. She is still a "miss". Speak, Unice. I wish to know all about her.'

'Well, you won't,' said Osmond on a note of satisfaction. 'For no one does. It's a dashed mystery, if you wish to know.'

'I do wish to know,' Denzell retorted. '*What* mystery? Come, Unice!'

Mrs Ruishton capitulated, lifting the coffee pot and refilling his cup. 'It is not a mystery precisely, although she is very close and will not chatter about herself. She lives in lodgings not two doors from here—'

'Then you are neighbours. Better and better.' He frowned then. 'Lodgings? What, alone?'

'No, no, she resides with her mother. I believe that is why they came here. Mrs Pateley is in the poorest of health.'

Denzell lowered the coffee cup from his lips. 'Pateley? I thought you said Chaceley.'

'Yes, Verena is Chaceley, but her mother is Mrs Pateley.'

'All part of the mystery,' put in Osmond darkly. 'The mother must have remarried, but no one has been able to discover the details.'

'Not even Mrs Felpham,' agreed Unice. 'She is the most inveterate gossip, you must know, and always has the news before anyone else. These two came here in September, just after the close of the Season. No one saw them arrive. They just appeared among us one day. Even Mr Tyson—our Master of Ceremonies, you know—was taken aback. He usually presents newcomers to the town, and this time he could not.'

'You've never seen anyone so put out,' added Osmond on a laugh. 'Or he would have been, only that he succumbed in minutes.'

'As did every other male in the community, including Osmond, whatever he may say. She is so serenely beautiful that it is hardly surprising.'

'I admire her looks, yes,' conceded her husband. 'Any man would. Too cold and placid, though. I prefer a cosier armful, by Jupiter!'

His eyes rested with a great degree of warmth on his wife's face as he spoke. But Denzell did not notice. The image of Verena Chaceley's animated countenance was playing in his vision. He frowned, nursing his cup between his hands.

'Cold and placid? Surely not. I give you my word, I have rarely seen a glow of such warmth, such freshness and sparkling enjoyment.'

Both the Ruishtons stared at him blankly. Then they looked at each other.

'He cannot mean Verena,' Unice said with conviction. 'It must be some other female he saw.'

'It can't have been, dash it! Who else could have bowled him out?'

Unice shook her head, her gaze returning to Denzell's face. 'Verena is very beautiful, very calm, and exquisitely polite. But I have never seen her display any sort of animation such as you describe.'

An odd look crossed her features, of disquiet, Denzell thought. He remembered then that earlier moment, when she had seemed flurried. This was indeed mysterious. Putting down his cup, he leaned towards her, asking persuasively, 'What is it, Unice? What are you thinking?'

'I have sometimes wondered. . .' she began, and stopped, shaking her head. 'Osmond thinks me fanciful, but she is so very serene that I have sometimes thought there is a strangeness about it—as if it is not quite right.'

Denzell's interest intensified. 'What is not right?'

'I don't quite know. It is only something that I feel, without knowing precisely what it is or why I should feel it. It is as if I sense something underneath. A feeling, or a touch of—yes, melancholy.'

'So that is why you used the term "poor girl"?'

But Osmond was laughing. 'Pay no heed to her, Hawk. My darling, you always imagine melancholia in others when you are in your present condition.'

'I know, my love, but in this case—'

Denzell withdrew his attention from the burgeoning squabble and addressed himself to his breakfast. To say that he was intrigued would be putting it mildly—this female became more and more alluring.

To be sure, he had indulged in a good deal of raillery in discussing the matter with his hosts, for, of course, he was not really in love. He had enough experience to know that these little *tendres* were transient in nature.

He had not yet met the woman with whom he might fall truly in love, but he knew that when he did so there would be far more to her than a beautiful face—animated or otherwise.

But a little harmless flirtation with an exquisite creature of the name of Verena Chaceley would certainly enliven his visit. Besides, Osmond seemed to think he must inevitably fail, and that in itself was a challenge. He must find a way to meet her as speedily as possible.

Miss Verena Chaceley, not aware either of having been observed or of being a subject for discussion, was hurrying home to Mama. She was feeling more than a little guilty, for she had been gone over an hour, forgetful of the time in her preoccupation with the children's games. She hated to leave Mama, even for this short time—although Betsey might be trusted to see to her rising. Only the fresh brisk air had beckoned, and the children's joyful cries had drawn Verena like a magnet.

How different from her own childhood! Laughter had been rare. Oh, she and Adam had played, yes. Had forgotten even, sometimes. But the shadow had pervaded their lives and could not often be set aside.

She had hoped to eradicate it here, thinking that with distance the scars would heal, the fear die. She was wrong. Mama seemed to be worsening, and Verena herself, instead of being reassured by the passing of time, felt every day more hunted, more at risk. She shivered, her gloved fingers clasping tighter within the brown bear muff that hung from a cord about her neck.

Then she set her teeth, annoyed with the little loss of control. Well might she shiver, she told herself defiantly. It was cold, was it not? Thrusting the thought away, she sped lightly in her snug kid half-boots across the snowy square of ground that separated the Ruishtons' house from her lodging.

It had been Verena's deliberate choice to move up here once she got the lie of Tunbridge Wells. The Ruishton property lay between two other plots on the one side, while closest to the lane—a curved departure from the main London Road that led down past the Common towards the centre of the town that clustered about the chalybeate spring and the Pantiles—were a number of houses with smaller areas of land about them.

The lodging house, of which Verena and her mother had hired the better part, lay more or less opposite the Ruishtons', largely hidden from general sight within some fencing against other houses round about, yet open to the fields. It had the merit of isolation, Verena felt. For although it had not been possible to remain aloof in a town like Tunbridge Wells—and for Mama's sake Verena had overcome her own disinclination for company—people were discouraged from forming a habit of visiting.

Several gentlemen had done so at first, but Verena had, she flattered herself, so well succeeded in damping any hopes of her interest that they now contented themselves with clustering about her only when she went down into the town.

It was Betsey, whose fierce loyalty had frustrated the landlady's attempts to pry into the mysterious circumstances surrounding her peculiar visitors, who let Verena into the lodging-house. Mrs Quedgeley's own apartments comprised the ground floor of the house, and she provided such services as the ladies required only under the forbidding eye of the faithful Betsey. Although she was able to report abroad that the ladies' linen was of the appropriate quality for the gentility, she could not satisfy Wellsian curiosity as to why these ladies had come to the spa town.

'They won't believe as you're here only for the mistress's health, they won't,' as Betsey had informed the daughter herself, 'but you needn't fear me, Miss Verena. That there Quedgeley won't learn nothing from my lips.'

Verena had every trust in Betsey on that count. She was much of an age with Mama and had maided Verena since her childhood. She had come with them on her own insistence—'as if I'd leave you both to fend for yourselves, Miss Verena! If not me, who's to look to your needs, I'd like to know?'—cheerfully taking on the burden of Jill-of-all-trades to them both. She was bustling and sharp, a buxom dame with a hectoring manner, and more than a match—as she pridefully boasted—for any number of Quedgeleys.

Verena accepted her loyalty without question, but could be little comforted to hear of the gossip. The hard necessity of defending her very small island from prying eyes only added to the strains and stresses that beset her: the well-nigh impossible task of keeping Mama's spirits up, and the haunting dread that Nathaniel might find them out.

'I was on the watch for you, Miss Verena,' Betsey whispered as she let her in, softly closing the door.

'Oh, dear. Is she up already, then?'

'If you can call it that,' uttered the maid in a severe undertone as she hustled the easier of her two charges towards the staircase. 'I tried to make her stay abed, indeed I did, Miss Verena. But she would insist on dressing. Now she's in a fair collapse on the day-bed, like I knew she would be.'

'She had a bad night, then,' Verena guessed, hurrying up the stairs.

'Tossing and turning,' confirmed Betsey, who always slept on a truckle-bed in her mistress's room. 'Twice she woke up crying. And I'm that sorry, Miss Verena, to have to add to your troubles, but she must have been at the laudanum again, unbeknownst. For when I woke and found her flat out, snoring, I looked at the bottle, and the level is down.'

'Oh, no, Betsey,' Verena groaned, stopping on the landing to turn and gaze at the maid in distress.

The maid nodded, setting the frill of her large mob-cap dancing. 'Oh, yes, Miss Verena.' She set her arms akimbo of the unrelenting black bombazine gown, its strict severity relieved only with a white apron. 'If you ask me, we should up and throw that bottle in the dustcart.'

Verena sighed, untying the ribbons of her bonnet. 'I would, Betsey, except that there are any number of physicians in this town only too ready to supply her with another.'

'Physicians!' snorted Betsey, relieving Verena of the bonnet as she removed it and brushing automatically at the flecks of snow still adhering to the bronze velvet. 'Much they know. It ain't any bodily ill that ails the mistress.'

'I know. Not now, in any event.' In an absent-minded way, Verena ran her fingers lightly through her honey-coloured tresses to fluff out the crushed curls. 'I had better go in to her.'

The accommodation that served for the ladies' parlour was a large chamber to the front of the house, which looked out of a square bay upon the short drive below, and from a rather smaller window to the far side of the room upon the vista of trees that sat in the square that Verena had just left. Before this window, to take advantage of the light, stood a small writing bureau that was Verena's particular domain, for she always conducted any business there might be. Two large armchairs facing the larger window took up most of the space in the bay, and beside a small fireplace opposite was an old-fashioned giltwood day-bed with worn damask upholstery, just now occupied by the frail and exhausted frame of Mrs Abigail Pateley, thin with prolonged griefs.

Verena's entrance seemed to sweep a breath of freshness into the stuffy atmosphere, and Mrs Pateley turned her head from contemplation of the fire and put out a wavering hand.

'Dearest!' she uttered faintly. 'I am sorry—so sorry.'

'Don't be, Mama,' Verena said bracingly, swiftly crossing the room and leaning down to plant a kiss upon her mother's cheek.

It was a faded cheek, upon which only the faintest traces of the beauty it had once held remained, eroded by long years of suffering. Furrows were etched into features once smooth and a sallow shade now overlaid that peaches and cream perfection. About the eyes a haunted look had chased away all vestige of joy, and the myriad tiny lines that nestled there gave the lie to the lady's forty summers.

Mrs Pateley groped for her daughter's hands and a rim of redness gathered about her eyes. 'So good to me. . .I am so very sorry, my dearest.'

'Mama, pray hush,' Verena begged, perching beside her mother on the day-bed, and lifting the folds of the dove-coloured swathes of muslin gown that were slipping to the floor.

It was like Mama to forestall criticism by a show of contrition, Verena thought. She would guess that

Betsey would see and report on the lowered contents of the laudanum bottle.

'I could wish you had not taken it,' Verena said gently, 'but it does not matter now.'

Mrs Pateley dissolved into tears. 'I c-could not sleep, Verena. I tried so hard. Indeed, indeed I did. But what was I to do? Such dreams. . .such horrible visions. . .'

'Hush, Mama, hush,' Verena crooned, lifting out from an all-enveloping woollen shawl the trembling fingers that feebly clutched at her hands.

It was some time before Mrs Pateley could overcome her emotion. Verena had expected this the instant Betsey mentioned laudanum. The wretched stuff might help Mama to sleep, but it always rendered her tearful and maudlin. If only she could arrest Mama's fears permanently! But how, when she felt them as acutely herself?

'You'd best let me take your pelisse, Miss Verena,' came briskly from Betsey, who had followed Verena into the room.

'In a moment.'

But Mrs Pateley emerged from her handkerchief, and looked enquiringly up towards the maid.

'Been out in all this snow, she has, ma'am,' said Betsey deliberately. 'A miracle it is she isn't sneezing the place down already.'

Mrs Pateley reached out anxiously to feel the sleeve of Verena's coat. 'Oh, you are quite damp, dearest,' she uttered in a much stronger voice. 'Do, pray, get out of that at once. I dare say your boots may be wet through. Betsey, pray. . .'

The maid hid a grim smile of satisfaction and took the brown furred pelisse as Verena peeled it off, revealing a pearl gown of figured French lawn, waisted lower than was generally modish, with wrap-over bodice and elbow-length sleeves, and worn over a round gown of muslin with sleeves to the wrist and closed at the neck with a frilled ruff.

Verena caught a wink from Betsey and understood. Anything to divert the mistress's mind. Bustling, the maid pulled up a footstool conveniently to hand to one side of the day-bed, and, pushing Verena down to sit on it, removed her boots and ordered her to warm her stockinged toes at the fire.

'I'll fetch your slippers to you, Miss Verena.'

'Oh, yes, do so, Betsey,' begged Mrs Pateley from her languishing pose, adding with concern, 'and a shawl. I could never forgive myself if you caught cold.'

Betsey threw her a glance of scorn. 'I'll fetch a shawl to her, ma'am, but what call you have to blame yourself for Miss Verena's gallivanting about in the snow, I'm sure I don't know.'

'Nor anyone else,' agreed Verena, laughing. Betsey's tactics were masterly, and it would not do to allow Mama to fall back into her vein of self-reproach. 'Now, Mama, you must not scold. I have been helping the village children to build their snowman. Oh, and the little Ruishton boys came out to join us, too. Such a darling pair! I know Mrs Ruishton dotes on them, although she is hoping for a girl this time, she says.'

This turn in the conversation proved unfortunate, however, for Mrs Pateley sighed deeply. 'Ah, Verena, how much I long to see you with your children about you!'

'Yes, well, for that I must needs be married first, and you know how I feel about that.'

There was an edge to Verena's voice, she knew, and she wished very much that she might manage these discussions better. But she could not. The very idea of marriage sent quivers up her spine and caused her chest to feel hollow. How Mama could even expect her to contemplate tying herself up in matrimony, heaven only knew.

But Mrs Pateley's eyes were swimming again. 'It grieves me so dreadfully, dearest, that I am standing in the way of your future.'

'Mama, we have been over all that I don't know how many times,' Verena said impatiently.

'I know, and I will never cease to bring it up until you give up this foolish notion,' cried her mother, her tears brimming over. 'How can I bear to be such a burden to you?'

'But you are not a burden, Mama. Do you think I would have taken this step if I thought that?'

'Yes, I am. Oh, I know you did not think so at the outset, but I *know* I am making your life a misery.'

'Nonsense!'

'Do not say it is nonsense. Look at me now! Unable to support myself through a night of memories, and you have warned me time and again against the taking of that drug.'

'Hush, Mama,' begged Verena. 'Heaven knows you have enough reason for a sleepless night or two!' She smiled warmly. 'I never expected it would be easy to overcome the pain of all those years. But together we can do it, I am persuaded. Thanks to Grandpapa's bequest, at least I am in a position to take you out of that life, and keep you out of it.'

'But think of your future,' begged Mrs Pateley distressfully. 'Already you are one and twenty. Why, you are quite on the shelf! It will not do, dearest.'

Verena laughed. 'How can you talk so? Do you suppose I care that I am on the shelf? My future is with you—and always shall be.'

'No, Verena,' said her mother sadly. 'There is little

future anywhere for me. I am convinced that I cannot last long, and then what will happen to you?'

Betsey's scandalised voice, as she came back into the room, broke in before Verena could reply. 'That will do, that will. I never heard such fiddle-faddle in all my born days. Talk as if you was a hundred, you do, ma'am. And you not a day above forty, as I know.'

'Exactly, Mama,' Verena agreed in a bracing tone. 'Come now. I know you are feeling poorly at this present, but once you have recovered your strength, you may expect to survive another forty.'

'Nathaniel will have discovered us long before then,' prophesied Mrs Pateley gloomily, 'and I know he will drag me home again.'

'That he will not! I am of age, don't forget. He will find he has more than he bargained for if he tries his tricks on you again, for he will have to reckon with *me* now.'

'Bravo, Miss Verena,' Betsey said, placing a bulky woollen shawl about Verena's shoulders. She stooped to thrust the young lady's feet into a pair of olive-coloured slippers with low heels and silver clasps, addressing her mistress the while. 'Never you fret, ma'am. Miss Verena will see him off if he does come. And I'm here to lend a hand, if need be. He ain't never going to take you back.'

She rose, nodding with satisfaction. 'There, that's done. Now I'm going down to see if that there Quedgeley has got your breakfast ready.'

'Thank you, Betsey,' Verena said warmly. 'I do not know what either of us should do without you.'

The maid grunted as she left the room, but Verena knew she was pleased. It was only the truth. They would have been lost, and exposed, without Betsey's care.

Mrs Pateley's plaintive tone drew her attention. 'Verena, dearest.'

She looked round to discover a worried frown in her mother's face. 'What is it, Mama?'

'Verena. . .if—if he should come—'

'I hope he won't. He does not know where we are.'

'But if he should,' insisted Mrs Pateley.

Verena eyed her doubtfully. What now? She was not going to make another futile attempt to extract a promise that her daughter would not interfere, she hoped. She had spent years not interfering, and had suffered in consequence agonies of guilt and remorse. Now that she had done so to some purpose, nothing would persuade her to alter her determination.

Mrs Pateley seized one of her hands and grasped it in a surprisingly strong grip. 'Dearest, my only fear is that you may provoke him beyond bearing. You have such strength, Verena. Much more than I ever had.'

'I may well provoke him,' Verena answered lightly. 'It does not take much, as you well know. But what of that? There is nothing he can do, Mama. Not now.'

Her mother appeared unconvinced. 'Still, I could wish that you would leave me to deal with him.'

'That I shall not, Mama,' uttered Verena indignantly. 'How could you ask it of me?'

'I ask it because—' She broke off, sighing deeply. 'Oh, Verena, I wish I knew how to explain. You think you know Nathaniel, my darling, but you *don't*.'

There was a serious look in her face that gave Verena pause. Yet what was there more to know? She thought she had been a party to all Mama's troubles, all that secret life that must be hidden from other eyes—for pride's sake, if nothing else. The thought of it hardened her.

'I know him as well as I wish to, Mama, believe me.'

Mrs Pateley's lip trembled, but her grip on Verena's fingers did not relax. Rather it tightened. 'Yes, you may speak in that stony way, Verena, and I cannot blame you for that with what you have witnessed. But—but you don't understand.'

'What more is there to understand,' Verena asked bitterly, 'beyond the evidence of my own eyes and ears?'

'There is more,' pursued her mother fervently. 'You have compassion for me, Verena, but you should feel it for Nathaniel also. You see, he cannot help himself. If you had ever cared for a man, you must have understood it. You will do so, when it happens to you. Nathaniel *loves* me.'

Verena stared at her in sheer disbelief. Compassion? He could not help himself? Then heaven help him, for she would see him dead before he dragged Mama back. And if *that* was 'love', then Verena would cut out her heart before she gave it to any man!

CHAPTER TWO

THE Lower Rooms, whither Denzell Hawkeridge, on the very next evening, dragged his hosts in search of the lovely Verena Chaceley, were situated at the back of the Sussex Inn. They were relatively thin of company at this time of year, opening for assemblies twice a week only for the benefit of the increasing number of residents settling in Tunbridge Wells.

The cold this Friday night had driven everyone to seek refuge in the smaller of the two plain, unadorned rooms where a good fire blazed, creating an illusion of a greater gathering than was actually present. But the weather did not prevent the inhabitants from appearing in the silks and muslins of full dress, as Unice had warned Denzell. He was himself attired in town gear of a suit of claret-coloured cloth and a black Florentine waistcoat, with stockings striped in black and white, his cravat knotted in an intricate bow. Not, he told himself, that he had taken extra special care with his appearance this evening!

Since the Ruishtons were among the very few of a younger element that the town could boast, and had been missed during their absence in London for some part of the autumn Season, they received an enthusiastic welcome, which was extended equally to the charming young man who accompanied them.

'Ah, yes, Hawkeridge, is it not?' mused Sir John Frinton, the elegant old roué who led the Wellsian gentry. 'I fancy I knew your father.'

'Indeed?' responded Denzell, smiling. 'I will not say

that I have often heard him speak of you, Sir John, for I am sure you will refuse to believe me.'

The old gentleman laughed. 'I should. It is far more likely that you will have heard your mother speak of me.' He twinkled at Denzell's surprised look. 'You need not look at me so, my young friend. I have been, in my day, quite as much a devil of a fellow as are you—with the ladies.'

Denzell grinned. 'I don't doubt it, sir. But unless my friend Osmond has been giving me away, I cannot see how—'

'My dear boy,' interrupted the elder man, 'you must not think that we are all of us unacquainted with your exploits, merely because we no longer have the energy to show our faces in town. We contrive to keep up with the world, you know, despite being quite out of it.'

'Oh, indeed?' Denzell muttered, faintly grim. The scandalmongers had been at it again, had they? He should be used to the tattling tongues of the old town tabbies by now, but it could not but gall him to find himself a subject for speculation even in this out-of-the-way place. 'And who is your particular informant, sir, or shouldn't I ask?'

In fact, there was no need to ask, for at that moment he saw a rather sturdy dame, alarmingly garbed in lilac and yellow with a heavily feathered turban, clearly moving in on Unice, her interested glance flicking in his direction. Sir John's wry smile was all the intimation needed that this was the local gossip whom Unice had mentioned at breakfast.

The inflection of distaste in his voice had been noted. Sir John's smile grew. 'There is a price to be paid, my young friend,' he said softly, 'if you pursue the path you are treading, as I know.'

Denzell eyed him. Yes, he had heard of this man,

now he came to think of it. There was that about him
that stirred a vague memory. The air of elegance
exuded by the grey silk suit of ditto, with its fine
embroidered waistcoat; the white toupée, the powder
and paint, now so outmoded as to be ridiculous; and
the wry, twinkling humour.

But Sir John Frinton had ever been a rake, according
to Lady Hawkeridge, which Denzell himself was not.
His own flirtations were harmless enough. He frowned
at the man.

'Even when it is merely a pleasant game?'

Sir John nodded, the teasing gleam in his eye pronounced. 'Even then. To those with an ear for tittle-
tattle, motive has no meaning. But you may easily stop
it, you know.'

'May I, sir? How?'

'Take a wife, my dear boy, take a wife.'

Denzell burst out laughing. 'Sage advice, sir, and of
course I must do so in time. But I shall indulge myself
a little more yet, despite such wagging tongues as
your—what the devil is the woman's name?'

'Mrs Felpham. And I'll wager there is not one item
about you that is in the public domain of which she has
not already made herself mistress.'

'I would not take you, Sir John,' Denzell responded,
grinning. 'There cannot be the least doubt of it. Oh,
deuce take it,' he added in an undervoice, 'now I am
for it.'

He had just caught sight of Unice heading his way,
with the wretched gossip in tow. Her quiet, dead-leaf
muslin gown, despite the disadvantage of her shorter
stature, looked remarkably well against the overpower-
ing Mrs Felpham.

Denzell turned instinctively for help to his com-
panion. 'Sir John—'

But the old man, with an adroitness that Denzell envied, had melted away. With an inward sigh, he braced himself to counter a series of impertinent questions that he could see forming behind the eager eyes drinking him in from within a raddled countenance, yellow with age and the ruthless application of cosmetics.

As he fielded the probing of Mrs Felpham with practised charm, he found himself wondering at Unice and Osmond's having decided to settle here.

To be sure, it was close to Unice's parental home in a more easterly part of Kent, and Osmond having no estates of his own—his small fortune deriving from the will of a favoured uncle—it had been prudent of him to purchase an affordable house and invest the remainder of his capital to provide a reasonable income. But to seek a home amongst this elderly and valetudinarian company was not what he himself would have chosen.

'Regretting your visit already, are you?' murmured Osmond's teasing tones in his ear, the instant Unice had borne Mrs Felpham away.

Denzell turned to his friend, resplendent in a suit of purple cloth, and spoke his mind in a disgusted undervoice.

'Deuce take it, Ossie, how can you bear it? That female for one. Not to mention an old bore of a playwright—Richard Cumberland, is it?—and your ancient nabob Martin Yorke, to name but two trials I had already undergone. It is small wonder that you come posting up to town at every opportunity.'

Osmond grinned. 'I suppose your opinion has nothing to do with the fact that you find Verena Chaceley to be absent from the company?'

A reluctant laugh was drawn from Denzell. 'On the contrary,' he admitted, 'it has everything to do with it.

Were my beautiful maiden of the snow here, I am sure I should be in raptures over the entire population. But in truth, I cannot blame her for absenting herself.'

'No doubt if she had known you were to appear, she would not have done so,' said Osmond ironically. 'Don't know what you're complaining about, however. Everyone is in such a flutter over you, I should think even your appetite for attention must be satisfied.'

Denzell grinned. 'Indeed, dear boy, I am quite set up in my own conceit. According to Sir John Frinton, my fame goes before me in these parts.'

'Ha! Nothing special about you, Hawk. Anyone new is welcome here, if they had a hunchback and a crippled leg.'

'I thank you. Now that you have thoroughly deflated my pretensions, let us, for pity's sake, extract Unice from that busybody of a female and leave this place forthwith. The light of my life is clearly not coming here tonight, and I have no mind to spend the rest of the evening in this insipid fashion for nothing.'

How he managed it even Unice was unable to tell, but in a very short space of time Denzell had whisked them away from the company with only a word here and a word there, and nobody in the least put out. Apart, that was, from Osmond.

'It is too bad,' he complained as, wrapped in greatcoats against the winter night, they walked briskly home beside the chair that carried Unice. 'First you tell me you have come here on a repairing lease. Then, merely because you catch sight of a pretty face—'

'Not just pretty, dear boy, a face of stunning beauty.'

'—you insist on hauling us out in the cold from our comfortable home just so that you may parade about in the vain hope of attracting her interest—'

'We shall see about vain!'

'—and as if this was not enough, when you don't find her, you dash out of the place as if all the devils of hell were after you!'

'They are,' retorted Denzell, as if his friend's ridiculous exaggeration had some truth in it, 'and will be until I meet Verena Chaceley. I will not give up, dear boy. I have conceived the most cunning plan.'

Osmond scoffed when he learned that Denzell meant to enlist the aid of his godson Felix.

The very next morning found Denzell Hawkeridge up and about at a most unseasonable hour for a Saturday, and ascending the stairs to the nursery.

Young Felix was only too delighted to oblige his godfather, and set off happily through the back garden with Nurse Dinah and Miles in tow, to show him the famous snowman. Sadly, there having been no further fall, it was somewhat the worse for wear. The flakes that had lain most of Thursday and Friday had now turned to ice underfoot, and the thaw showed patchy areas of rough ground through the white film.

Disappointed, Felix nevertheless embarked on a description of the snowman as it had been at the zenith of its short life, while Denzell contemplated the remains. He was listening with only half an ear, while his eye searched this way and that about the square whenever his godson's gaze was engaged with the melting snowman. But no glimpse of a brown pelisse rewarded his covert diligence, and no sign of Felix's friends appeared to relieve him of his self-imposed charge.

He was obliged to hear his godson out, to make what he might of the additional information fed to him in baby prattle by Miles in concert with his elder brother, to admire what was left of the unfortunate man of snow,

and to endure a barrage of hardened icy balls thrown
by both boys in the fit of exuberance induced in them
by his presence.

It was left to Dinah to call a halt to the proceedings,
decreeing that the breakfast hour was upon them, and
that the boys must return to the nursery forthwith.
Denzell, with one last forlorn look around the area,
desolate now with the lack of his fairy princess, allowed
himself to be dragged back to the house with one
shrieking child clinging to either hand.

His hosts, he learned from Mayberry, the manservant
who combined the duties of butler and footman with
innumerable other functions, were not yet in the breakfast parlour, and might be found in the green saloon
next door.

This large term described, as Denzell knew, the small
chamber where the family were wont to gather infor-
mally through the day, being comfortable enough for
sitting in, with a good fire in the wide grate, and yet
sufficiently well appointed, with its green brocade wall-
paper and toning upholstery to the Sheraton sofa and
chairs, for receiving any visitors who might chance to
arrive.

'Thank you, Mayberry,' Denzell said, with a smile, as
he handed the man his greatcoat and brushed down the
dark blue coat beneath.

Osmond, who was warming his plum coat-tails before
the fire as Denzell entered, moved quickly forward to
greet him. 'Ah, Hawk. You are up betimes, old fellow.
I wonder why?'

'You know very well why,' Denzell retorted, provoked. 'I told you I meant to use Felix to effect an
introduction to that glorious creature. Didn't you
believe me?'

Osmond grinned wickedly. 'Oh, I believed you. Your mission did not prosper, I take it?'

'No, and I'll thank you to refrain from cheap gibes.'

'Gibes? Me?' said Osmond, all innocence. 'I was only going to say that the gods favour you after all, Hawk.'

He stepped aside on the words, and Denzell looked past him and stopped dead, staring stupidly at a vision seated in the round armchair to one side of the fireplace. A vision in a furred brown pelisse, with a bronze velvet bonnet set at a charming angle above the most beautiful face in the world.

'Chaste stars!' gasped Denzell, shocked out of his customary sangfroid. 'Verena Chaceley, as I live and breathe!'

'None other,' murmured Osmond beside him. 'I found her visiting Unice.'

The vision's features did not stir, although her eyes were turned in Denzell's direction. Without conscious thought, he found the word that Unice had used playing in his mind: serene. Beautiful, calm and serene. She might have been carved in marble.

Then Mrs Ruishton spoke from the sofa opposite Verena, pulling Denzell back to reality. 'Miss Chaceley, allow me to present to you our guest, Mr Hawkeridge.'

She moved then. The slightest nod of the head, the faintest of polite smiles. 'How do you do?' A musical tone, but flat with disinterest.

Denzell could not respond. He was utterly disconcerted. He must seem the completest fool! An odd laugh shook him. He shrugged helplessly, his eyes riveted on her face.

'I am—confounded,' he managed.

It was Osmond's low laughter, redolent with glee, that snapped him back to himself again. He took a breath, smiled and moved forward, holding out his hand.

'Miss Chaceley, I am *enchanted* to make your acquaintance.'

She lifted her hand, and the ends of her bare fingers—for her gloves were held loosely in her other hand—clasped his for the briefest instant. There was no change in her expression, however. But her fingers, Denzell felt, had been warm. He took courage, moving back a step.

'Miss Chaceley, I confess I am so discomfited that I know not what to say.'

Her brows lifted very slightly. 'Indeed? Why so, Mr—?'

'Hawkeridge,' he supplied, as she hesitated.

'Why so, Mr Hawkeridge?' repeated the pleasant voice, although Denzell could descry no real interest in any answer that he might make. No matter. He would force her to notice him somehow. He must. She had been fashioned in heaven, no doubt about it!

But Unice, who had been fidgeting uneasily with the many folds of her muslin gown that spread about her, broke in swiftly. 'Denzell has been looking at the snowman you were building with the children the other day, Miss Chaceley. Felix insisted upon it, you know.'

'Nothing of the sort,' argued Denzell, seating himself in the chair closest to Verena. 'It was I who insisted upon Felix taking me there.' He smiled winningly. 'You see, Miss Chaceley, I was in hopes that I might find you.'

'Hopes!' muttered Osmond, taking his seat beside his wife on the sofa.

'And so you have met her after all,' Unice interrupted bracingly. 'Such a fortunate chance that you came to visit me this morning, Miss Chaceley.'

Again Denzell smiled, leaning towards Verena's chair. 'Unice would have me dissemble, but I vow I will have none of it. The truth is that I saw you from my bedroom window when you were playing with the children—oh, an eon ago!—and instantly conceived the strongest desire to meet you.'

There was nothing in her face to encourage him to continue in this vein. She made no attempt even to reply to him, but sat calmly, the wide-set gaze clear on his face, apparently unmoved. This close, her features, still as they were, showed to even more perfection, and the frame of curling tresses that surrounded them, peeking beneath the bonnet's ornamented brim and trailing their way onto her shoulders, were of the colour of warm honey.

It took an effort for Denzell to think about what he was saying. Yet having taken the bull by the horns and told the precise truth, there was nothing for him to do but to go on. He was hardly aware that he was smiling, that his eyes glowed with warmth at the sheer enjoyment of her beauty.

'Was it presumptuous of me, Miss Chaceley? Failing to discover you at the assembly last night, I went out into the snow expressly to try to scrape acquaintance with you. I cannot begin to tell you how much disappointed I was not to find you there.' He was aware that he was rattling off his words, but he could not stop. The very lack of response impelled him to continue. 'And then—to see you sitting in this very room. Now do you see why I said I was confounded?'

A very slight smile curved her lips, but there was no reflection of it in her eyes. 'What can I say but that I am deeply flattered, Mr Hawkeridge?'

'Oh, no, no!' he exclaimed. 'I protest I am not flattering you.'

'He isn't,' put in Osmond, adding his mite. 'Miss

Chaceley, you have not heard the half of it, I promise you.'

'Osmond, pray hush!' begged Unice. She turned to Verena. 'Pay no heed to either of them, Miss Chaceley. They are rascals when they get together. You have no notion what I am obliged to contend with from the two of them.'

'Indeed?' said Miss Chaceley politely.

Denzell could not tear his gaze away from that lovely face. Not a flicker! Not the faintest trace of amusement. It was fascinating. Unice had been right. Where the deuce had all that warmth and laughter gone? He had not imagined it—had he? The memory of her animated countenance hovered in his mind, battling with the present placidity. No, he had not imagined it. There was a joyous creature somewhere inside this apparent shell. He set himself to draw it out, exerting every ounce of his considerable charm.

'You have never visited London, Miss Chaceley?' Verena's gaze turned back towards him and his eyes invited her smile. 'I am persuaded I could not have forgotten had I seen you there.'

She did not smile. 'I have not been there.'

'It is our loss,' Denzell said, with a gleam that would have thrown any other young lady into confusion. It was met, on this occasion, with a bland note of indifference.

'You are too kind.'

'May we look forward to the expectation of seeing you at some future time? During the coming Season, perhaps?'

'I think not.'

He was daunted, but he tried again. 'But surely you cannot mean to hide your charms away here in

Tunbridge Wells forever? What a shocking waste that would be, Miss Chaceley.'

'My plans are as yet uncertain.'

Deuce take it, she could not even raise a simper! Deflated, Denzell sat back. Was she so vain that his compliments meant nothing to her? Or was she merely stupid? His gaze, moving away, met the unholy glee in Osmond's features. He threw his eyes faintly to heaven, casting his friend a rueful smile. Osmond was obliged to turn quickly away, biting his lip on laughter. Unice intervened swiftly.

'Mr Hawkeridge, you must know, is a confirmed man of the town. It is a rare privilege to have him here, for you will hardly find him away from London. Unless he is at home in Hampshire.'

'Indeed?'

'In fact, no,' Denzell cut in, glancing across. 'At home in Buckinghamshire, Unice.' He turned back to Verena, speaking in a more natural way. 'It chances that my father's estates are on the border, at Tuttingham. Just a village, but the barony extends widely around it. It is near Aylesbury.'

Rather to his surprise, Verena turned to look him in the eye. There was nothing in her voice to suggest anything but politeness, but the words she spoke struck him like a douche of cold water.

'You are plainly extremely eligible, Mr Hawkeridge. I imagine there must be any number of young ladies only too ready to receive your advances. I hope that it may not be long before your friends are wishing you happy.'

Denzell was so taken aback that he scarcely knew how to reply. By George, but what a masterly stroke! She was certainly not stupid. Before he could gather his wits to find a suitable response—not that he could have thought of one even had he done so!—Miss Chaceley was drawing on her gloves. Then she was rising.

'I must go, Mrs Ruishton,' she was saying, crossing to take Unice's hand. 'No, do not get up. I am happy to find you looking so well.'

Both the gentlemen had stood up automatically, and Verena turned to hold out her hand to Osmond. 'Goodbye, Mr Ruishton. Do you take care of her, pray.'

'Oh, I will,' said Osmond cheerfully. 'But there is no need for concern. She manages these matters very well, does Unice. But let me see you to the door.'

A faint smile was all his answer, and Verena turned her head to Denzell, saying in a voice utterly devoid of expression, 'I am happy to have met you, Mr Hawkeridge.'

The next moment, she had left the saloon. Osmond flung a speaking glance at his friend before following her from the room, and Denzell grimaced at Unice who was looking at him rather anxiously. Neither of them spoke until the front door had closed and Osmond walked back into the room.

'What did I tell you?' he demanded, grinning widely. 'Unice, did you see his face? I've never enjoyed anything so much in my life!'

'For shame, Osmond. Poor Denzell, she was quite *brutal* to you, I think.'

'No such thing,' argued Osmond, hugely entertained. 'After being given due warning, he flung himself to the wolves, and he has only himself to blame.'

Denzell sank back into his chair, shaking his head. 'You are quite right, Ossie. I am deservedly set down.'

'Oh, don't say so, Denzell,' protested Unice. 'I do think she might at least have acknowledged the compliments you paid her. Really, I am quite out of charity with her. I had no idea she could be so horrid.'

'No, no, Unice. She was politeness itself, just as you predicted would be the case.'

'I'm dashed if I've ever seen you so crestfallen, Hawk!' observed Osmond, raising his brows. 'Giving up the notion already, are you?'

Denzell frowned. 'No, not giving up. Just—oh, I don't know. Yes, I do, though. I'm *confused*. When I saw her yesterday, she was so. . .'

He paused, at a loss for words to describe the difference between the girl he had seen in the snow and this cold statue. He looked from one to the other of his friends, and suddenly smote his knee. 'I don't believe it! I simply do not believe that this was the true Verena Chaceley.'

He might have been cheered could he but have seen Verena at that moment, left alone outside the Ruishtons' front door. Breathless, she put a hand to her breast, as if to still the fluttering there within. Dear heaven, but what charm there was in his smile! Had she not trained herself all these long years to suppress even the slightest outward display of emotion, she feared she must have given him the satisfaction of knowing how much he had moved her. Her control had never been so severely tested.

She drew a steadying breath, and came away from the door, her half-boots crunching along the worn path that was once again showing beneath the dissipating snow and ice. Lost in her thoughts, she had forgotten the short cut and began along the longer trail that led back to the road.

Heavens, but she did not wish to have *any* man affect her this way. Least of all, such a man as that. Eligible, indeed. Heaven send Mama did not get wind of his interest! If there was any substance to it, which she frankly doubted. That winning smile, the limpid gaze from those misty eyes, had all the hallmarks of the accomplished flirt.

She had not been so out of the world that she could not recognise these signs. The society of Fittleworth might be limited, but she had not been the reigning belle for several years without schooling herself to nip these sorts of pretensions firmly in the bud. It would surprise her very much if Mr Denzell Hawkeridge took the matter any further.

A sneaking regret caused her to quicken her pace, lashing herself mentally. None of that, Verena Chaceley! Did she so easily forget the horrors that lay in store for the unwary female who allowed herself to be beguiled by such men as this? How could she forget? She dismissed the idea. She was but human, and a comely countenance, accompanied by such an onslaught of determined charm, was bound to have its effect. She need not concern herself over that. Particularly when she guessed him to be singularly experienced at this game.

All at once she checked her pace. No harm in arming herself, just in case Mr Hawkeridge should not have been sufficiently deterred by this one meeting. Turning away from the route home, she passed back along the row of houses that bordered the lane and crossed beyond them towards the New Inn. Two houses down, she stopped and knocked at a certain door.

Mrs Felpham, her sturdy frame planted firmly in a chair by her own fireside, expressed herself as being delighted to welcome Miss Chaceley. Of course she was! She had been trying these few months to penetrate the wall Verena had erected to keep out just such intrusions. Verena could almost feel sorry for her. This was her only purpose in life.

A widow, settling here some few years since, she had nothing to do but busy herself in hunting out all the little details that made up the lives of those around her. What else had she, except a very obvious pride in her dress—up to the minute in a spotted lawn open robe whose high waistline could not be said to be becoming to a flat chest in a square frame?

There was no need for Verena to touch upon the subject of her visit, because the lady herself brought it up the instant the greetings were over.

'A most *charming* young man, and quite eligible. His father is Lord Hawkeridge, and I believe the estates are in very good heart. No other sons to be provided for. There is only a sister, I believe, and she is out already so that she must soon be off their hands.'

'Indeed?' Verena said, maintaining the cool company manners that stood her in such good stead.

'What a pity you were not there last night, Miss Chaceley, for I am sure you could not fail to catch his eye.'

'As it chances,' Verena said blandly, 'I have just met him at the Ruishtons'. I called to see how Mrs Ruishton did, and am happy to report that she seems very well.'

'Oh, yes, dear Unice carries her children most comfortably. And, pray, what did you think of Mr Hawkeridge?'

Verena met the eager gaze under the large lacy cap with a show of complete unconcern. 'I do not know that I thought very much about him at all, Mrs Felpham. Except perhaps to form the impression that he is a practised flirt.'

'Quite accomplished, so I have been informed,' averred Mrs Felpham avidly. She leaned forward in a confidential way. 'Dear Miss Chaceley, allow me to put

you a little on your guard, although I am persuaded it
is not necessary, so sensible as you are.'

If it was not necessary, Verena thought drily, why
bother to say it? But outwardly, she was all polite
attention. 'How thoughtful of you, Mrs Felpham.'

Excitement showed in the woman's eyes. 'You are so
young, my dear. You can have no notion of the sort of
tactics that young men such as Mr Hawkeridge are apt
to employ.'

'What sort of tactics, Mrs Felpham?'

'Well,' said the dame, settling down to enjoy herself.
'I am led to believe that there have been few female
hearts held proof against him. Do you know what is his
practice?'

'No, Mrs Felpham,' said Verena, though she was sure
the lady was going to tell her!

'What will he do, dare you imagine, but select some
poor wretch, and then tantalise and tease until she does
not know whether she is coming or going.'

'Indeed? How might he do that?'

Mrs Felpham's avid eyes sparkled. 'Why, pay her a
battery of compliments and attention. Then, the very
next time he sees her, what will there be? Nothing but
indifference and withdrawal.'

She stopped, eyeing Verena as if waiting for some
comment. There was much Verena might have said!
But she waited politely, allowing no change in her own
expression. Mrs Felpham sighed faintly, and resumed.

'Of course it means nothing. For on the next occasion,
he will be all smiles and charm, declaring that it had
been *her* rebuff and he only feared to approach her.
Once she is softened by such mouthings, he will desert
her once more, sometimes for days—not paying court
elsewhere, you know, but keeping company instead
with his particular cronies.'

'And that is the end of it?' asked Verena, unable to help herself.

'No, no, no!' exclaimed Mrs Felpham, brightening at this show of interest. 'He returns again. For by now, as you may imagine, the unfortunate female is on tenterhooks and positively tearing her hair out with yearning.'

The more fool she! thought Verena, as Mrs Felpham sat back with an air of utter satisfaction.

'What do you think of that, Miss Chaceley?'

There could be no doubt what Verena thought of it. She had never heard of anything more shabby! Disgust rose in her at the thought of such arts being employed, so as to turn some poor girl's head into a whirl of confusion. Dear heaven, she ought to know how dangerous a pastime was being played here! So he blew in turns hot and cold upon his victim, did he? All to satisfy his own vanity, no doubt. What a conceit! Little did he know how well aware was she of the effects of such erratic conduct.

Mrs Felpham was waiting for her answer, a look of such comical anticipation in her face that Verena must have laughed had she not been so disappointed. Disappointed? Well, she had as well admit to it. It *had* been flattering to be the recipient of such strong attentions. To hear now that it was but a prelude to a practical campaign could only drop Mr Hawkeridge in her estimation.

'I think,' she said calmly, 'that any female who is taken in by such blatant posturings must be a complete fool.'

Damped, Mrs Felpham was silenced for a moment. But she rallied quickly. 'Then I have only to say, Miss Chaceley, that London is full of a great many fools.'

Verena permitted herself a faint smile. 'In that case I

must be happy that I have no place there, Mrs Felpham.'

She left the widow dissatisfied, she thought, but herself secure in the knowledge that her words would be carried through the town as swiftly as possible, so that none would be able to suppose her to be falling under the spell of Mr Hawkeridge. It would rather be the gentleman himself they would watch, waiting to see his failure with the female whom no one in the spa town had as yet succeeded in touching.

Hurrying home, Verena resolved that she would remain aloof, nevertheless. She might be disenchanted, but she already knew herself to be vulnerable to him, and she had seen too much of Mama's sapped strength not to suspect her own.

She was able to maintain her resolution for several days, Mama thankfully offering her the best excuse possible by her current bout of weakness. They did not attend Sunday service at the King Charles Chapel, and Verena caught herself out wondering whether Mr Hawkeridge had missed her, instead of she being compelled—according to Mrs Felpham—to miss him!

Furious at herself for even this slight show of interest in the man, she spent Monday at her bureau in the parlour, handling overdue accounts and some belated correspondence with the lawyer who had charge of Grandpapa Whicham's trust fund, to which she owed her present independence.

It was Mrs Pateley who undid her daughter's best-laid plans *not* to appear in sight of the flirtatious Mr Hawkeridge. Having spent Monday resting contentedly on the day-bed, reading one of Miss Burney's romances culled from the circulating library, she greeted Verena as she came to breakfast on Tuesday morning with what was, for her, a deal of enthusiasm.

'Dearest, I am feeling much more myself today. I should so much like it if we were to go down to the Rooms tonight. Do you not feel we might enjoy keeping company for a change?'

Denzell, happening to be deep in conversation with Sir John Frinton, did not see Verena and her mother enter the room. But a sudden break in the old man's attention alerted him.

'Ah, there she is at last!' uttered Sir John on a note of satisfaction. 'Would that I were forty years younger.'

Turning to follow the direction of the old man's gaze, Denzell at once espied Verena, and his breath caught. If she had been beautiful in a brown pelisse and a ribbon-trimmed bonnet, she was positively ravishing in full dress.

An open robe of white muslin with a low pleated bodice, sleeved to the elbow with beaded trimming covering the long gloves of York tan, was worn over a dull yellow petticoat. The shade perfectly complimented the honeyed tresses, simply dressed with only a ribbon-bandeau threaded through so that one or two curling locks fell loosely across her white breast.

A fairy princess, truly! Staring in wonder, Denzell became aware of a sense of hushed expectancy pervading the room. It held a moment, and then broke, as every male in the place seemed to converge upon Miss Verena Chaceley.

Denzell did not move. With difficulty, he brought his gaze to bear upon the woman standing by Verena's side. The resemblance was plain, although the mother—there could be no doubt of her identity—was but a pale echo of the daughter, a waif-like creature in violet silk. She was of slighter stature, seeming so frail that she might break.

Before the various gentlemen could reach her, he watched Verena turn to her mother, solicitously drawing her towards a chair by the fire. Then she was engulfed and he could no longer see her plainly.

'Well?' came Osmond's probing voice at his side. 'What are you doing standing there? You will never make any headway if you do not thrust your way into the mêlée.'

'What, and make one of a crowd?' said Denzell scornfully, turning his head. 'You know me better than that.'

Both gentlemen were suitably attired for the occasion, Osmond in his favourite purple, while Denzell once again sported the claret suit with its black-silk accoutrements.

Osmond had his attention on the area by the fire where the portly Mr Cumberland and the wheezing Mr Yorke were vying with a number of other gentlemen who tried, regardless of the proprieties of rank or station, to be first with Miss Chaceley. It was Sir John, Denzell saw, who succeeded in procuring her smile, however, for he was so adroit as to set the chosen chair for Mrs Pateley, thus evidently earning the beauty's gratitude. The little circle widened as Miss Chaceley herself took a seat, enabling Denzell to watch her as she turned, from one to another gentleman in turn, to answer whatever sallies they might be making.

'I cannot see that she favours any one above another,' he observed in a pleased tone.

'Told you so. She always metes out exactly the same treatment to all—just as she did to you.'

'For pity's sake!' uttered Denzell suddenly. 'What is she made of, ice? Or is she just soulless?'

Osmond grinned at him. 'Love dying already, eh?'

Slowly Denzell shook his head. 'Growing, Ossie. I

tell you, I am intrigued past any bearing! I swear to
you, she was so vital, so *alive*. This is—well, I don't
know what this is, but I can see that it is apt to drive
me insane.'

'You're piqued, Hawk, that's all. Too used to having
your own way in these matters, and you can't abide to
lose.'

Denzell looked round at him, eyeing him consider-
ingly. 'Is it that? Did I imagine it then?'

Osmond raised his brows. 'Phew! Taking this a mite
seriously, ain't you, Hawk?'

'Am I?'

'Come on, man. What is it to you, barring a trifle of
fun and gig? You're as bad as Unice, laying some
fanciful notion of your own on the girl's head. Face it.
She's a handsome piece, but cold. That's all there is to
it.'

'No, it isn't,' said Denzell with decision. 'I know what
I saw. She's acting—wearing some kind of public mask.
Only look at her! How could any female remain indifferent, being so fêted and fawned over? It's unheard
of.'

'It don't sit well, I must admit,' mused Osmond
thoughtfully. 'What do you mean to do, then, if you
won't join the throng?'

Denzell grinned. 'Draw her attention, of course.'

'Ha! Playing that game, eh? A bow and a smile, and
not a word said, in the hopes you'll pique her vanity. It
won't work.'

'You've tried it, of course,' returned Denzell
sarcastically.

'No, but I've seen you at it. I know you, Hawk. But
I'm telling you. This time it won't work.'

Denzell remained unconvinced. If he was right, if
Verena Chaceley was presenting a façade to the world,

then it was incumbent upon him to find a chink in her armour. He bided his time, waiting until the crowd about her thinned a little, giving meanwhile his attention to the elegant Sir John Frinton—blue silk tonight with silver lace at his waistcoat—who, having paid his respects to the beauty, wandered close by apparently for the sole purpose of twitting his junior slyly.

'Do you believe her to be aware of your absence, my dear young friend?'

Denzell cocked an eyebrow. 'By "her" you mean. . .?'

'Come, come, Hawkeridge, do you take me for a fool?'

'No, sir,' said Denzell, laughing. 'But I'm damned if I know how—'

'I should imagine the whole room must know how, my dear boy,' chided Sir John gently. He added, as Denzell, looking rather startled, glanced swiftly round, 'No, no, you will not find them advertising their interest. But if you do not wish the world to know where *your* interests lie, then you must become more master of your eyes, my friend.'

'Chaste stars, but how can I?' Denzell uttered unguardedly.

Sir John's smile grew. 'She is very beautiful.'

'In this case, sir, I find the word inadequate.'

'But it is a surface beauty,' continued the elder man blandly. 'Or don't you think so?'

Denzell met his eyes, a frown in his own. Was he being quizzed? Had Sir John also seen beyond the veil of that polite serenity?

'I don't, sir,' he said bluntly. 'And I mean to seek what there may be beneath it.'

A soft laugh came from the aged exquisite. 'I wish you well. Though the odds, I fear, are against you.'

'I care nothing for the odds, as long as it is not Miss
Chaceley who is against me,' retorted Denzell, grinning.

Sir John glanced across to where Verena could be
seen listening politely to Mr Cumberland's ponderous
speechifying. He said drily, 'I imagine you must inevitably receive a welcome if you were to rescue her from
our poet, poor girl.'

But Denzell had no intention of rescuing Verena
Chaceley. He had quite other plans in mind. When at
last he moved in Verena's direction, he did not look at
her, but kept his gaze firmly on Mrs Pateley instead,
who had risen from her chair and was weaving a slow
path through the room, chatting with a number of
acquaintances.

As he passed close to where Verena still remained
seated, with now both Cumberland and Martin Yorke
vying for her attention, Denzell paused in his way,
turned his head and looked her full in the face quite
suddenly.

She caught his eye, and blinked, but her features did
not alter. Denzell gave her his most dazzling smile and
nodded a greeting. Very slightly, she inclined her head.
Before she could turn away again, Denzell deliberately
averted his own gaze and continued on his way.

He had reached the circle containing Mrs Pateley
before he dared to glance back to see how his treatment
of Miss Chaceley might have affected her.

Deuce take it, but she looked quite unconcerned!
The statuesque vision was speaking to Mr Yorke, her
gaze wholly concentrated upon the old man. Piqued,
Denzell turned to greet the mother with an excess of
enthusiastic charm.

'May I introduce myself, Mrs Pateley? Denzell
Hawkeridge. I am staying with the Ruishtons. I was

fortunate enough to meet your daughter a few days since.'

Pasty features looked up at him, gaunt and shadowed. Deuce take it, but the woman was shockingly ill! Frail, too, if he was any judge. But she answered him readily enough.

'You have met Verena? She said nothing of it to me.' A smile came, echoing very slightly the look he originally saw in Verena's face. 'I have heard of you, Mr Hawkeridge, if only tonight. One does, you know. So few newcomers in a place like this. Not that we are. . .'

Her voice faded, and she seemed to sway very slightly. Denzell put out a hand, catching at her arm to steady her.

'May I see you to a chair, Mrs Pateley?'

But the Master of Ceremonies, Mr Tyson, bustled up. He was a dapper gentleman of middle years, with a respectful manner that diminished a trifle the air of self-importance that he assumed from his position in the town. This, his attitude seemed to say, was peculiarly his own task.

'Mrs Pateley, allow me! You should be keeping your bed, ma'am.' He shook his head at Denzell, including him even as he ousted him from the lady's side. 'She is not in the best of health, not at all.'

Personally tucking the lady's hand into his proferred arm, Richard Tyson guided her towards one of the sofas that were ranged about the sides of the room, chattering as he went. Denzell watched them go, and then glanced back at Verena suddenly. She did not appear to have so much as moved a muscle. Deuce take it, she had not even noticed! Perhaps Osmond had indeed gauged her correctly. Such an apparent carelessness of her sickly parent argued a lack of feeling, as well as a cold heart!

CHAPTER THREE

VERENA, for all her apparent unconcern, was acutely aware of everything that had passed. Aware, and indignant. What was his design in seeking out her mother, she would like to know? How dared he flash that look at her as if to censure her for not taking better care of Mama? Or did he suppose that she had not seen that piece of byplay? Little did he know!

No doubt he would be astonished to learn of her mastery of a particular art she had acquired over the years. Had been obliged to acquire it. Swift and unremarked were the glances cast from under her lashes, and from the corner of her eye she was well able to note the whereabouts of anyone she chose.

She had mastered this secretive trick from sheer necessity. Heavens, but had she not had her back to the wall for as long as she could remember? Had anyone informed old Martin Yorke, for instance, that his listener, seeming to be looking directly in his face, was in fact checking quite other places, she was sure he would not have believed them.

At home she had never entered a room without a swift and comprehensive glance about, and had always taken care to sit where she might slyly observe the room and the doors. How else could she have fathomed Nathaniel's moods?

She caught herself on this thought. Reverie in public was too dangerous a pastime! She could not afford an instant's relaxation of her extreme vigilance. Besides, she did not wish to think about Nathaniel.

She did not wish to think about Mr Hawkeridge either! But his antics—accosting Mama in that manner and evidently embarking on the vaunted flirtatious campaign by ignoring her!—were forcing him upon her notice. She tried to ignore him and put her wayward attention back on Mr Yorke.

'Pity you were never in India, Miss Chaceley. You would have liked it extremely, I am persuaded.'

'I am persuaded I should, Mr Yorke,' she agreed, although she scarcely took in the sense of his words.

'Why, we had splendours never dreamed of in England.'

The wheezy voice droned on, but Verena found that she could pay no more heed to it than was needed for the interjections she could make that would keep him content. For one thing, she was carefully assessing Mama's condition, and for another—much to her chagrin—was keeping track of Mr Hawkeridge's progress about the room.

Ah, but that would serve him out! He had been accosted by Mrs Felpham. Grim satisfaction settled in her breast, and she eyed the old nabob with an air of interest, only to find that Sir John Frinton had appeared behind him.

Verena permitted the ancient roué one of her marginally warmer smiles. She liked Sir John. He had an acerbic tongue, and he did not pay her fulsome compliments, allowing only an appreciative glint in the eye to speak his admiration.

'Are you boring on again about India, Yorke?' he demanded wearily. 'How tedious of you! Poor Miss Chaceley is glassy-eyed.'

Verena put a dismissive hand out to the old nabob, nevertheless saying politely, 'Your stories are most interesting, Mr Yorke.'

'My dear Miss Chaceley, don't encourage him!' protested Sir John in an undervoice as the wheezing old man wandered away. He sat himself down in a chair beside her. 'Now then, Miss Chaceley, to some serious business.'

She looked enquiringly. 'Yes, Sir John?'

'You are sought after, my dear.'

'Indeed?'

He laughed. 'You need not sound so disinterested. I am not speaking of the plethora of tedious old men — myself excepted! — who constantly badger you for attention.'

Verena's expression did not change. 'You are speaking of Mr Hawkeridge.'

'Ah, so you have noticed.'

'I am neither blind nor inexperienced, Sir John. Besides, I have already been approached by the gentleman himself. I think he will not long waste his time on me.'

A knowing gaze watched her carefully. 'Is he wasting his time?'

'Yes,' she said tranquilly, 'but that is his privilege.'

Sir John's brows rose. 'Why, this is truly hardhearted, Miss Chaceley.'

'I truly hope so.'

'Do you indeed?' The aged exquisite laughed softly. 'I wonder.'

He glanced about the room to locate Denzell, and Verena with difficulty refrained from looking towards the precise spot where she knew him to be standing. He was engaged with the Ruishtons in close conversation.

A little pulse beat a trifle unevenly in her veins all of a sudden. Had she seen aright? Did Mr Hawkeridge cast a quick glance across at her then? She had the

distinct impression that he had, and an eerie sensation
swiftly followed. She was under discussion!

'Denzell,' Unice was saying low-voiced, 'did Mrs
Felpham say anything to you?'

He shook his head. 'Nothing beyond pointing out
how lovely Miss Chaceley looks tonight—as if I had not
already noticed. She must have searched the ware-
houses to match so perfectly her hair colour with that
gown!'

'Never mind that,' said Unice, brushing aside the
unimportant matter of dress. She was herself, as always,
discreetly fine, cleverly drawing attention away from
the bump below the waist of her simple gown of
Canterbury seersucker, with a fancy Cabriolet bonnet
perched on her dark curls.

'Mrs Felpham has certainly said something to me,'
she declared. 'And I should think she has said it to
everybody else also, judging from the veiled remarks
that have been passing around.'

Denzell cast another glance across to where he could
see Verena talking with Sir John Frinton. 'That must be
what Sir John meant. What is being said?'

'It seems that Miss Chaceley has pre-empted you,'
she told him in a hushed voice.

'What do you mean, Unice?'

'She went to see Mrs Felpham that day you met her.'

'And?'

Unice sighed deeply. 'She made it very clear, so Mrs
Felpham says, that she was not going to succumb to
your charms.'

'So that is why she has been invisible!'

'And,' pursued Unice, 'Verena must have intended
that Mrs Felpham would see to it that the whole town
knows.'

'Ha!' uttered her husband happily. 'Spiked your guns, Hawk!'

'Has she indeed?' said Denzell softly.

Once more he looked over at Verena. She appeared to be listening to what Sir John was saying, if not intently—for who could tell what lay behind that expressionless face?—at least with her full attention.

Then, miraculously, as if she felt Denzell's regard, her head tilted very slightly his way, her lashes flickered briefly and by some trick of the candlelight that brightened the room from two modest chandeliers, he caught a flash from her eyes. It was over so quickly that he almost thought he must have been mistaken. Intently now, he continued to survey her, quite forgetting that he had not meant to show her any further attention tonight.

Then her hand suddenly came up and her fingers brushed lightly at her hair, slid down her cheek, hovered at her lips, and were swiftly returned to her lap.

Triumph leapt in Denzell's chest. 'Chaste stars!' he murmured. What a giveaway! A slow grin split his face. 'So, Miss Chaceley. You are not as indifferent to me as you would have me believe.'

Verena, quite as aware as he of the ruinous nature of the slip, was inwardly cursing herself. To all outward appearances, she was listening with interest while Sir John talked of indifferent things. But inwardly, she seethed.

What a stupid blunder! How *could* she have given way to such an obvious gesture of self-consciousness? Her position had not altered, but she was quite able to see Mr Hawkeridge grinning in that fatuous way. How silly to have allowed herself to become flustered by the conviction that he was talking about her. Now he would know that she *had* noticed him. There was all her work of the evening gone for nothing.

It was infuriating. How hard she had worked since coming to this town! How difficult it had been, day after day, guarding her every expression, maintaining an iron composure that deflected all efforts to penetrate beneath her cool surface. It had been so much simpler at home.

A picture flashed into her mind. Herself a very mouse, quiet and still in a corner, all her concentration on remaining unnoticed—by Nathaniel. She could see him now, those hooded orbs passing indifferently over her, to her relief. Outwardly obedient she had ever been, showing nothing of the rage and defiance that burned in her breast.

Yet it had been much easier to maintain that front, she decided, the image fading out of her inner vision, than to hold this one. For here so many sought to probe where they scented mystery.

To fail at this moment! Oh, she could *weep* with frustration. She did not want his interest. She did not want his attentions. All her concentration had been on making him see that. Surely to heaven Mrs Felpham must have done her work? And all, all to be ruined by one instant's failure.

She caught herself up suddenly. What in the world was the matter with her? Why should she be so overset at having made one insignificant gesture? It *could* have been insignificant, could it not? He might choose to think otherwise, but she would very speedily show him that he had misinterpreted the moment—even if he had not! All she had to do was resume her pose of indifference.

Pose? What nonsense was this? She *was* indifferent. She could not be so vulnerable that she could be set in

a whirl by one man's charm. Could she? If that was the
case, then there was only one thing to do. Remove from
his vicinity forthwith, and *stay* aloof for the future.

Without seeming to move more than slightly, she
flicked a look towards her mother, widening the area of
her vision. It was brief, but comprehensive, enabling
her to take in that Denzell Hawkeridge was still keeping
her under observation. She noted also that Mama, still
seated in the sofa where she had been led, but now
conversing with an elderly couple, was looking distinctly
peaky.

Resolutely, she interrupted Sir John. 'Pray forgive
me, sir, but I believe my mama is unwell.'

'Then you must go to her, my dear,' he agreed at
once, rising to his feet.

Deftly excusing herself, Verena rose and went
straight across to Mrs Pateley. One full glance at her
mother, and all concern over Mr Denzell Hawkeridge
flew out of her head. She knew that look.

Mrs Pateley's features were drawn, and beneath the
apparent idle chatter—for Mama was almost as accomplished as herself at maintaining a company face, and
heaven knew how much she'd had need of it!—Verena
recognised the tragic note that signalled the onset of a
hysterical outburst.

Throughout the mercifully short carriage drive home,
Mrs Pateley, wrapped in a woollen mantle, hung on
convulsively to the cloaked figure of Verena at her side.
Her breathing was shallow, and she was barely able to
obey her daughter's vehement plea.

'Softly, Mama, softly, I pray you! Not here. Not yet.
Only hold yourself in until we reach home.'

'Home!' uttered Mrs Pateley in a breaking voice. 'We
have no—home.'

'Hush, Mama!' begged Verena urgently. 'Don't, pray.'

'Oh, Verena. . .oh, my love. . .'

'Mama!'

'I know. . .I know. . .I b-beg your p-pardon, dearest.'

'*Don't.*'

Nothing was more painful than that Mama should apologise for what she could not help. But at all costs, she must keep her countenance until they were safely indoors. Even Mrs Quedgeley must not hear the lamentations that were bursting to erupt at this very moment. Fortunately, the woman slept like a log and was always abed early, and would besides be unlikely to hear anything through the two floors that separated her own apartment from Mrs Pateley's bedchamber on the second floor. It was thankfully rare that Mama was subject to these fits in the daylight hours.

Nevertheless, Verena's heart raced with anxiety, and she was obliged to croon and to plead what seemed like a thousand times before the carriage finally set them down at Mrs Quedgeley's door.

As always, Betsey opened to them, holding up an oil lamp which she kept lit against their coming. The redoubtable maid took in the situation with one glance at her mistress's face.

'Oh, lordy, not again!'

'Betsey. . .oh, Betsey,' uttered Mrs Pateley brokenly.

'Up you come, ma'am, there's a good girl,' ordered Betsey in a brisk whisper, putting a stout arm about the thin mantled shoulders and drawing Mrs Pateley quickly towards the stairs. She added over her shoulder, 'I'll see to the mistress, Miss Verena. Do you get yourself out of that fancy gear, quick as you can. It's going to be a long night.'

By the time Verena had changed, donning a thick

flannel dressing-robe, and hurried from her own chamber that was situated next to the parlour, and up the one flight of stairs to the larger room above, Mama's heartrending sobs were already filtering through the closed door.

'Don't—let him come! Oh, Betsey—don't let him hurt me!'

'That's enough now, that is. He won't be allowed to come,' the maid was saying, gruffly passionate.

Verena entered the room and swiftly closed the door behind her, crossing to the bed where Mama was lying hunched in a pathetic heap, weeping into Betsey's copious lap.

'Just such a gathering—just such pleasures,' she jerked out. 'They look! They look! But they do not *see*.'

'Hush, Mama!' Verena soothed, exchanging a speaking glance with Betsey over her mother's head, as shudders shook the thin frame.

The significance of her words did not escape either of them. 'It's the company,' whispered Betsey grimly. 'She ain't ready for it.'

'Too much remembered pain,' Verena uttered compassionately.

For it was all too obvious that the memories had come crashing back and Mama was not capable of the sort of control that Verena herself had mastered.

'She is too weak, too worn down,' she said, low-voiced.

'Is it any wonder?' snapped the maid grimly.

Verena shook her head. 'No, and I know what triggered it.'

'Don't we both, Miss Verena?'

For Nathaniel, as they were all too well aware, would use precisely this kind of occasion to twist the knife, hell-bent on whipping up his own demon of jealousy.

'He f-flatters me,' quavered Mrs Pateley through pathetic little sobs. 'He calls on them—praising me—speaking of my b-beauty...what *beauty*, Betsey?' A wail of agonising distress left her lips. 'What beauty have I left?'

Her sobs intensified, and tears started to Verena's own eyes. That ever-present rage burgeoned anew. Readily could she have pulled the trigger this time were Nathaniel to be in front of her now! This time her courage would not fail her. To what had poor Mama been reduced, so that even here, even now, when everything must be behind her, she could still be so easily overset? Oh, but to have him here at this moment! Verena's hatred of him would serve to make her execute the fell deed—though she should *hang* for it.

The charm of him in company! she raged. Waiting only for the moment when his flattering attentions to his wife drew others to congratulate his good fortune. And then heaven help Mama! Hot and cold...hot and cold...and here was she, knowing full well the effects of such conduct, allowing herself to be even vaguely moved by the machinations of Mr Denzell Hawkeridge.

But the task of soothing Mama into quiet—a task that occupied the two females most concerned with Mrs Pateley's welfare for the better part of the night—left little leisure for reflection, and her annoyance with Mr Hawkeridge was relegated to the back of her mind to be dealt with at some more convenient time. When she sought her own bed at last, she collapsed into an exhausted sleep, yet waking again too early and very little refreshed.

Dragging herself upstairs, Verena cautiously opened her mother's bedchamber door. Finding both Mrs Pateley and Betsey still sunk in deep slumber—Mama

always slept like one dead after these draining
emotional outbursts—she carefully closed the door and
left them. Poor Betsey needed her rest, too. Would that
she might have slept as soundly herself! Sighing, she
crept quietly downstairs and dressed quickly in the cold
chamber—the ashes in the fireplace not having had the
benefit of Betsey's early morning attention. She hardly
cared what she put on, as long as it was warm, quickly
choosing an old cherry gown of kerseymere with a low
waist, long sleeves and closed to the throat.

Mrs Quedgeley had already lit a fire in the parlour,
which was warming up nicely, but Verena found herself
too restless, her mind churning raggedly, to remain
indoors. Glancing out of the window, she saw that
although the skies were overcast there had been no
fresh fall of snow in the night. It must be safe enough
to venture forth.

Donning her pelisse and bonnet, she set out, hands
tucked within her muff, fighting a brisk wind as she
headed not for the square patch where the snowman
had been built—and where she might come under
undesirable notice from a certain unnamed pair of
eyes—but crossing the London Road to fetch up at the
Common. She did not want to meet anyone—not
anyone. She wanted to think.

Trudging with some care across the grass, for it was
still patchy with iced snow, her thoughts were not
happy. Could Mama ever forget? How long would it
take? *What* would it take? Absence was not enough, it
seemed. Mama was becoming daily more agitated at
the prospect—which she appeared to consider inevitable—that Nathaniel would catch up with them.
Should they consider going abroad? Verena had
thought of it. Italy, perhaps, where the sun might more

readily wash away the bleak memories than it appeared this winter emptiness could do.

For herself, Verena was haunted less by the memory of the painful years of Mama's misery, and more by the nightmare of that hideous last day—it seemed a miracle now that they ever had managed to get away!—and those appalling final moments, when Nathaniel had unexpectedly returned.

They had been creeping down the stairs, both clad suitably for travelling, but lightly for late summer's warmth, Verena in a cloth riding-habit and a beaver hat, Mama in a linen greatcoat dress with a straw bonnet, adorned simply with ribbon. Betsey had called to them from the hall below that the coach had been loaded up and was ready to go.

'Come, Mama, quickly,' Verena had begged, easing her mother down with an arm firmly about her waist.

Mrs Pateley, hustled into taking this terrifying step towards a freedom that she had only expected in death, was in a state of benumbed anxiety, hardly able to believe that this was really happening.

'The servants,' she muttered consciously. 'You know Nathaniel insists that our differences remain strictly private.'

'Have no fear, Mama,' Verena soothed. 'They all believe we are going to the seaside for your health.'

But inwardly she fumed. Differences! Well, let him call it by that innocuous name if he wished. It had mattered no longer. In a few moments they would be gone, free of his influence forever, and the wilting flower that had been Mama would bloom again. As for the servants, how dared Nathaniel demand privacy? By rights, his activities should have been shouted to all the world that they might have known of Mama's wrongs.

None the less, it had ever been Verena's care to attempt concealment from the domestic staff, though she had believed they must have been both blind and deaf to be unaware of the unnatural events that had taken place in this house!

'Do get a move on, Miss Verena!' Betsey hissed from the bottom of the sweeping stairs, straightening her own black pelisse that had become disarranged from her exertions.

'We are coming,' Verena returned, but oddly the staircase began to seem endless. Mama's physical weakness slowed her down, and her progress, step by painful step, began to rack Verena's nerves.

She must have sensed the danger! For barely had they reached the last stair, Mama setting her foot to the patterned quarry-tiled floor of the wide hall of the Manor, than a flurry of activity and a hoarse shout outside startled them both into immobility.

'Dear heaven, what is it, Betsey?' Verena whispered, clutching at the maid's arm.

'*Nathaniel!*'

The cry, shot through with alarm, issued from Mrs Pateley's lips. The three women froze at the foot of the stairs, three pairs of eyes fixed fearfully on the open front door. Verena herself, thrown by Mama's voice of conviction, found herself temporarily devoid of resources. Her thoughts whirled.

It could not be Nathaniel! Not *now*. Oh, pray heaven, not now. He was meant to be away until this afternoon. Adam had told her so—*promised* her. Though indeed he was ignorant of their plans. She'd had to keep him ignorant, for he would be left to face Nathaniel's wrath. And she could not permit him to become involved. Fittleworth was Adam's inheritance, his future. She could not have jeopardised that. But he had seemed so *sure*—she had invented the only too plausible excuse that Mama was in need of a day of quiet. There was no need to explain further to Adam. It could not be them!

But Squire Pateley was now even walking through the front door, his son at his heels. Both were in riding dress, booted and spurred. Nathaniel stopped dead, glaring upon his wife—all but fainting at sight of him and clinging to her daughter—as he took in the significant apparel in which she was dressed. Verena saw consternation in Adam's face. Should she have told him? Had he known, he might have done more to keep his father away.

Nathaniel found his tongue. 'What in Hades are you doing, Abigail? That coach outside—is it awaiting you? Where are you going?'

Long habit, or perhaps present necessity, moved Mrs Pateley to be the first to speak.

'P-pray don't be angry, Nathaniel,' she quavered, releasing her daughter, and holding out suppliant hands.

The abject sound, the sight of her mother cringing before him, forced Verena out of her immobility. Not that! Not one more time could she bear to see Mama's pride in the dust.

Stepping forward, she threw a protective arm about her mother's shoulders, and faced Nathaniel, showing him a countenance blazing with determination, underlaid with the fierce rage that consumed her. It was, although Verena had for the moment forgotten her habit of docility in his presence, an expression that he had never previously seen.

'I am taking her away from this house. Away from this life. Away from *you*.'

Nathaniel frowned briefly. Then he laughed—a disbelieving laugh. 'Have you run mad, girl?'

'No, I have not run mad,' Verena told him in a shaking voice. 'But I will do so if I allow Mama to remain in your power for one moment longer. We are going. We are going this moment. And there is nothing you can do to stop us.'

His face changed. Verena saw the lean cheeks darken, and shock come into his eyes. He believed her! What would he do? Her heart began to pound. Could they still go? They *must*, for if not, they would have lost the advantage of surprise and he would be on the watch for another escape. But how? *How*, when he stood there looking like a gaoler?

A familiar scowl had drawn Nathaniel's thick eyebrows together, and his lips were twisting into a snarl. Like a wild beast, Verena thought frenziedly. Mama had married a beast! Mrs Pateley, recognizing these signs, visibly quailed, giving vent to a protesting whimper as the thunderous gaze she knew so well, feared so acutely, was turned upon her.

'Going?' came in a guttural tone from Nathaniel. His chest heaved. His stature was not above the average, tending to the lean hardness of muscle rather than fat, but aroused he appeared to grow, a menacing force standing squarely in the path of escape. 'You dare to say you are going?'

'No, Nathaniel, no...'

The feeble response, hardly an answer, more the plea for mercy that Verena had so often heard on her mother's lips, sliced through her own fear, strengthening her will. She could not stop now. She *dared* not, for fear of the consequences to Mama.

'We—are—going,' she reiterated, clenching her teeth against the trembling at her mouth, her hold on her mother tightening.

Nathaniel ignored Verena as if she was of no account,

his eyes burning at the shivering form of his spouse. His voice grated on her name. '*Abigail*. Would you leave me, Abigail? I am your husband. You belong here. What of your vows? You owe me a duty, Abigail.'

At that, all the pent-up emotion in Verena erupted. 'You vile monster!' she threw at him. 'She owes you *nothing*. You have destroyed her life!'

Nathaniel barely glanced her way. 'You are not leaving me, Abigail!'

Then, wasting no more words, he moved, striding towards his wife. Mrs Pateley cried out in fear, and Betsey screamed. Verena, knowing only that she could not afford to fail now, tried hastily to shift Mama away that she might avoid him. But Mrs Pateley, terrified, was rooted to the floor. In seconds, Nathaniel was upon them. Hardly glancing where he struck, he flung the back of one hand at Verena's face, beating her aside. Then he seized his wife.

Half-falling, Verena caught at the maid, who steadied her, clucking in fright and anger, and then grabbing at Verena's beaver hat that dropped from its place and rolled. But Verena had no ears for this, no eyes for anything but Mama, held between two iron fists of a man insane with fury.

'Adam!' she screamed desperately. 'Help us!'

Her brother had seemed to stand transfixed, hardly able to take in the scene. But as his father struck out at Verena, something snapped in his head. Filial duty was forgotten. By the time his sister called for his aid, he had flung off his beaver, tossed aside his whip and gloves, and was already halfway across the hall.

At nineteen, Adam had not the half of his father's physical strength. But a flying leap threw onto the man's back, the sheer weight of the impact driving Nathaniel to the floor. Verena shrieked in unison with Betsey, for his hold was so strong that he took his wife with him. But Adam, scrambling free, wrenched his mother out of the now slackened grasp, and shoved her to one side with some violence.

Verena was on her haunches, dragging Mama to bring her to her feet, the maid at her side in an instant. She saw, with a sense of shock, her brother fling himself on top of Nathaniel, holding him down only by virtue of the fact that the breath had been knocked from his father's body by his fall.

Hardly had Verena and Betsey drawn the shocked and bewildered Mrs Pateley back onto her unsteady feet, her bonnet awry and her dress disarranged, than Nathaniel was seen to be recovering, letting out a roar more frightening than the earlier menace of his angry tongue.

Adam drew back a fist and slammed it into his father's face.

'Adam!' Verena shrieked in shock.

'Go!' he yelled, as Nathaniel's head recoiled under the blow, hitting at the hard tiling of the floor. 'Go, Verena! Take her, for the love of God! Go, go, *go*!'

Gathering her wits, Verena caught at her mother's shoulders. 'Come on, Mama! Betsey, quick! There is no saying how long Adam can hold him. Hurry, we must hurry!'

Betsey was quick to follow her lead, catching at her mistress on the other side, still clutching Verena's beaver in one hand, as Squire Pateley's fist rose up against his own son, the two of them writhing desperately on the tiled floor.

'God bless you, Adam!' Verena shouted as, with Betsey's help, she half-carried Mama, the grunts and thuds of the continuing fight ringing in her ears, and ran her out of the wide hall, and into the blaze of sunshine where the coach awaited to take them into a new life.

But it was a life, she thought, coming back to the present, that was not having the effect she had envisaged. Mama had not bloomed. Far from it. They had left, in the end, like animals fleeing a forest fire, the coach rattling down the drive at breakneck speed.

How Mama had wept, even as Betsey had tidied her with frantic haste—as if it had mattered how they looked at such a moment! How she herself had sat, shuddering in the aftermath of that horrid scene, barely aware of the pulsing throb in her cheek, beset by visions of Nathaniel, riding like the devil in pursuit, afraid every moment that all would have been in vain. Verena could only suppose that Adam must have got the better of his father, for there had never been any sign of his coming after them, and since no one knew where they were, there was no finding out the truth of what might have happened at home.

Home, she thought bleakly. In that, Mama had spoken truth. They had no home. Was it that? Was it the loss of all she had possessed, all the familiarity of the world she had known, that precluded her recovery? It could not be the loss of Nathaniel. It *could* not be that. No, no, Mama. That she would never be brought to believe. But if not that, then why, why, *why* could Mama not rest easy? It was almost as if she had abandoned any idea of life, had lost the will to live. Or was her spirit so broken that she *wanted* to die?

The thought was so painful that Verena drew raggedly on a sobbing breath, putting up a hand ready to dash at the threatening tears. The movement of her

own fingers threw her eyes into present focus, and she
gasped out loud.

She had halted stockstill in the middle of the
common, and standing directly before her was Mr
Denzell Hawkeridge, his figure exaggerated in size by a
greatcoat with several capes, and a curly-brimmed
beaver atop his tied-back fair hair. He was staring in
blank astonishment at her unguarded face.

For an instant or two, Verena stared back, still so
enmeshed in her own dismal thoughts that she did not
even remember that she must drag herself back into
that habitual iron control. But as the expressive face
before her began to react to the fact that she was aware
of him, a look of concern replacing the amazement, and
his lips forming as if they might speak, Verena struggled
to master her own countenance.

She felt inside as much turmoil as ever, but the
habitual blankness to which she had assiduously trained
herself reasserted its stamp upon her face.

'How do you do, Miss Chaceley?' Denzell said,
doffing his hat, and watching with close attention as the
ravaged features regained their former serenity.

He could scarcely believe the evidence of his own
eyes. Had he not seen it for himself, he would never
have imagined that a face could alter so radically. But a
moment ago, there was a world of distress reflected
there. Now one would have sworn that there could be
not a ripple of emotion that would disturb these placid
features.

'How do you do, Mr Hawkeridge?'

Not a tremor! Not the faintest quiver in the calm
voice with which she responded.

'You are about early, Miss Chaceley,' he pursued.

'So also are you, Mr Hawkeridge,' she returned
pleasantly.

Denzell felt curiously disorientated. How could she do that? Switch in an instant from that rigid pose, a look in her face that was almost—yes, tragic. There was not the least suggestion in her of the storm that must have been in her mind. He had seen it. He could not have imagined it—could he? Moved to test her out, he smiled.

'I confess I had no notion that my luck had changed so radically.'

'Has it?'

Did he detect a vagueness in her tone? Perhaps she had not really heard what he had said.

'From last night, I mean.'

'Last night.'

It was not a question, but a statement. And he thought a shadow crossed the still features.

'Yes, Miss Chaceley. I was too unsure of my welcome to risk a rebuff by approaching you. In any event, there was no getting near you in the Rooms, you know.'

She was not taking it in! Where was the nicely calculated response to depress his pretensions? Oh, she had every outward semblance of normality, but he would swear to it that her mind was elsewhere as she glanced up at the sky.

'It appears the sun may be breaking through.' Her gaze came back to him, and there was once again that faint trace of a disinterested smile on her lips. 'If you will excuse me, Mr Hawkeridge, I will resume my walk.'

'By all means,' he agreed, stepping to one side, and leaning on the cane he carried. He had to let her go, although everything in him urged him to hold her there, that he might probe this mystery to its depths.

Yet how in the world was he to effect any sort of communication with her? Was she truly so contained, so much mistress of herself? He allowed her to pass on, and watched her walk away, her quickened pace perhaps the only sign of agitation visible.

Shaking his head in wonder, Denzell turned his steps towards the Ruishton home, all his ideas about Miss Chaceley turned upon their heads. He had been persuading himself otherwise—or trying to!—but in reality he had begun to think her truly dull, even soulless as he had said to Osmond. But here was a change indeed!

Who could have looked upon that face unmoved? Who could have watched those unseeing eyes, reflecting all unaware the distraught message of her heart, and not been conscious of a rush of sympathy?

Seeing her pacing slowly on the Common, he had instantly recognised her. Filled with a new determination after the little triumph last night he had approached her, ready with a teasing quip that, if it had not covered her in confusion, should certainly have provoked some response. But by the time he had reached her, her steps had ceased, and he had found her so deep in thought that it was a good many minutes before she had become conscious of his presence.

Minutes in which he'd ample time both to observe the well of emotion that she evidently thrust down in company, and to discover in himself a tug of sentiment that had nothing to do with the surge of admiration that had attacked him on first setting eyes on her. He *had* felt something more. Something that had piqued his curiosity, his interest—not merely his sympathetic concern. Miss Chaceley was not what she would have them all believe. He could be certain of it now, after that first image, of laughter and warmth—and now this well of concealed emotion. What was it that had brought about that extraordinary reflection of melancholy?

The word struck him. Unice had been right! Melancholy exactly described it.

On reaching the Ruishtons' house, and finding his hosts awaiting the breakfast summons in the family saloon, he lost no time in relaying to them what he had seen.

'You see now that your instincts were right, Unice. There is something distinctly strange under the calm exterior.'

Fascinated, Unice gazed at him. 'Did I not say so? There now, Osmond. And you would have it that it is just my condition.'

'I still say so. Hawk is merely finding excuses because she will not look at him,' said Osmond from his customary position before the fire.

'I thank you, dear boy, but I had already thought of that for myself. The difficulty about it is that I cannot argue with my own evidence. I *saw* it, Ossie, as clear as I see you at this moment.'

Osmond's brows went up. 'Phew! She's hit you hard, I perceive.'

'Nothing of the sort,' said Denzell impatiently. 'Unice, I appeal to you. Is it not natural that this whole mystery should intrigue us both?'

'Oh, pay no heed to Osmond,' she said from her position on the sofa. 'He has no curiosity. I promise you I am agog, Denzell. What can have happened to her, I wonder?'

'Exactly. So do I wonder. So would anyone of sensibility wonder—' casting a darkling glance at his host who merely grinned back '—and all I can tell you is that whatever it may be, it distresses her very much.'

'Poor girl!' uttered Unice, with ready sympathy.

'Probably lovelorn,' chimed in Osmond.

'Chaste stars, no!' uttered Denzell, a sinking in his chest.

But Unice was shaking her head. 'It can be nothing of that sort. There is Mrs Pateley to be accounted for, recollect. Whatever it is must concern them both.'

'I devoutly hope you are right,' said Denzell.

'How dreadful, though, to be obliged to hide her unhappiness before us all. She must be very lonely.'

'Fiddle!' came from Osmond, but he was ignored.

It was not an aspect that had previously occurred to Denzell. It did so now, forcibly. 'By George, yes, Unice! Poor princess. I wish she was not so determined to keep me at a distance.'

'But she might not do so with me,' suggested his hostess.

'The very thing!' exclaimed Denzell. 'You befriend her, softening that icy front, and then I may—'

'So Unice is to pave your way now,' cut in Osmond sarcastically. 'Beware, Unice! You will catch cold at it if you make yourself a party to Denzell's amours.'

'Amours nothing!' snapped Denzell, with a faint resurgence of that unwanted idea of some other love affair. 'I am sorry for the poor girl.'

'Pooh!'

Denzell addressed himself once more to Unice. 'I promise you I am not looking to set up a flirtation with her. I don't think I could—now. I am touched, that is all.'

Unice regarded him in some doubt. 'Is it, Denzell? Truly?'

Even Osmond, although he grinned expectantly, refrained from comment, merely massaging his rear under the plum-coloured coat-tails and awaiting his friend's response to this. He was somewhat startled by

the vehemence with which Denzell answered, and the
serious look in his face.

'If you had but seen her! There was that in her face—
no matter its cause—that would have melted the hard-
est heart. I did not even think of her beauty then.'

Osmond shook his head. 'Seems incredible to me.
And I tell you what else seems incredible, Hawk. That
anyone could change all in a minute, as you say she
did.'

'I must say,' mused Unice, 'I find it a trifle hard to
believe myself. You are quite, quite certain that you did
not imagine it, Denzell?'

He threw up exasperated hands. 'Do you think I have
not asked myself the selfsame question? No, I am not
certain. Yes, I am, though! I swear to you, it was as if a
mask descended upon her face.'

'But, Denzell,' protested Unice, 'do you realise what
it is you are saying—that her whole manner is just a
façade?'

Denzell nodded, frowning at the vision of serenity in
his mind. 'A façade, yes. Or perhaps a shield.'

CHAPTER FOUR

THE shell of Verena's composure deserted her the instant she noted, with a swift glance backward, that Mr Hawkeridge had continued on his way. Somehow she kept her feet moving, but she was conscious, under the heavy thudding of her heart, that her knees had weakened. Indeed, she felt quite faint, and would have been glad to sink to the ground regardless of the icy clumps that crunched beneath her plodding boots.

To have been discovered thus unshielded was bad enough. That the curious eyes which witnessed the exposure of her innermost thoughts should turn out to be the eyes of Mr Denzell Hawkeridge was disastrous! Last night's little error might have been brushed aside. But how was she to pass off this dreadful display of emotion? Her private thoughts were no concern of Mr Hawkeridge, but that did not offer any comfort. *No one* must be permitted to penetrate beneath the mask of her disguise, least of all a man who had professed himself a pretender to her affections!

Her hand crept to her bosom, as if she might by this gesture quieten its uneven pulsing. She had thought herself safe this early on the Common, with scarcely a soul about beyond one or two trudging labourers. But no. *He* must needs venture out at this unseasonable hour—and in this very direction. It was almost as if he had planned it!

Although he had made no attempt to detain her when she chose to move on. The thought calmed her a little. Perhaps she was allowing herself to become unnecessarily disturbed. What had he said? Something about the previous evening. She had been too much agitated to take it in. Had he perhaps a deal more sensitivity than she would have credited?

For she could not pretend to herself that her recovery had been quick enough to prevent him seeing much of her distress mirrored in her countenance. Yet he had said nothing, nor shown that he had noticed. Indeed, she had been too much discomposed—by his very presence, so unexpected!—to fathom his reactions.

At least his appearance had been of some use—in driving away those painful memories. Mr Hawkeridge receded from her mind as the thoughts he had interrupted crept back. They had, she supposed, been inevitable after Mama's long night of tears. Hardly surprising that she had awoken so dispirited. She was still conscious of tiredness, although the fresh air had done much to brush away the cobwebs that had been clinging about her brain. How long had she been out? She had better return quickly, for Mama might have awakened by now and she ought to be there to offer what comfort might be required.

But when Verena slipped quietly into the parlour, she discovered that her mother was up, and since she was in an old muslin chemise of lilac, evidently must have dressed in as much of a hurry as her daughter had. She was, considering last night's events, in extraordinary spirits.

'Dearest!' she greeted her daughter on a joyful note, rising from one of the large armchairs before the bay. 'I have been on the watch for you.'

She seized Verena's hands in a convulsive grip, and her faded eyes, for once in a glow, pleaded as did her words. 'Now you must not scold, Verena, though I know you have cause. I *could* not confess it to you, indeed I could not. But now there is no concealing it from you any longer, and I can only beg—nay, *implore*—your understanding, my dearest love.'

Verena stared at her, a chill of apprehension sweeping through her. Mama could not have—oh, dear heaven, surely she could not have. . . The thought died. Could not have *what*? The idea she had almost allowed was rigorously suppressed as too hideous to be borne.

'Mama, you are raising the most dreadful possibilities in my mind,' she uttered involuntarily. 'What is it? Pray tell me at once!'

A new voice spoke, as a figure emerged from the other armchair in which it had been concealed, for its back was towards the door in front of which Verena still stood.

'I will tell you, Verena.'

Verena fairly gaped. The visitor was a young man of slight stature, in whose countenance the resemblance to the dread spectre that hovered over her mother's life was marked.

'Adam!' she gasped.

All through the greetings, the moments of explanation, Verena felt as if she wandered in a daze. Mama's pleading tones, joined with Adam's as between them they attempted to assuage her expected wrath, seemed to pass by her in a dream.

It appeared that Adam had driven himself here by easy stages in the gig which Nathaniel permitted him to use, to which his dark riding frock-coat, buckskins and boots, and the great-coat and beaver thrown carelessly across the chair before the bureau, bore witness.

Only half aware, Verena allowed herself to be drawn to the day-bed to sit, with Mama close at her side, and her brother taking up a position on the little footstool that she herself was wont to use, and sitting before her with an expression of great anxiety playing across his features.

'For my part,' he was saying vehemently, 'I am only too thankful that Mama chose to write to me. You cannot imagine how it has been for me, racked with worry over the welfare of you both, and having no knowledge of your whereabouts.'

'But did you look, then?' Verena asked vaguely. 'Did he?'

Adam shook his head, tutting and sucking in his cheeks so that he gave his face a look much like that of his father. 'I did not, no. I made it abundantly clear that I would neither assist him to make a search, nor make one myself. I hoped it might cause him to desist.'

'And did it?'

'No. He did stop, but it was not that that made him do so. We were barely speaking, in any event.'

At that, Mrs Pateley's eyes filled and she squeezed his fingers convulsively. 'Oh, dearest, I am so sorry! Never, never would I have sought to cause a breach between you and your papa.' A thought struck her. 'Oh, my darling boy, I never thought to ask! Did he hurt you very badly? When we went, I mean.'

'Oh, nothing very serious,' said Adam stoutly. 'At least, I promise you I gave as good as I got.'

'But he is so *strong*, Adam. I am sure you must have taken the worst of it.'

'Don't you fret, Mama. I can stand a knock or two better than you ever could.'

Mrs Pateley's hand went to her mouth in a little gesture of distress, and Adam, suddenly conscious of his own words, coloured up.

'Beg your pardon, Mama. I didn't mean to mention that, I swear.'

Verena found herself angry all at once, the fog induced by the double shocks of the morning receding fast. 'Why in the world shouldn't you mention it? If there is to be any further evidence of quite unnecessary secrecy in this room, I give you my word I shall scream!'

Mrs Pateley promptly dissolved into tears, and Adam flushed even more darkly. But he was quick to jump to his mother's defence.

'For shame, Verena! Has not Mama explained? Has she not begged your understanding? If this is the way you mean to go on, I am not surprised that she kept the matter from you.'

Verena rose swiftly, moving away from them both to stand before the fireplace, gripping the mantel with both hands. Behind her, she heard Mama hushing at Adam, as if she might prevent him from provoking his sister further. And why should she not feel provoked? Had she not reason enough? No wonder Mama had been so much on edge of late, saying repeatedly that Nathaniel must inevitably come to remove her from Verena's care. Of course he might come, since she had put the means for him to do so into her son's hands! It was not that she did not trust Adam's fidelity. Of course he would not dream of a deliberate betrayal. But he had far less control than she—a lack which had earned him many a beating that she had escaped—and she would not put it past him to alert his father inadvertently to Mama's whereabouts.

Controlling her annoyance with an effort, she turned to face them both. 'I do understand, Mama.'

'Do you indeed, dearest?' uttered Mrs Pateley piteously. 'I *would* have told you, only I so much feared to distress you—and your burdens are heavy enough. But I found I could not endure to be without my boy—' reaching out to clasp her son's hand between both her own as her voice trembled on the once again threatening tears '—without even a word from him, let alone never to have a sight of him.'

Verena sighed. 'Could you not have spoken of it to me, Mama? Have I been so unfeeling towards you that you could not find it in you to confide in me?' She regretted the hurt in her tone, but she could not help it. As she might have expected, it had the effect of making her mother's tears flow all the faster.

'Dearest, it is not that, indeed it is not.'

It was Adam who put his finger on the nub of the matter. 'Verena, you ought to know how hard it is for Mama to speak out—on any matter. Her feelings have been so crushed.'

Yes, that was true enough. It must have been hard indeed for her to dare to speak of something which she knew must meet with disapproval. But Verena was uncomfortable with the thought that, even slightly, Mama should think of her as an authority to whom she must kowtow.

'Forgive me, Mama,' she uttered contritely, moving swiftly to sit beside Mrs Pateley once again. 'I had no intention of reproaching you.'

'Oh, no, no, Verena,' protested her mother. 'You have every right to be angry. I know it was foolish of me, but—'

'Let us say no more about it. Adam is here now, and we should rather enjoy his unexpected presence. For how long do you mean to remain, Adam?'

It appeared that her brother could only be here a few days, for he had informed his father that he was going on a visit to an old school friend in order to exchange Christmas greetings. They settled it that he should take a room at the New Inn close by, but spend his days with them, Mrs Pateley extracting his promise to remain at least until Friday when she might show him off at the Lower Rooms.

Over breakfast, of which Adam partook, he was persuaded by Mrs Pateley to give an account of what had transpired after their removal.

'I'm afraid we continued fighting until the two of us were incapable of anything further. We had drawn the entire domestic staff out upon us by then. None of them dared to interfere, of course, but at the last Papa demanded his valet and they staggered away together.'

'Did he not say anything—about us, I mean?' asked Verena curiously.

'Not a word. So I did not either. The servants were left to make what they might of the whole incident. You had set it about that Mama was gone to the seaside for her health, Verena, but I don't think they long believed that. Not after the way Papa was carrying on.'

Mrs Pateley's eyes widened. 'Carrying on? What do you mean, dearest?'

'Was he drinking?' asked Verena bluntly.

Adam nodded. 'Heavily, I'm afraid. That was after he rushed around searching for you. I found out from the grooms where he went—all over the south coast, I think. For some obscure reason, he seemed to be convinced that you must be in Little Hampton, Mama.'

'Little Hampton!' repeated Mrs Pateley on an odd note.

'Yes, is it not the strangest thing?'

But Verena thought Mama looked a little conscious. What could there be in that name to bring such a reaction? A moment later she had forgotten it, however, for as her brother resumed, a more horrible possibility reared its head.

'Has he been very miserable?' asked Mrs Pateley quietly.

Adam laid down the cup from which he had been sipping chocolate, and looked at her. 'Mama, he is a changed man.'

She clasped her hands together, resting her fingertips against her lips. 'Tell me.'

Her son shrugged slightly. 'I don't quite know how to describe him. He has gone quiet—despairing almost, as if the life has gone out of him. He is drinking, yes, but he remains quite sober. I believe—' He paused, glancing a trifle uncertainly at his sister's face.

Verena placed her knife and fork carefully to one side of her empty plate. 'Say what you wish to, Adam. I had rather you did so in my presence than that you saved it for Mama's private ear so that she felt obliged to keep it from me.'

'Don't say that, my love!' uttered Mrs Pateley distressfully. 'There will be no more secrets between us, I promise you. Come, Adam. Verena will hear it with patience, and I *must* hear it. What do you believe?'

Adam drew a breath. 'That he is missing you dreadfully, Mama. If you could but see him! He has lost flesh, his eyes are constantly shadowed—I suspect he is not sleeping. He—he mutters over his glass. We do not converse, you see, apart from what must be said. He has not forgiven me, that is sure. But what I truly think, Mama, is that he cannot now forgive himself. He has had a salutary lesson, which he will not readily forget.'

'No, for he will not be permitted to forget it,' stated Verena in a hard voice, seeing the evidence in Mama's eyes of her tender heart melting already. 'It is a lesson he will remain at, though he rue the day lifelong!'

Adam's gaze came around to her, and he frowned in perplexity. 'I have never heard you speak so harshly, Verena. I know you hate him, but have you no compassion?'

'None at all,' returned Verena, adding bitterly, 'and I wonder at it that you can have any either.'

Mrs Pateley intervened. 'But I have, Verena. I do not like to imagine him in such a state as Adam describes. Perhaps I should think of going back.'

'Going back!'

Verena's heart sank. This was just what she feared! To have Nathaniel insinuate himself back into Mama's heart—in spite of all. Oh, she could scream with frustration! Now she must use all her arts to persuade Mama against so ruinous a course. Adam! She must speak to him in private. He *must* stop painting this pitiful picture—a picture that only served to harden her own heart. If Nathaniel was suffering and remorseful, so much the better!

It was some little time before she could find a moment to get Adam to herself, but at last Mrs Pateley's tiredness overcame her and Verena called out for Betsey to take her up to her bed to sleep for a while.

There was silence for a short time after the two elder females left the room. Adam, his slim fingers playing a fidgety rhythm on his thigh as he moved restlessly about the parlour, cast his sister an uneasy glance where she stood still at the door that she had closed behind Mama. Verena turned to look at him.

'Oh, Adam!' she sighed, and quickly crossed the room to embrace him, resting her head briefly on his shoulder. 'I'm so glad you're here.'

The young man hugged her close, and then took her shoulders and drew her back a little so that he might look into her face. Verena was above average height, but Adam, for all his slight build, had a little the advantage of her. His features were of a more severe cast than his age warranted, already set with lines edging shadows under his eyes—an effect accentuated by the hereditary overhang of his brow that gave to both his father's orbs and his own a hooded appearance. In Nathaniel, it was almost sinister. In Adam, Verena found it touching for the loss of the boy he should still have been.

'I've missed you,' he said.

Verena's eyes misted at the sorrow in his own. She reached up and took his thin cheeks between both her own. 'Darling Adam.'

He clasped the hands and held them tight, bringing them down to hold at his chest. 'How are you managing?'

She lifted her shoulders slightly and smiled. 'Well enough.'

'No, I mean, here—this place.' His glance travelled about the parlour in a disparaging way. 'You can't mean to live like this forever!'

Verena withdrew her hands, reserve entering her voice. 'It may not be what we are used to, but it is what we can afford on my grandpapa's money.'

Adam frowned. 'Papa ought to make you an allowance.'

'For that he must needs know where we are, Adam, and that he must not.' She grimaced. 'It must be hell for you—alone with him.'

Her brother shrugged. 'He doesn't notice me. He never did.'

'Except when you would try to save Mama.'

'I couldn't stand for it. I know Mama hated me to intervene, but—'

'I know, Adam.' Verena drew a breath. Now was her opportunity. She must make him see reason, that he would cease to speak to Mama of a return. 'And you must also know that nothing has changed.'

'Yes, but—'

'Adam! He may be as remorseful as you please. I have seen him so before this—many times. I have heard him make his promises to Mama, promises made with tears streaming down his face. But did that prevent him, the very next time he chose to suppose himself jealously injured by some imaginary slight, from raising his hand to her again? You know it did not.'

'But that was in the past,' her brother protested, releasing her fingers and pacing restlessly away. 'That was before he knew I might retaliate on her behalf. If she returned—'

'She will never return!'

'But if she did, Verena, I swear I would never permit him to touch her.'

'How could you prevent him?' demanded his sister, moving to stand in his path, forcing him to face her. It was evident that he missed them both, that he wanted Mama home. But he must be made to see how impossible it was. 'How, Adam? Oh, I believe you are utterly sincere, my dear, but only think a little. Could you be with her day and night, guard her incessantly?'

'You are,' he countered. 'I dare say there is scarce a moment when you are not together.'

'But we are only living in lodgings. Besides, I am a female. What, will you stand sentry by her bed, preventing his entry there?'

'Verena!' he gasped, shocked.

'Let us have no mealy-mouthed pretences about this, Adam,' she said impatiently. 'You know as well as I that it is precisely in those circumstances—in her very bed—that these hideous beatings begin. That is just how he managed to conceal the matter from so many eyes—even ours, Adam!—for so long. Come, how old were you when you knew of it first? How old was I?'

'Nine, ten—I don't know,' he uttered, his voice ragged with distress.

'Well, I know,' Verena told him deliberately. 'I was eight years old before I knew why my mother was so often indisposed. Why we were kept from her presence for so many days together, why everyone was excluded—except Betsey.'

Adam shifted hurriedly away, moving to stand before the big bay window, looking out with unseeing eyes. She knew why. He could never bear to speak of these matters, even when she had tried to discuss them with him at home.

'You need not recite to me all the circumstances,' he said bitterly. 'I know them well enough.'

'Yes, you know them, Adam. So don't talk to me of her going back to that life!'

He swung round. 'But she does not look any the better for being here, Verena! I swear to you, I was shocked at her appearance.'

Pricked in her vulnerable spot, Verena turned away, putting up an agitated hand to smooth at her own honeyed tresses, which she had left loose in her haste this morning.

'That is because she had a bad night. It is no use expecting her to recover from a lifetime of torture all in a minute. She is bound to suffer bouts of distress.' Glancing back at her brother, she saw a frown across his brows, heightening the hooded look.

Desperately, she added, 'Adam, she is worn down with years of suffering and dread. She is only forty years old, but she looks ten years older than that. She— she needs time, that is all. Time to. . .rest, to heal, to forget. She will bloom again. She *will*, Adam.'

She was aware of the uncertainty in her own voice, and knew that her brother recognised it. There was a hardness in his face, and his tone was almost contemptuous.

'Here? Here, Verena? Where she has no home—no life, no friends.'

Quietly, Verena answered, 'She has me.'

She read a retort in his eye, and the stresses of the past hours overtook her all at once. Her voice shook, and tears stood in her eyes.

'Don't—don't say that I cannot be enough. Pray don't say that, Adam. If I could not believe that, live with that hope, I could not go on. . .'

Her voice failed, but Adam was already across the room, his arms hard about her. 'Don't cry, Verena! I know how much you have to bear. Mama, too.'

He released her a little as he felt her struggle, and she looked up into his face, the threatening tears arrested.

'What has she said to you?'

'Verena, she knows how hard it is for you. She wants you to have your own life, as any young girl should. Marriage, a husband.'

Verena pulled away sharply, all desire to weep leaving her. 'A husband? Yes, I thank you, that I may be beaten and cruelly insulted at every hand in my turn! No, Adam. You will not persuade me that Mama could be better for a return to *hell*. And I promise you, if you tell your papa of our whereabouts you will never see Mama again, for I shall take her abroad where neither you nor Nathaniel will ever find us.'

It was not a satisfactory interview, for Adam, refusing to take this threat seriously, persisted in his arguments, painting a portrait of his father's current state that made Verena almost want to hit him. Could he not see, did he not understand, that Nathaniel's conduct was all part of the same pattern? But then Adam had ever tried to brush away what he could not bear, and being away at school had relieved him of the necessity to confront these things.

Verena, on the other hand, had borne witness to every assault as she anointed her mother's bruises afterwards; witness also to the aftermath of remorse that completed the circle of Nathaniel's vengeance. A vengeance that was, to Verena, incomprehensible—except that she knew it was provoked by 'love'. No, Mama would not go back, no matter what Adam said.

Even now, she found herself scheming how she would leave Tunbridge Wells for some other refuge, although she doubted her ability to persuade Mama to move—not now that she knew Adam would visit her here. Verena had not realised how much Mama had missed him.

If she could only have trusted Adam's unruly tongue! But he had his father's intemperate nature—though not his cruelty—and deeply though she loved him, she *dared* not have faith in his ability to keep this all-too-important secret.

The appearance of the new young gentleman at the Lower Rooms on Friday evening created more than the usual sensation. At last there was something to be learned of the mysterious sickly mother and her exquisite daughter. Not that anyone could be said to learn much, beyond the fact that young Mr Pateley was his mother's son and a source of joy and pride to her—perhaps even more than was her daughter.

'He is not nearly as handsome as his sister,' Unice reported, having been one of the first to be presented, 'but he has a good deal more of animation, let me tell you. A very pleasant boy. His mother is clearly besotted with him.'

'And what of Miss Chaceley?' demanded Denzell, who could not see his snow maiden in the press of persons gathered about the family.

'What do you mean, what of her?'

'Is she besotted?'

Unice tutted. 'How in the world could I tell? You don't suppose she is demonstrating anything more than her usual company face, do you?'

'Probably not,' he agreed, glancing across to where the knot of people was beginning to disperse a little. 'Aha! There goes Mrs Pateley, determined no doubt to introduce the paragon all around. Now is my chance!'

'Your chance for what?' asked Unice frowningly. 'I thought you said you were not meaning to flirt with her.'

'I am not.' He grinned wickedly. 'But that does not mean I will not use what weapons I possess. I mean to probe the mystery of Miss Verena Chaceley to its very depths.'

Verena, finding herself superseded by her brother as the object of public interest, slipped thankfully into the other of the two rooms which, although still remaining open, had been largely abandoned by the company who tended to congregate in the warmer one. She had not wanted to come tonight, knowing Adam's presence would give the locals more food for gossip. But Mama had insisted, and Verena could not find it in herself to cast a damper over her uplifted spirits.

She did not share her mother's mood. On the contrary, every moment that Adam remained here only brought her more anxiety. True, he had refrained, adhering to the promise she had managed to extract, from speaking of Nathaniel's state and made no further attempt to suggest to Mama that she should go back.

It was not fear of what he might say and, although

she had been on tenterhooks in case Nathaniel should have followed Adam unbeknownst, it was not a nervous anxiety that beset her. It was, she admitted reluctantly to herself, Mama's very vivacity that was making her anxious.

Finding herself alone in the room, but for two old tabbies conversing in low tones in a chair in a corner, she was conscious of a chillier atmosphere and was glad of the short vest of sky-blue velvet she had chosen to wear over the round gown of white muslin with its long silk-lined sleeves.

She moved towards the much smaller fireplace that gave out too little warmth to make the place inviting. Resting her hand on the mantel, she looked down into the glowing embers below and allowed herself to relax the stern mastery of her features.

A small sigh escaped her. Here had she toiled these few short months to give Mama some semblance of normality, to keep her from too much brooding on the past, with, it had to be admitted, but indifferent success. And yet Adam, making a wholly unexpected appearance, had thrown her into alt and kept her there in a mere two days! She could not help feeling disheartened, even while she rejoiced at it. Worse was the growing conviction that Adam's departure would bring on Mama's deepest gloom. And then what was she to do? Would Mama begin to dream of a return, if only to be near her son again?

Conscious of her own growing distress, she fought for a resumption of her usual control. Barely in time!

'It seems to be my fortune to catch you out in reverie, Miss Chaceley,' said a familiar voice.

She was so startled at his having the audacity to refer to the other morning that she looked round before she had completely mastered her features. Mr Hawkeridge, in a coat of bottle green, with black cloth breeches and waistcoat, the latter relieved only with a tracing of gold embroidery on its lapels, was smiling pleasantly. There was no mischief in his expression. What had he meant by it then?

'I do not understand you,' she said, coolly she hoped, but conscious of a tremor in her tone.

Denzell's smile grew. 'Oh, come, Miss Chaceley. You looked charmingly, posed as you are so tastefully by this fire, but you will never bring me to believe that you were not expending thoughts upon this brother you have been concealing about you.'

It was so apt that Verena let out a spurt of astonished laughter. What, could he read her mind? Swiftly recovering as best she could—though she felt as if she dragged her features back under control!—she gave him what she trusted was at least a semblance of her usual polite smile.

'I have indeed. It is some time since we have met.'

Denzell silently triumphed. She was flustered! Oh, it was all too quickly concealed, but he had got under her skin. He must pursue his advantage while he might.

'Mrs Pateley seems to be deriving great benefit from this visit. She is looking so well.'

'Yes,' was all Verena could manage.

Eyeing her, Denzell thought he detected a spasm in her cheek. Was she jealous then? Impulsively, he offered, 'It is often so with sons and mothers, you must know, Miss Chaceley. My own sister has frequently complained of the selfsame thing. She speaks disparagingly of our Mama's apparent partiality for myself, declaring that I am spoilt by it and that whereas she must struggle for Mama's good will, I myself have only to whistle and she is all affection towards me.'

Oh, but this was all too near the bone! He said it, as

he thought, to comfort her. Ironic that his words but twisted the knife. She hunted in her mind for some suitable response, all effort concentrated on keeping her countenance.

In vain. Close as Denzell was, he could clearly see the wavering of the rigid control. What had he said? Somehow he seemed to have hit upon the very thing that touched the surging emotions within her. She spoke, and he was able to define a faintly forced note in her vocal tone.

'Your sister has all my sympathy,' she said, dampingly calm and—to the casual eye—quite unaffected.

But Denzell's eye was far from casual. He was, on the contrary, on full alert, aware that to catch Miss Chaceley's truth, he must read beneath the surface. There was something between the brother and sister, of that he was certain.

He was prevented from probing any further, however, for Verena, all too conscious of the trick he seemed to have of penetrating her thoughts, was already moving away.

'If you will excuse me, Mr Hawkeridge,' she murmured, and turning, headed purposefully towards the door to the other saloon—more crowded and therefore much safer.

Disappointment gripped Denzell in a wave. Only half intentionally he called out, 'Why are you always running away from me, Miss Chaceley?'

She stopped dead. He saw her shoulders stiffen under the blue velvet and her head come up. Very slowly, she turned a little, glancing back at his face. Denzell took a step or two towards her.

'Do you fear me so much?' he said quietly.

At that she turned fully round to face him, the polite mask struggling a little. 'What should I fear?'

He did not hesitate. 'My amorous intentions.'

Verena's pulses were running riot, and she was hard put to it to maintain her calm. No man had dared to address her so openly! Nay, to *challenge* her. How should she answer him? But that was obvious. With equal candour, if she was going to match him on his own terms. She forced herself to speak in the best imitation she could summon up of her usual style.

'I have no interest, Mr Hawkeridge, in the flirtatious games you appear to enjoy. Have I not made that clear?'

'Abundantly, Miss Chaceley.' He smiled. 'Yet I only wish for your better acquaintance. Is that so wrong?'

To her own consternation, Verena found herself severely discomposed by this question. It was wrong. Wrong for her. She did not wish to become better acquaintanted. But any hint of that must make her instantly vulnerable in his eyes.

'Not—wrong.'

'Merely unacceptable.'

'No!'

Dear heaven, why must he make these wholly disconcerting remarks? It was so typical of the man, all of a piece with this habit he was forming of coming upon her unexpectedly.

Denzell moved to one side of the fireplace and set a chair for her. 'Won't you sit down?'

Feeling somewhat dazed, Verena did so. She was beginning to wish that she had not allowed that provocative remark to call her back. She should have pretended not to hear it.

To her further inward confusion—though she trusted that her well-trained countenance did not betray her!— Mr Hawkeridge did not himself take a seat near her, but remained standing to one side of the mantel, leaning his elbow thereon, and watching her steadily, his glance playing over her face and up to the golden crown which she had dragged up tonight into a chignon, banded in blue velvet, a knot of ringlets falling behind. It gave her features a piquancy that belied the steel shell of her control.

There was a silence of some moments' duration, during which Verena pleaded with the blood in her veins not to build a blush in her cheek. But it was Denzell who gave a self-conscious laugh.

'What am I to say to you, Miss Chaceley? Having succeeded in capturing you thus, I find myself at a loss for a subject.'

Amused despite herself, Verena looked up with an involuntary—and very natural—smile. Denzell caught his breath. *That* was the look. Oh, the warmth of her when she forgot the need to hide her feelings!

To his intense disappointment, it was gone again in a second. Damn this infernal mask! But she was speaking, the control more secure now.

'In that case, Mr Hawkeridge, I will introduce one myself. How long do you intend to remain in this vicinity?'

Now why ask him that? 'I shall have to go soon. I am expected home for Christmas.' Dared he? After all, he had dared so far and she was still sitting here. 'Why do you wish to know? So that you may put a limit to the extent of my importunities?'

Again her countenance relaxed. Almost she laughed out, he thought. But all too quickly she had buried it again, once more politeness itself.

'I am sure Wellsian society will be sorry to see you go.'

'Will you?'

Damnation! He had not meant to say that. But a

fleeting—very fleeting!—look of consternation rewarded him in spite of the slip. She was rattled by the question. He was willing to wager that she would not acknowledge as much in words, however. Nor did she. She did not even answer it.

'It looks as if you will be fortunate in the weather for your journey.'

'Ah, the weather,' he murmured. 'How safe a topic!'

Verena choked on a laugh. Really, this man was impossible! How unfair of him it was to attack her with humour in this unscrupulous way. It was so much more difficult to maintain one's countenance against laughter than against anger or pain. She gathered her skirts, making ready to rise.

'Don't go!'

But Verena was on her feet. 'My mother will be wondering what has become of me.'

'No, she won't. She is far too busy parading your brother around for the world to gawp at.'

Back it all came in a rush. Too fast for Verena's now lax control. Denzell glimpsed the distress before she could fully resume the mask, and cursed himself. What in the world had possessed him to bring that up? Deuce take it, how careful one needed to be with this girl! He saw her preparing to depart, and knew he had lost her for now. The oddest sensation attacked him. He wanted to seize her hand and forcibly prevent her leaving him.

'Excuse me, Mr Hawkeridge.'

He bowed, watching her go as the strange feeling began to recede. What in the devil's name was the matter with him? He had managed to hold her for a moment or two, succeeding, if not in probing beneath the mysterious façade, at least in cracking it a little. What was there in that to make him experience that intense sense of loss?

All at once he got it. Of course! It was like a reversal of his own tactic. The closer she kept her secrets, the more intrigued he became. He almost laughed at his own simplicity, becoming confused because he was caught in the selfsame trap he was wont to use on females.

But Miss Chaceley was a honeyed trap! Not only beautiful, but with depths that just begged to be explored.

As he followed her back to the other room, he was waylaid by Mrs Felpham, the eager eyes, under another preposterously feathered turban, scanning his features and casting glances to where Verena was rejoining the circle about her mother.

'Mr Hawkeridge, I am so happy to have caught you! How do you find Miss Chaceley enjoys her brother's company?'

There could be no doubt that she had seen him conversing with Verena next door. Then let him give her something to chatter about! He smiled winningly.

'Do you know, ma'am, I forgot to ask. We had other matters to discuss.'

Her eyes popped. 'Do not tell me you are succeeding!'

'In entertaining you, ma'am? Oh, I hope so.'

She coloured at his sarcasm, and swiftly excused herself. Denzell found Sir John Frinton, resplendent as ever in grey and salmon, at his elbow.

'You cannot believe you have silenced her thus, my young friend,' he said, amused.

'The woman is impossible!'

'And so am I,' said Sir John, twinkling.

Denzell grinned. 'I don't mind your probing, sir.'

'Just as well. I take it you have not abandoned all hope?'

'Far from it!' he answered swiftly, watching Verena's polite serenity circling the room. Involuntarily he added, 'Osmond thinks she is lovelorn.'

'Lovelorn? No!' came Sir John's voice without hesitation. 'A female in that condition is all too susceptible — to rebound affections, you know.'

Denzell was conscious of a sighing away of unnamed anxiety. He looked round, asking abruptly, 'Then you do not still think I am wasting my time, sir?'

Sir John raised his brows. 'How will my opinion serve you, my dear boy? You will take your own road despite it and so you should.'

'I don't know that,' Denzell said, still with a crease between his brows. 'There is *something* here. If not an amour, then — I don't know. She is beyond my experience, Sir John. I am at a loss.'

The old man's lips were thin with age, but the smile on them widened a moment. 'I know. I find it excessively amusing.'

'I am happy to afford you and Mrs Felpham entertainment,' Denzell said ironically.

'No, you are not, and who shall blame you?'

Then the powdered and painted features became serious all at once, and Denzell felt a friendly hand tucked into his arm, and a murmur close to his ear.

'One word only, my young friend. There is a fragility of which you may not be aware. Take care, in your enthusiasm for the chase, that the vessel does not break.'

The next moment, the old man was gone from his side, leaving Denzell staring after him in a good deal of perplexity.

Verena had not intended to visit Unice Ruishton again while Mr Hawkeridge was staying at her home. But

Adam's constant presence in her own parlour afforded her so much inner agitation that she found herself seeking some excuse to go out. He had adhered to his promise, speaking to Mama neither of Nathaniel's depressed state nor of a possible return, but it was Monday already, and he was still in Tunbridge Wells.

It seemed as if Mama could not let him go. A fresh fall of snow on Saturday had provided a legitimate excuse to delay his departure, and of course Mama could not think of him travelling on Sunday, and they had all gone down to the Chapel for the service. But worse than this, Mama was asking all manner of questions, and it appeared to Verena's jaundiced ear that there was far too much gossipy news from home.

The Fittleworth circle had apparently accepted the story that Mrs Pateley and Verena had gone away for the former's health, but it was clear from Adam's discourse that many had guessed the real reason behind the unprecedented departure.

That was bad enough. But the eager note in Mama's voice as she sought news of her friends and neighbours, the wealth of detail she demanded about the affairs of her household, were like tiny pinpricks in Verena's tender spot. *Could* Mama ever be happy away from all she knew? Adam had made his opinion of their present living conditions clear enough. Verena had rescued her from a life of tortured misery—but how little she had to offer beyond sheer survival!

At last she could stand it no longer, and she rose from her chair, forcing a smile. 'Mama, I will leave you with Adam for a little.'

Mrs Pateley looked up, a trifle conscience-stricken. 'My dearest, forgive us! We have been talking so hard, and forgetting all about you.'

'Oh, she don't mind,' said Adam with a grin. 'Do

you, Verena? After all, you have had Mama all to
yourself these three months.'

'But you must not feel yourself driven out, dearest,'
urged Mrs Pateley, throwing out a remorseful hand.

'Nothing of the sort,' objected Verena. 'I am only too
glad that Adam can keep you company, Mama. It
happens that I have something that I must—' thinking
fast and seizing at random the first idea that came into
her head '—I have been meaning to call and see how
Mrs Ruishton does. She has so few female friends of
her own age here, and—'

'That is like you, Verena,' said her mother warmly,
'to wish to befriend her.'

Verena disclaimed, feeling something of a fraud, but
she took comfort from the fact that Mama was perfectly
satisfied. Even enthusiastic.

'Such a friendly soul she is. It must be good for you
also, dearest. You are far too much with me. Yes, go,
Verena. Spend the morning there, if you will.'

There was nothing for it after that, but to carry
through the plan, although a full morning was scarcely
in question. She might put Mrs Ruishton out.
Besides. . .

Heavens! Could it be only now, when she was already
stepping across the drive towards the trees that
bounded the square patch of ground between the two
houses, that she remembered Denzell Hawkeridge? She
hesitated, conscious of an uncomfortable sensation in
the pit of her stomach.

A whole morning! Oh, dear, no. Not with *that* danger
to face.

But perhaps he would not be there, she thought
hopefully, moving on again. And if he were, what was
it to her? Nothing at all! If only he did not take her visit
for encouragement. Denzell Hawkeridge, she now

knew, had an arsenal of weapons to trap the unwary female—and laughter not the least of them! But she was on her guard against him. He would not worm his way under the hard carapace of her armour.

But when she was admitted into the green saloon of the Ruishton home, she found only Unice herself, busily embroidering a garment for the forthcoming infant.

Conscious of a most unwelcome sense of disappointment, Verena greeted her in her usual polite company fashion and took a place beside her on the sofa.

'I am sorry that I have not been to visit you for some little time, Mrs Ruishton.'

Unice smiled. 'Why in the world should you be sorry, Miss Chaceley? You owe me no special observance, you know.'

'Perhaps not,' agreed Verena, relaxing just a little of her stern self-command. Her smile contained more warmth than she usually permitted herself. 'But it occurs to me that we must be the only two females in the town under five and thirty, and—'

'Five and thirty!' echoed Unice, bursting into laughter. 'I defy you to find another under five and fifty.'

Verena was betrayed into a laugh. 'You may be right.'

Unice reached out an impulsive hand and laid it on Verena's arm. 'I am so very happy that you came. I wish you will do so more often.'

'If you wish it. Though it may not always be possible to remain for long.'

'Your mama! Of course, she has great need of you.'

This was a little too near the bone for Verena, and she quickly changed the subject, asking after Unice's health and the progress of her two boys. She was relieved when her hostess launched into these matters with enthusiasm, for she was able to listen with only half an ear, while keeping a wary eye on the door. She did not dare to enquire after Mr Hawkeridge, for that would imply an interest that she was far from advertising—far from *feeling*, she corrected herself.

She remained a little over half an hour, rising to leave only when Unice ran down, apologising for boring on about her offspring in a way that her visitor could only find tedious. On a sudden impulse, Verena dropped her mask for a moment, a smile flitting across her face.

'Never mind it, Mrs Ruishton. I shall feel free to retaliate one day, and you may hear instead the tedious ramblings of an offspring about her mother.'

Unice laughed, reflecting that perhaps Denzell was right, after all. There *was* warmth within the shell.

But Verena was on the move, anxious to go before *he* should make an appearance. She made a rather hasty farewell and left the house in somewhat of a hurry. She could not imagine what had possessed her to allow her mask to slip—to Unice Ruishton of all people! Might she not be depended upon to encourage Mr Hawkeridge to suppose that she *could* be beguiled into. . .into what? Flirtation? No!

But the conviction that Denzell Hawkeridge, left to his own devices, might well beguile her into *something*, remained with her as she took a route beside the house and into the ground behind, stepping between the icy patches of what remained of the last snowfall.

She had gone only a short way when the unmistakable sound of running footsteps halted her. Turning, she beheld the man himself, chasing through the back garden, his feet crunching as he came. Heavens! He was coming after her.

CHAPTER FIVE

ARRIVED at the low back gate in his path, Denzell
vaulted lightly over it, and hurried up to his quarry, a
touch out of breath, but blue eyes quizzing her from
their misty depths.

'How could you be so unkind—Miss Chaceley? Visiting the place—and then leaving before I could so
much as catch a glimpse of you!'

Verena found her own breath catching in her throat,
as if she had been running as hard as he. Her pulses
were flurried, and it was all she could do to maintain
the outward cool reserve that *must* distance him.

'Good morning, Mr Hawkeridge,' she managed,
refusing to be drawn into responding to his provocative
speech.

He grinned, bowing slightly, as he flung aside the
folds of a greatcoat that hung open. He had obviously
seized it and thrown it on all anyhow in his haste to
follow her, and taking no time at all to find his hat, for
his head was uncovered.

'Good morning, Miss Chaceley. May I escort you
home?'

She blinked, saying stupidly, 'Thank you, I know my
way.'

'No, do you?' he countered, on a spurious note of
surprise. 'Why, then you must have come this way
before.'

The spurt of laughter could not be contained. She
controlled it swiftly. 'You are absurd, sir.'

'I know,' said Denzell, and the grin vanished. 'It has

become a habit with me. And for that you should take pity on me, Miss Chaceley, and indulge me just a little.'

'What, by allowing you to escort me home?'

His face lit. 'You are so quick, ma'am.'

Again, Verena was obliged to bite down on a quivering lip. 'And you, sir, are remarkably slow.'

'How so?'

Verena drew a breath. 'What does it take to convince you, Mr Hawkeridge?'

He raised his brows. 'Of what, Miss Chaceley?'

Disconcerted, she snapped, 'You know perfectly well.'

Denzell eyed her for a moment, his gaze roving her features under the bronze bonnet. He had succeeded in rattling her, but that was not what he wanted. Yet if that was what it took to shake her out of that infuriating façade, then what choice had he? There was only frankness left.

'I don't know what it takes,' he said coolly. 'I can only suggest that we pursue the matter until we find out.'

'We?'

A slow grin entered his face. 'Why, I think so. Though I admit that for you, Miss Chaceley, it seems to be a case of willy-nilly.'

She almost laughed out again. Really, the man was too much! In spite of herself she warmed to him, saying in a friendly way that she had not meant at all, 'In that case, I will be on my way, and you may do just as you please.'

'How magnanimous!' he murmured, turning to keep pace beside her as she began to plough across the uneven ground.

A hidden dent under a pocket of snow undid her, catching the heel of her boot. She gasped as her step faltered. But Denzell put out an instant hand, grasping her arm strongly.

'Steady!'

She straightened, glad of his support. The gratitude in her smile, as she turned to him, was genuine. 'Thank you.'

His lips quivered at the edges. 'That will teach you to try and run from me!'

Verena's laughter bubbled up, but she nevertheless drew her arm from out of his grip, retorting, 'It ought rather to teach you not to trouble me!'

Denzell's features at once became serious, and his gaze held hers. 'Do I trouble you?'

A flurry of confusion was set up in Verena's chest. The automatic rebuttal came out before she could stop it.

'No!'

'I wish I might!'

Verena became aware of a tattoo battering in her bosom. She thrust down the burgeoning emotions, unaware for the moment that, though her features were composed, her eyes gave away more than she would have wished.

'Mr Hawkeridge, pray leave off this incessant badgering,' she said in the severest tone she could muster. 'I am aware that you are merely passing the time in a fashion which you apparently find agreeable, but believe me, sir, it is not agreeable to me.'

'Because you will not allow it to be so!' he hit back, out of a sudden frustration that welled up inside him.

Verena's instinct was to slam back at him, but she controlled it rigidly. She knew it for the truth, but that did not make his saying it any better! She could feel the tremor in her own voice, and only hoped that it did not reach his ears under the calm manner in which she answered him.

'That, sir, is no concern of yours.'

'I am all too well aware of it,' he retorted.

'Then I think we understand each other. Good day, Mr Hawkeridge.'

Denzell watched her walk away, cursing himself for that instant's foolish show of revolt. Chaste stars, but her control was ten times more effective than his own! How little she gave away. And how swiftly she covered over every tiny lapse. It was maddening!

He sighed, turning a trifle disconsolately for home. He hardly knew now why he was persisting. She clearly did not want anything to do with him. Why, then, should he force himself upon her notice in this ruthless fashion?

And yet. . .and yet she *had* warmed to him. Briefly, yes. But she had laughed at his sallies as she had the other night, never mind that she had swiftly damped down upon her mirth. Given time, he could succeed with her, he was sure of it.

Only, why bother? He must leave for Tuttingham soon, in any event. He had set out only to beguile the time, just as Verena Chaceley had accused. But she had proved so intriguing that some other motive seemed to have set in, and Denzell was not at all sure he knew what it was. He was not at all sure, moreover, that he liked it!

What, was he so set up in his own conceit that he could not endure—just as Ossie had said—to be thwarted in his interest in a female? It was a chastening thought.

However, it did not serve, he discovered later, to deter him from renewing his explorations into Miss

Chaceley's hidden interior. At the Lower Rooms on the following evening, whither Denzell repaired with his hosts, telling himself that he would ignore Verena if she turned up, he no sooner caught sight of her exquisite beauty—radiant, if statuesque, in a gold-spangled muslin gown that seemed to make her loose tresses glow in the candlelight—than he straight away abandoned his resolve.

Deuce take it, she was intolerably beautiful! How the devil could a man be expected to keep his distance, when everything she was beckoned to his deepest desires? Oh, but that was fustian! Everything she was? He did not know what she was! How could he, when she would open nothing of herself to his sight?

A thought struck him. The brother, now! Why not investigate there? Had not Unice spoken favourably of him, of his animation? Might he not then be more forthcoming than Verena herself? He could hardly be less so! But how to beard the boy?

His ingenuity was not called upon, as it turned out, for as he glanced about the company in the large room, he discovered that the mother having apparently been ousted from the boy's side, he was being quizzed by none other than Unice Ruishton herself.

'Unice, present me at once!' he ordered, coming up smilingly and holding out his hand. 'Or better still, go away and allow me to present myself. Hawkeridge, dear sir, and delighted—' leaning towards the boy with a confidential air '—to welcome a like-minded spirit in this aged desert!'

Adam shook hands, grinning. 'Adam Pateley, sir.'

Unice looked from one to the other of them. She had chosen to beard the boy for Verena's sake, feeling that the bud of a possible friendship with her might be reinforced if she showed interest in the family. It might

serve Denzell quite as well. Finding herself already
excluded from the conversation, she shrugged slightly
and left them. She could readily quiz Denzell later for
the gist of their conversation.

'Yes, yes, I know who you are,' Denzell was saying.
'I was commiserating with your sister only the other
day on giving place to a newer, brighter star.'

The young man shook his head, saying in a deprecating way, 'I could never compete with Verena. Mama
says that she gets at least half her looks from her
paternal side, although Mama is—was—herself v-very
handsome. . .'

Denzell carefully ignored the conscious way he corrected himself, and the stammer as he petered out.
Capital! The youth was clearly loose-tongued.

'You are then her half-brother, I take it?'

There was reserve in his voice now, but he answered
readily enough. 'Yes, on Mama's side.' He gave a light
laugh—forced, Denzell thought. 'There is little beauty
in the Pateley family.'

'But you have taken your colouring from the other
side, I think,' Denzell said easily, glancing at the bur-
nished glow of the boy's hair that was cut to rest on his
collar. Keep it casual. Keep him relaxed.

'That is true.'

The lad was not at all bad-looking, he thought, and
he dressed to advantage. The suit was all of a piece in
tones of brown, if rather too tight-fitting. Denzell,
himself attired once more in his claret coat, but ringing
the changes with black satin breeches and the cloth
waistcoat with the embroidered lapels once more,
thought that the boy would do very well in a few years
when he gained a man's figure.

He smiled at him in a friendly way. 'So you are on a
visit? Don't you find this place intolerably slow?'

Adam shrugged. 'Oh, well. It is not much different from Fittleworth, I suppose. Except that there are far more of us in the younger bracket.'

'Fittleworth? Is that far?'

'Sussex. It is near Petworth.'

'Has not one of the racing men a stud there?'

'Yes, but we don't race. We hunt, though. My father is the Squire, and so he is Master in the area.'

So Mr Pateley was alive! Then why was his wife living with her daughter in Tunbridge Wells? And how to phrase this innocuously enough that he did not put the boy on his guard?

'So you have a decent inheritance.' He grinned. 'I know what that can be like. No doubt you have all the girls of Fittleworth on the hunt for you.'

Adam flushed, stammering, 'No—at least—well, I am not much of a catch, you know. Not like Verena, though she has never shown the slightest preference for anyone. And we don't entertain—very little, in any event. Not at all now that—' He broke off in some confusion.

'Of course not,' Denzell agreed, with a leap of something in his chest. Verena had no lover! 'With your mama away, recuperating, no doubt your father has no mind to it.'

The boy looked so conscious that Denzell was almost sorry for him. How readily he showed that this interpretation of the circumstances fell far short of the truth! And how little control he had in comparison with his sister. He was tempted to let the matter rest there, but something—he knew not what—drove him to pursue it. To his cost.

'Do you find your mother in better heart now?'

An icy voice spoke behind him. 'Yes, he does, Mr Hawkeridge.'

Denzell turned quickly. Verena Chaceley was at his elbow, her features quite composed, but such a blaze of anger in her eyes that astonishment struck him to silence.

She paid him no further attention, but turned at once to speak to her brother. 'Mama is asking for you, Adam.'

'Is she? I mean—yes, of course. I will go to her at once.'

Too discomposed even to take his leave of the other gentleman, the young man departed. Verena's glance returned to Denzell, scorchingly, and her voice took on a metallic quality that was distinctly unnerving.

'I do not know, Mr Hawkeridge, if you are merely indulging in vulgar curiosity, or if you have some other end in view, but I will thank you to keep out of the affairs of my family.'

Quite taken aback, Denzell stared at her for a moment in silence. Then, from sheer amazement, he laughed.

'Bravo, Miss Chaceley! That is the first time I have heard anything on your lips other than polite inanities. Am I to take it that the thaw has set in?'

Without any warning, Verena's anger dropped right out. There was delight in his tone! Dear heaven, but had she given so much of herself away? Thaw! Then he supposed her to be melting towards him. Was it his mission to thrust through her carefully cultivated control?

Denzell watched the fury vanish into consternation. She had forgotten her countenance! There was puzzlement, too. She did not know how to take him, that was certain. He could not help but smile.

'There is far more to you than you would have us believe, is there not, Verena?'

He had used her name involuntarily, not even noticing that he did so. But Verena noticed. She noticed also a quality of tenderness in his voice. It touched something within her. Something that seemed to thrust straight into her chest so that it seemed to burst asunder, depriving her of breath. It was powerful, frightening. All her control deserted her.

Her lips trembled. Her eyes misted. And everything was in her face. The spangled gown seemed suddenly to envelop an ethereal creature, vulnerable and confused.

Remorse gripped Denzell. Without any thought, he put out a hand. 'Miss Chaceley—'

'Don't touch me!'

She stepped smartly back. The action purely instinctive, the words ripped from the panic within. She met his eyes, her own luminous, reproachful, matching the faint note of it in the husky voice with which she addressed him.

'Does it amuse you, Mr Hawkeridge, to prick at the frailties of your fellows?'

He was silenced, shattered by the appalling reaction to this lightest of teasing quips. She had laughed before! How in the world was he to guess that she might break apart like this? What could he say?

But even as he watched, unable to utter a word—for what word might not worsen the work he had already done?—the mask was resuming as she turned from him to walk deliberately away into the thick of the throng.

He watched her for some time, conscious of the most wretched sensation somewhere deep inside himself. For all her outward appearance, however, the incident might never have been. Miss Verena Chaceley was once again the polite serene beauty, shutting him out.

At length he was accosted by his hostess, interested

to know what he might have discovered from the Pateley boy. She was destined to disappointment.

'Nothing very much,' Denzell told her shortly.

Unice looked up at him, struck by his manner. 'Why, what is the matter, Denzell?'

He met her anxious gaze, conjuring up a smile. His answer came from the heart, without any previous consideration of the question, the decision ready made.

'The matter is that I must leave you tomorrow, Unice. I am going home.'

Denzell tossed off his wine and dumped the glass down unceremoniously onto the green baize table. He was beginning to loathe this incessant wining and gaming. Not that tonight's game had been serious, not when he played with his particular cronies.

He was aware that his boredom had communicated itself to his friends, for there was silence about the table, and no one had offered to begin another rubber. Denzell was thankful for that at least. Chaste stars, but this Season was tedious!

Reaching out, he lifted the half-full bottle and poured himself another glass from one of the better offerings from the club's cellars. He did not notice two of his companions exchanging significant glances.

Despising the stuffy political correctness of both Brooks's and White's, Denzell and his cronies were in general to be found, on those evenings when no other interesting entertainment presented itself during the busy London season, enjoying the more convivial atmosphere of Boodle's. Its aspect might be modest compared with those of its chief rivals, but within the arrangements were agreeable, promoting a relaxed and easy camaraderie among its *habitués*. They might enjoy its amenities in comfort, frock-coats, buckskins and topboots being acceptable wear even in the evening.

It had offered tonight, to Denzell, a respite from the incessant round of socialising that he was beginning to find irksome. And the females thrust into the *ton* for the picking! An insipid collection with a sameness that could only pall on his jaded spirit. Why it should seem so, why he should feel so bored, so restless, he could not imagine. Deuce take it, it was barely March! Yet he was conscious of a sense of frustrated irritation that grew ever stronger with the arrival of each new gilt-edged invitation.

Lounging like this—Denzell was in the *déshabillé* of shirt-sleeves—with his three particular friends, about a gaming table in one of the smaller rooms, was at least less demanding than the rest. Yet the cards lay abandoned from the desultory game of whist. A moment later, however, he wished they had gone on playing.

'Now, lookee, Hawk,' said Mr Aldous Congleton suddenly, leaning across the table and wagging an admonishing bony finger, 'ye've a deal of explaining to do.'

Denzell glanced across the table at the lean-featured face of his friend, with its long thin nose that was poking at him in a manner that filled him with dismay. Oh, no. He had been expecting this. It had been too much, of course, to hope that his lack of interest in the current Season would pass unnoticed. He made no attempt to deflect the question, but the belligerence of his voice was intended as a warning.

'Have I now?'

It did not deter Mr Congleton. He jerked the nose in a bird-like nod. 'Ye have, Hawk. Been meaning to tackle ye this age.'

'That's right,' agreed the deep voice of another gentlemen to Denzell's left.

Mr Cyril Bedale, whose large bulk formed a stark contrast to the stick-like stature of Congleton, did not attempt to move from the chair where he was sprawling, his hands folded comfortably across the protrusion of his belly under a double-breasted waistcoat, for the moment unbuttoned.

'Can't expect to hoodwink your friends, old fellow,' he observed in a tone not untinged with sympathy.

'Indeed?' Denzell said dangerously.

The word struck with stunning force in his own head. '*Indeed.*' Deuce take it, he could almost hear her saying it! The recognition blanked out all his earlier antagonism, leaving him with an inward, groaning protest.

Not *again.* If there was one thing more galling than the tinsel emptiness of this Season, it was the persistent, unwanted, remembrance of a certain person whom he had several times over sworn that he would forget! And just at this moment, when his friends were making ready to quiz him on matters upon which he preferred to remain silent. Damnation!

He pushed the thoughts away. Very well. Certain people—unspecified—did not have a monopoly on keeping their countenance in public! He maintained his languid stance, allowing his glass to dangle loosely in his fingers.

He was sitting leaning his forearm on one raised leg, which was supported on a rung of the chair occupied by Frederick Lord Rowner, the fourth member of the group, who had pushed himself back and was resting his booted feet on the seat of another chair filched from an adjoining table.

Before either of his two friends could pursue their queries, this gentleman, a puzzled frown gathering in his rather vacant, if handsome features, looked round at Denzell.

'What must you explain, Hawk?'

'It's no use asking me, dear boy,' Denzell told him lightly, and quite untruthfully. 'I haven't the remotest guess what they would be at.'

And if he had, he decided savagely, he was damned if he would explain a thing! Especially as he did not understand himself.

But Mr Congleton, his thin countenance drawn into lines of careful severity, rapped the table. 'It won't do, Hawk. Ye know perfectly well.'

'Do I?' Denzell drawled, wondering how he could find a way to turn the subject. It wanted only an opportunity.

'That's right,' repeated Cyril Bedale, blinking somewhat owlishly. 'And if you don't, we do.'

Denzell dredged up a laugh, and deliberately cast up his eyes. 'You're foxed, Cyril.'

'No, I ain't. Only on the second bottle. Can't possibly be foxed yet.'

'Never mind that,' put in Congleton impatiently, once again smartly rapping the table as he addressed himself this time to Lord Rowner. 'Lookee, Freddy. When have ye ever known Hawk to absent himself from a ball, eh?'

'What ball?'

'He means Lady Breachwood's party,' Denzell explained, adding testily as he turned back again, 'And why the devil shouldn't I absent myself, Cong? Can you seriously suggest Lady Breachwood's daughter to be an attraction?'

'Lady Breachwood's party?' Freddy repeated before the other gentleman could reply. 'Is that tonight?' He glanced down in consternation at his own person, clad like the others in raiment quite unsuitable for a ball. 'Lord, I think I accepted that one!'

Lord Rowner was known for his vagueness, and Congleton said so. 'No one could be in the least surprised that you don't turn up, Freddy—too late now, in any event—and everyone knows Cyril don't dance. But Hawk? Now I ask ye, is it like him not to present himself where he is bound to meet every debutante on the town? Not to mention the Breachwood girl, though I grant ye, Hawk, she ain't your style.'

'How do you know what is my style, Cong?'

'Ought to, damme!' exclaimed Bedale. 'Been watching you at your tricks for years.'

Mr Congleton leaned across the table again, a smile of sly triumph under the pointing nose. 'Ah, but there's more to it than that. Got the whole tale from Ruishton in a letter.'

'The devil you did!' Denzell swore.

What had Ossie told him? With Unice so close to her time, Osmond had put in no appearance in town this Season. But deuce take him for a confoundedly literary fellow! Why he must needs engage so avidly in the epistolary arts with Cong was a matter passing Denzell's comprehension. What the devil did he mean by this base betrayal?

Honesty compelled him to toss away this thought. Ossie had thought the whole affair to be merely a matter upon which he might exercise his wit at Denzell's expense. Could he reasonably blame his friend for that? It was precisely in such terms that he had begun it—to his shame and regret. Only he had not known then with what he was dealing.

Still, willingly could he have strangled Ossie! The last thing he had wanted was for his cronies to get hold of the story. Bad enough that he had thought they were seeking a reason to explain his unutterable tedium. Disastrous that they should have already found it!

Chaste stars, but how could he turn it off? He *must* turn it off. Make light of it. Could he possibly bear to be the cause of her name being bandied about the gentlemen's clubs? Deuce take it, no! He would not have that on his conscience—not in addition.

'I have no doubt at all,' he said easily, 'that Ossie has exaggerated the matter out of all recognition.'

'Stuff!' scoffed Bedale. 'If I know Ossie, I'd wager he understated the case.'

Lord Rowner was looking utterly confused. 'Hey! What is all this? What case are you talking of?'

'Pay no attention, Freddy. They're both foxed.'

'No, we ain't,' grinned Congleton. 'And there's no need thinking ye can turn it off. Ye see, Freddy, Ossie says our boy here tried a fall with a female he calls the Ice Maiden. Tried—and failed. Had to retire defeated after the first two rounds.'

'What—Hawk? I don't believe it!'

But Denzell was smiling in sudden relief—exaggerated relief, out of all proportion to the event. What had he been concerned about, after all? The matter was of no *real* interest to him. Not any more.

But if that was all Osmond had said, there was no harm done. He could admit it, pretend it meant nothing. Pretend? What was he thinking of? It did mean nothing! Brushing aside the thoughts, he drained his glass and laid it down.

'You may believe it, dear boy,' he said on a wry grin, 'because it is quite true. She wouldn't look at me.'

'Told you,' said Congleton smugly. 'Most beautiful girl in the world, too. Or so Hawk would have it. Ain't that so, Hawk?'

'Stunning!' uttered Denzell involuntarily, as the

image of Verena Chaceley leaped into his mind. Unbidden—and totally irremovable.

Verena laughing and golden, warm and vital against the winter world of white.

He was hardly aware of speaking as he added, 'But not ice. A fairy princess. . .a snow maiden.'

And she had thawed towards him! Yes, she had. An inward groan shook him. She had—until that last horrible encounter! A moment that he had tried to rend from his memory, but that still pierced him with remorse. Chaste stars, but he had argued himself silly, declaring that he could not have known that a simple joke would upset her so! But it would not do. Had he not been witness to that earlier unwitting display of intense emotion? Had not Sir John Frinton even *warned* him? He should have guessed. That he had not must be to his everlasting reproach.

Not that there was anything to be done about it. Not since he had been idiotic enough to have left the place so precipitately. Why he had done so, no amount of churning the matter in his mind could discover. He had made a stupid blunder, but it might readily have been mended. Another day, a simple apology and the thing would have been done.

It was no good wishing now that he had stayed to do it. The simple truth was that at the time all he had been able to think about was—escape, deuce take it! What sense did that make? None at all. From what was he escaping? He was at a loss to imagine! He knew only that nothing Unice or Osmond could say had moved him from his determination.

The very next morning he had left, having chafed impatiently even at the delay occasioned by the necessary partaking of breakfast. A quick farewell, and he had driven away from Tunbridge Wells as if the devil himself were after him! The only conclusion he had been able to come to since was that he had taken leave of his senses.

He became aware that his friends were eyeing him, in a mixture of wonder and suspicion. The memories faded and he frowned. 'What the devil are you all staring at?'

'You said she is not ice,' accused Bedale, 'and then you went off into a dream.'

'I did nothing of the kind!'

'He said "fairy princess",' added Congleton severely. 'And then he said "snow maiden".'

Lord Rowner jerked up in his seat. 'Snow! You're talking of Christmas. You don't mean that female you was chasing down at Tunbridge Wells?'

'So ye do know about it,' commented Congleton.

'Only what Teresa says.'

'Oh, the deuce!' Were all those closest to him determined to undo him? 'What the devil has my sister been saying?'

'Says you're obsessed,' reported Freddy with devastating candour, provoking instant glee in the other two.

'Aha, I knew it!'

'Caught at last, Hawk!'

'Says you talked of nothing else all through Christmas,' pursued Freddy. 'Says she thinks you're in love with the girl.'

'Chaste stars!' Denzell exclaimed, outraged. 'Has Teresa run mad?' In *love*? What an utterly stupid idea! And his sister was setting it about! 'When I next see Teresa—'

Dropping his foot to the floor, he leaned forward to snatch up the bottle from the table and refill his glass yet again, his thoughts tumbling in confusion and fury.

That was a female all over! Merely because he had

mentioned the matter once or twice, Teresa must needs take it into her head that he was 'in love' with the wench. Oh, he knew he had said so to Ossie and Unice, but that was in jest. Just because Verena Chaceley chose to thrust her image into his head time and again, it did not mean that his heart was touched!

Deuce take it, even he could understand why that happened! It was that last look of her—that spangled gown, the honey locks: a fairy princess, *broken*. His heart contracted, but he flung the thought away. That could not be helped. It was done and he could not change it now.

It was hardly worth oversetting himself. Verena Chaceley was—*had* been, he reminded himself wistfully—lovely to look at, and quite uninterested in Denzell Hawkeridge. So what had he to do with Verena Chaceley? Because no female happened to have caught his interest this Season was no reason to imagine that his interest was already too caught up to be available to another. The whole idea was ludicrous in the extreme, and he would have something to say to Teresa.

Glancing around the circle of his friends, he discovered them to be obviously quite of Teresa's mind. 'You need not look at me so,' he snapped. 'It's nothing of the sort. In love, indeed!'

'Well, ye can't deny it explains a great deal,' said Aldous Congleton frankly.

'That's right.' Cyril Bedale was moved to unravel his hands from his stomach and lean across to pat his friend's arm. 'No need to be ashamed of it, old fellow. Bound to happen sooner or later.'

'Yes, but it has not happened,' said Denzell in a harassed sort of way. 'Merely because my sister chooses to take some romantical notion into her head—'

'Then how do ye explain your conduct these many

weeks?' demanded Congleton. 'Ye've not set up a single flirt since the Season began.'

'Well, deuce take it, I'm trying to avoid the match-makers! With the new crop of debutantes just out, every bachelor who wants to remain so has to be careful. Besides, it isn't true. I've been courting several chits.'

'Ah, but with what sort of enthusiasm, old fellow?' put in Cyril knowingly. 'Abstracted, that's what you've been. All noticed it. Haven't we?'

Congleton nodded. 'Noticed it from the first. Except Freddy, but he never notices anything.'

Desperation lent Denzell wit. Here was an opening. Let him, for pity's sake, deflect attention from this appalling nonsense! At the same time, he decided grimly, he would have a little of revenge on Freddy for putting the cat among the pigeons in that boneheaded fashion.

'You're in the right of it there, Cong,' he agreed. 'Freddy hasn't even noticed that he's about to enter parson's mousetrap himself.'

'Eh?' said Lord Rowner, startled.

'Well, you are going to marry Teresa, aren't you?'

The other two gentlemen roared with laughter at Freddy's astounded face. He blushed hotly, blurting out, 'How the deuce did you know that I am going to marry your sister?'

'Come, come, dear boy,' Denzell said gently. 'This is Teresa we are talking about. If you must have it in words of one syllable, it is my sister who says you are going to marry my sister.'

'But, dash it, I haven't even popped the question!'

'What has that to say to anything? If you don't get a move on, I have every expectation that Teresa will pop it to you.'

This remark not unnaturally provoked a deal of

hilarity in their colleagues, further embarrassing the unfortunate Lord Rowner, who would now be obliged to endure much chaffing.

'If I were you, dear boy,' Denzell advised him in a voice of mock kindness, 'I should run away as fast as you can. I have never met a stronger-minded female than my own sister.'

Except, he found himself reflecting privately as his friends turned their teasing attentions upon poor Lord Rowner, for Miss Verena Chaceley. Did it not take a strong character to maintain that iron self-control?

A fleeting idea crossed his mind that it was this strength that had made him depart in such haste— running away, as he had advised Freddy to do. Only what had he to fear? Verena did not even *like* him, let alone wish to catch him in matrimony! Her iron will could give him no qualms.

But she was not iron beneath, came the unbidden protest from somewhere deep within him. Oh, she was not. He would swear to that! She was as soft as the snowflakes she had caught at that day to build the children's snowman.

Verena awoke to the sound of violent knocking. Starting up in bed, she sat a moment, blinking in the dark, the shock reverberating in her head as the relentless rat-tat continued.

Abruptly the significance struck her. Nathaniel! Who else would come battering on the door in the middle of the night? He had come at last, just as she had known he must.

Even as the thought was forming in her mind, she had thrown off the covers. Sweeping aside the curtains of her bed, she flung herself out of it, snatching up her flannel dressing-robe from the chair nearby with shaking fingers. There was a candle on the bedside table, together with a flint to light it, but she had no time to fiddle with that now. Mama must be stopped from going down!

Groping her way to the door, she dragged it open and became immediately aware of voices in the hall below. Mrs Quedgeley had already opened the front door!

Verena flew for the staircase to the upper floor, almost bumping into Betsey's bulk as the maid arrived at an uneven stumble at the bottom of the flight, armed with the oil lamp that always remained burning low against Mrs Pateley's difficult nights. Verena saw her own confused anxiety matched in the maid's illuminated features.

'It must be him!' Verena uttered in a harsh whisper, grasping at the woman's arm. 'Go down, Betsey. At all costs, you must prevent him from coming up!'

'Who, Miss Verena?' The maid's tone was a trifle bleary still with sleep, but matching her urgency. 'Who is it?'

'Who? Who but Nathaniel!'

Betsey's large hands gripped the oil lamp tighter. 'Not the master!'

'It must be. Go down, Betsey, for the love of heaven!'

The maid needed no further urging. With a terse, 'He'll not get by me!' she was gone, lumbering off down the passage and clumping noisily down the stairs towards the voices below.

With automatic haste, Verena began ascending the second flight towards Mrs Pateley's room. Then she halted abruptly. What if Betsey failed? And if Mama had managed to sleep through the knocking, why should she wake her—to this?

If there was a tiny thought at the back of her mind

that Mama might insist on speaking to Nathaniel, despite her daughter's efforts to prevent it, she did not long allow it to worry her. Her determination was fixed. Nathaniel would *not* take Mama back!

A piercing whisper penetrated her thoughts.

'Miss Verena! It's all right, Miss Verena!'

All right? How could it be all right? Peering down, she saw the glow of the lamp moving up towards her.

'Betsey?' she called.

'Yes, it's I, Miss Verena,' came the answer. 'Don't fret now.'

Bemused, Verena crept back down the stairs and met Betsey in the passage outside her own room. There was an intensity of relief in the maid's voice and face, eerily lit by the shadowy spill of light from her lamp.

'It ain't him, Miss Verena, thank the Lord!'

Verena blinked dazedly. 'Not Nathaniel?'

Betsey shook her head. 'It's that there Mr Ruishton, and he's asking for you.'

'Mr Ruishton! At this time of night?' Then it struck her. 'Dear heaven, it must be Unice! What has happened?'

Even as she spoke, urgent now with a growing dread—a different dread, but none the less painful—she was moving towards the head of the stairs, Betsey close behind her, holding high her lamp to light the way.

All thought of Nathaniel, of the principal worry of her life, left Verena in seconds. She had become so familiar with Unice these last few months, so *fond* of her, that the thought that something might have gone amiss concerned her deeply. The baby was not due for another two weeks or more. What could have happened?

'Mr Ruishton!' she called, seeing in the flickering

light cast by Mrs Quedgeley's own candle below the outline of Osmond's figure waiting in the hall. 'What has occurred?'

He broke into speech before she could reach the bottom of the stairs. 'Miss Chaceley, I am sorry to disturb you at such an hour, but I did not know what else to do.'

As she moved forward, Betsey at her back, Verena saw at once, in the brighter glow, the distress of mind mirrored in Osmond's features, pale with worry and fatigue.

'Oh, what is it?' she cried, grasping urgently at his lapels. 'Is she ill? Oh, heavens, tell me at once!'

'No, no, she is not ill,' he said hastily. 'Only she is before her time, and we are all at sixes and sevens, not having expected—'

'Do you mean that the baby is coming?'

'At any moment! She thought it had been indigestion last evening after dinner, but—oh, Lord, Miss Chaceley! My mother-in-law always comes to us, but she had not planned to be here for another week.'

Verena's head was reeling as these words tumbled out. But their message was clear enough. 'You would wish me to come to her?'

'I should not ask it of you, I know, but there is only her maid and the midwife—'

'Of course I shall come, Mr Ruishton,' Verena said at once. 'I have no experience in these matters, but—'

'She will be comforted merely by your presence, Miss Chaceley, I know. *Pray* come. She is having a difficult time of it and I am...' His voice failed, and he was obliged to draw a painful breath. 'Miss Chaceley, I *cannot* lose her!'

Verena grasped his hands, gripping them convulsively, for she could not speak. There was no thought at

such a time for the company mask she still maintained
towards him, although for Unice there had been some
slight relaxation. It did not seem, however, as if he
noted its lack.

Another voice chimed in, dissipating the sudden
tension in the air.

'That will be enough of that, young sir!' said Betsey
with all the authority of her years in service to a mistress
who, like a child, needed more of a nurse than a maid.
'You won't lose her, not if I can help it.'

'You'll come, too?' asked Osmond eagerly.

'Try and stop me.' In command now, Betsey grasped
her younger charge's arm. 'Now then, Miss Verena, up
we go and make ourselves fit to step abroad.' Turning
to the landlady, she added, 'Mrs Quedgeley, you must
keep watch for my mistress in case she wakes and tell
her what is going forward.'

The landlady began to respond, but Betsey was
already wagging a finger at Osmond, whose countenance, Verena saw, had lightened a little in relief.

'As for you, young sir, do you go back to your wife at
once. We'll follow as soon as may be.'

'Oh, Betsey!' cried Verena, between tears and laughter. 'You may bully me, but don't bully poor Mr
Ruishton.' She put out a hand to Osmond. 'Go back
quickly. Assure Unice that we are close behind you.'

He grasped her hand and shook it warmly. 'Thank
you. Thank you a thousand times!'

CHAPTER SIX

'ALL is well, Unice,' Verena was saying, some hours later, stroking the limp hands that lay upon the coverlet. 'Rest now. Rest.'

It had been a struggle, for it was as if the tiny infant, who had at first seemed so eager to enter the world, breaking through the natural barriers too early, had appeared to think better of the matter and abandoned the onslaught for some little while.

By the time Verena and Betsey had entered the bedroom, where the panting mother lay already exhausted by these first efforts, the natural motions had stilled. Only Unice's own maid and the midwife were in attendance, and the latter had whispered worriedly to Betsey, while Verena had run to Unice's side, grasping her hands as the poor woman fell into tears from weakness—and some fear.

'She says my baby may be dead, Verena,' she gasped.

'Oh, no, Unice! No, *no*.'

But the redoubtable Betsey would have none of it. 'Fiddle-faddle!' she told the midwife stoutly, and marched over to the bed. 'Now, ma'am. There ain't no call for you to fret yourself to flinders. Gather your strength, my dove, for you've work to do!

'And—*push!*'

It had seemed to Verena that if Betsey gave this order once, she gave it a hundred times. Poor Unice, crying throughout, and screaming now and then as the painful process proceeded to its natural extreme, did as she was told. Verena held her hands, wincing as the

129

grip tightened almost unbearably, but making no complaint, and passing a damp cloth over the sweating face whenever Betsey permitted a respite.

The odd thing was that the midwife took no offence at the interference of the invading maid, but seemed rather to draw strength from her, doing all she might to assist, until at last the troublesome little package emerged—and began to howl in protest at the rude misuse of its tiny person.

All four helpers fell to laughing in relief, and Verena dropped to her knees and clasped the author of this miracle in her arms, crying out, 'It is just as you wished, Unice! A girl. You have a little girl.'

Unice, her dark hair plastered wetly to her skull and the pillow, laughed and cried together, albeit weakly.

'A girl? Oh, Verena! But I promise you she shall rue the day she put me through this.'

Betsey, busy with towels and the hot water that Unice's maid held ready, while the midwife did her own part, overheard this and looked up towards the wan face on the pillow.

'Likely she'll give you as much trouble her lifelong! Girls, ma'am, are ten times worse than boys in the bringing up, be they never so much sugar and spice.'

'Then shall her father be the sufferer, not me,' Unice uttered into the general laughter.

She was quiet for some time after this, dozing a little although she was not yet able fully to sleep, while Verena soothed and petted her, wringing out the flannel in the fresh bowl of water brought by Unice's maid, and wiping away the damp stains on the exhausted features, smoothing the lank hair, and stroking the lax fingers.

At length, Unice's eyelids fluttered open again. She turned her head to her friend. 'Verena, take her to

Osmond, pray. He does not say it, but he wanted a daughter so much.'

But Betsey insisted that Miss Ruishton must first be presented to her mama. And once the tiny squalling babe was put into her arms, Unice was indeed reluctant to allow her to be removed. This time it was the midwife who called the tune.

'Madam and I have some matters here to finish, miss,' she said to Verena. 'It would be a kindness in you to take the babe away for a spell. Your good nurse here and I will make the lady presentable for her husband.'

Verena might be unfamiliar with the business of childbirth, but she knew there were necessary things to be done after the baby was born. Unice, already a veteran, made no objection, although she kissed the infant and sighed as she reluctantly permitted Verena to lift the bundle from the bed.

'Don't fret, Miss Verena,' Betsey whispered. 'She needs her peace now, for all she may not think it.'

Outside the room, Verena abruptly realised that Osmond must still be worrying downstairs. They had none of them thought to send down to the poor man to relieve him in his concern. She hurried a little on the thought, the now sleeping baby tucked securely in her arms.

She found Osmond Ruishton standing in the middle of the saloon, in a listening attitude as if he waited to know if the footsteps betokened any more than Unice's maid once more going for fresh water. He no soooner saw the little bundle than his hand went up to his mouth. Verena saw him bite into his hand and instantly understood that he was unbearably anxious.

'All is well,' she said quickly, coming into the room. 'Have no fear, Mr Ruishton, all is well. See! You have the most beautiful little daughter.'

But Osmond's first glance passed over the tiny face that she uncovered almost unseeingly. With painful intensity, his eyes locked onto Verena's, and he uttered only the one word.

'Unice?'

'She had a severe struggle, but it is over. She will do very well in a few hours, I promise you.'

His shoulders sagged as a hoarse whisper left his throat. 'Oh, thank the Lord!' Then he dropped into the nearest chair and threw his hands over his face.

Moved, Verena gazed at him. How deeply he cared for his wife! So much so, that the baby was as nothing compared to his need to hear news of her.

But in a moment Osmond had mastered his emotion. His hands dropped and he looked up, a smile beginning in his eyes. 'Forgive me, Miss Chaceley. I have been so anxious.'

'Oh, pray don't ask my pardon! It is very understandable.' She paused, and then added hesitantly, 'You must—you must love her very much, Mr Ruishton.'

'She is my life,' he said simply.

Verena stared, tears gathering in her own eyes. *Could* a man feel so strongly? And if he did, could he be—she hardly dared to think the word—gentle?

Osmond was rising, coming towards her, his eyes on the infant whose passage into the world had been so very stormy.

'And so this is my daughter?'

Verena made haste to offer the child, holding it out towards him. But Osmond only reached out a finger and gently ran it down the smooth baby cheek, red still and tightly muscled from its recent exertions. Watching his face, Verena saw him smile. Then he turned his finger and the tip just gently brushed the minute lips.

'How do you do, Miss Ruishton?' he said softly.

'What shall you call her?' Verena asked.

'Oh, that will be Unice's privilege,' he said, his eyes still on the infant's mouth.

Then he drew back, and a great sigh escaped him as he looked up again to Verena's face. 'Will they have finished? Do you think I may go to her now?'

'Yes, of course. At least—' She gave an odd laugh. 'I beg your pardon, Mr Ruishton, but I do not know. I think it may be all right.'

'She will need me,' he said firmly. 'And, by Jupiter, I have great need of her!'

Then he turned, and walked quickly out of the room. Verena watched him go, feeling utterly confused. For the first time in her life, standing there in a soiled muslin gown—the first that came to hand in her haste—and left for the moment in sole charge of a newborn infant, she wondered if perhaps it might be possible that a man and a woman could enjoy true happiness in marriage.

A vision sprang full-blown into her mind. A vision of an expressive countenance, a teasing light in its eyes of misty blue, and a smile on its lips that turned her knees to water.

Verena sank down onto the sofa, nursing the baby against her breasts. Why him? Why his face at such a time? She had not thought of him in weeks. Or at least, she amended, she had tried not to think of him. She had banished him from her mind forever that day—the day that Unice and she had become a little more than acquaintances.

He had left abruptly, Unice had told her, obviously distressed. Verena had been unable, for the quite unforeseen emotions that she herself was experiencing on hearing of the man's departure, to respond in any suitable way. For her heart had stilled, and a hollow opened up inside her chest.

Unice had seen it, or had seen some reaction in her face—unguarded for a moment—and remarked upon it. Verena had ended by telling her just what had occurred that night, expressing her regret if any words of hers—stupid words, provoked by some strange emotion she did not herself understand—had been the cause of Mr Hawkeridge's decision to leave. Unice had been quick to pooh-pooh any such suggestion, saying that Denzell must have had reasons of his own of which neither of them knew anything.

It had been a small opening up on Verena's part. But it had been enough. Warming to Unice, she had found herself succumbing more and more to the temptation to drop the mask. Only once had Unice spoken of it.

'Dear Verena, I know there is some urge that makes you poker up in public. But pray don't feel you have to hide your feelings with me. I will ask no questions. Only do not shut me out, Verena. I so much want to be friends.'

Touched, Verena had only pressed her hand, and thereafter had resumed her mask only when others were present, including Osmond. They had not discussed Mr Hawkeridge again, although Unice would from time to time let fall an item of news concerning his activities in London.

Verena persuaded herself that she was not interested. *Had* so persuaded herself. Then why now, in these truly unusual circumstances, should he thrust himself into her thoughts uninvited?

She looked down again into the newborn features of the little lady in her arms, cradling the infant closer. To be sure, it had been a hideous entry, but it was over now—and the result! Oh, but what joy it must be to be entrusted with a tiny soul such as this. To hold a new life close, to nurture it thus, sweetly at the bosom, giving of oneself even to the provision of its daily food.

Her eyes pricked. This was not for her, could never be. For she had dedicated her life to Mama's salvation, and sworn never to marry. Never to permit that intimacy—of which, despite her maiden innocence, she knew altogether too much!—that might have given her *this*.

A shadow at the door brought her eyes up. Unice's maid stood there. She dropped a curtsey.

'I've come to take the babe up, ma'am.'

She came forward. As of instinct, Verena's arms tightened about the bundle she held. The oddest feeling of possession engulfed her. She did not want to let the baby go! But the maid was before her, arms held out expectantly.

Verena looked once more into the sleeping face. This is Unice's baby, not mine, she told herself. *Not mine*. She must give it up.

Her clasp loosened. The bundle shifted, and the waiting hands removed it from her arms. A pang shot through her, as she watched the maid walk from the room, taking the baby away. It was as if she took with her a part of Verena's heart.

Bereft and confused, Verena simply sat there, in a kind of daze. What was the matter with her? How could so little a creature be responsible for so great a sense of loss? The child was not even hers! She had never wished for children—had she? Not if it meant she must marry, put herself into the selfsame position in which Mama had suffered so.

But Unice seemed happy, a small voice whispered at the back of her mind. She could almost imagine the scene upstairs. Unice lying with the babe in her arms, and Osmond sitting at her side, looking down upon his wife with the eyes of love. She was his *life*. That was what he had said.

Abruptly the vision changed. Verena herself was lying there, the baby hers. And the man who sat beside them wore the face she had sworn she would not remember. Verena found herself shaking.

Movement on the periphery of her vision made her glance up, blinking. In the doorway stood two little nightshirted boys, their young faces pale and uncertain. Felix and Miles! They had woken, disturbed by the strange happenings in the night. Her heart contracted. Poor, frightened little boys! Instinctively she held out her arms, and they ran to her, nuzzling into her and bursting into sobs.

'Hush, now, hush!' she crooned, all thought of her own confusions swept away. 'There is nothing to be afraid of. Listen to me, both of you. Your papa will come presently, but he is with your mama just at this moment. And he has the most wonderful news. Do you wish to know what it is?'

Two small faces, the tears smudged away by knuckling hands, looked up at her expectantly. Verena smiled warmly.

'God has brought you a little sister.'

That was enough for Felix. Questions rained on Verena, and Miles climbed into her lap, sticking a thumb in his mouth and preparing to sleep again, satisfied with an explanation, even though its significance was beyond him.

A few moments later, when Osmond appeared in the doorway, the two boys leaped up and ran to their father, who lifted them bodily from the floor, both together, and hugged them, laughing in an excess of joy, repeating the momentous news.

Verena discovered that tears were pouring down her face. Osmond saw it, and hastily put the boys down, coming quickly towards her, his children at his heels.

'Miss Chaceley! Why, what is the matter?'

But Verena was smiling, even while she hunted in the hidden pocket of her gown for a handkerchief. 'Pay no heed to me, Mr Ruishton! It is—it is merely an expression of—of joy. I am so happy for you!'

Osmond reached out and, leaning over her, took both her hands in his. 'I cannot thank you enough, Miss Chaceley.'

'Oh, don't!' begged Verena. 'It may seem an odd thing to say, but I have—I have had so much *pleasure* tonight.'

She returned the pressure of his hands, and then let them go, using the handkerchief to dry her eyes. Smiling, she added, 'I think we may dispense with formality after this, don't you, Osmond?'

Osmond laughed. 'You are a remarkable female— Verena.'

Felix and Miles were clinging to his legs. Detaching the younger boy, he lifted him up into his arms again, and took the other by the hand. It was obvious that his joy in his family was unbounded.

'I can only say, Verena, that I wish fervently that you might one day know the happiness I am experiencing tonight. Marriage is bliss, you know. I can thoroughly recommend it.'

From a few feet away, Denzell watched his sister's face as she turned to whisper to her new husband. Chaste stars, but Teresa was radiant! He had thought her determined pursuit of poor Freddy to have been for the advantage of position, but he was clearly wrong. And Freddy himself. One only had to look at him!

Lord Rowner, receiving the murmurs of his bride into his ear, responded with a glowing look that told its own tale. An unexpected pang smote Denzell. This was a *love* match. Though why it should affect him in such a way he was at a loss to imagine. He should be happy for them. He *was* happy for them—for Teresa. At least one Hawkeridge could look forward to a rosy future.

He turned away on the thought, conscious that for some little time now he had himself been something less than happy. He was hanged if he knew why! Life had somehow become empty, meaningless. Deuce take it, but it was a ridiculous state of affairs! He had everything he could want, did he not? What more could there possibly be? Trying to shrug off the mood, he threw himself into the business of the day.

The wedding breakfast celebrating the nuptials of the new Lady Rowner was held, as was proper, at Tuttingham, in the home of the lady's parents. Hawkeridge Hall, the Baron's seat, was a pleasantly old-fashioned edifice, erected in the days of Queen Anne before the Palladian craze had swept the country. It was solid, but not imposing, of good proportions, and much more comfortable to inhabit than the windswept baronial hall that had preceded it.

The gardens, tending rather to the natural than the formal, were admirably suited to occasions of this kind, and the guests, having eaten and drunk of their host's plenty, had been invited on this warm summer day to amble the lawns, studded for the purpose with pockets of chairs and tables for the comfort of the less energetic.

Denzell's duties as son of the house—attired for the occasion in a suit that was for him unusually bright in colours of russet brown over apricot and cream—had kept him sufficiently occupied to set uncomfortable thoughts at bay for the moment. Later, as he was taking a respite, enjoying the idle jocularity of his particular friends—including Osmond who had travelled up for the occasion—he was hailed by another young man.

'Hawk, old fellow! I have not seen you this age. I suppose you have been gallivanting in London all winter.'

Turning, Denzell beheld a lad some years his junior, extremely smart in the blue coat with buttoned-back revers and white breeches of a naval lieutenant. He grinned and came forward to shake hands.

'And I must suppose that you, Kenrick, have been sailing the high seas.'

'Alas, yes. Nothing but the sea for us Chaceleys, you know.'

Denzell stared at him, stricken to silence. A hollow seemed to have opened up inside him. Deuce take it, why had he not thought of it before? Chaceley! Verena Chaceley. And here he had a whole swarm of that name on his very doorstep.

Pittlesthorp Place was but a mile or two away, near to Ivingho, but so close that all the Chaceley boys had been the neighbouring companions of his youth. So much a part of his background were they that their own names—Kenrick, Fulbert and Walter, to call but three to mind—were perhaps too familiar for him to be recalling their family name.

Kenrick Chaceley was blinking at him. 'What in thunder ails you, Hawk? Look as if you had seen a ghost!'.

Denzell felt almost as if he had. A need, urgent and compelling, forced him out of his abstraction.

He grasped the young lad's arm. 'Kenrick, bring me to your grandfather. I have the greatest desire to renew my acquaintance with him.'

'You must be mad!' uttered the young gentleman,

standing firm. 'My whole desire is to keep as far away
from the old tartar as possible. If you want him, you go
and find him for yourself.'

'Oh, come, he's not as bad as all that.'

'No, he's worse!' retorted Kenrick. 'He may not bite
your nose off, but then you ain't related to him.'

Denzell smiled over the unnatural impatience that he
felt. 'Dear boy, I am convinced he cannot even notice
you among so many.'

'That's just what I rely on. I thank God I am not the
eldest, for although a naval career is not precisely what
I would have chosen, at least it keeps me away. Poor
Fulbert is obliged to remain, just as my father is.'

Yes, and his reverend Uncle Hartley had the
Pittlesthorp living, Denzell remembered, so that his
cousin Walter must be much under old man Chaceley's
eye. There were several females, too, were there not?
They were all in attendance at the wedding, even the
Chaceley sisters, who had moved away on their
marriages, returning with their families to make an
appearance here.

'Lord, yes, I had not thought!' Denzell said. 'Your
house must be pretty full at this present.'

'Bursting at the seams,' said Kenrick cheerfully.
'Which is all to the good. Grandpapa has too many
distractions to be concerning himself over one insignificant naval officer.' He tapped his own chest. 'Me.'

Denzell glanced around them, saw with satisfaction
that his friends were all deep in discussion, and pulled
Kenrick apart, obliging him to walk as he said in an
urgent undervoice, 'I have something I particularly wish
to ask you.'

'What?' demanded Kenrick, intrigued.

'Have you any relatives down Sussex way?'

Kenrick frowned. 'Not that I know of. Why?'

'Are you sure?' urged Denzell, ignoring the question.

'Sure? No! How in thunder should I know all the ins and outs of the family? My grandfather was one of five, and I can't account for the half of them.'

'Oh,' said Denzell, slightly dashed. 'Damnation! Then it might go years back, and you would not know of it.'

'Talking in riddles, old fellow. I wish you'd tell me what's in your mind.'

Denzell suddenly wondered why he was doing this. If Verena Chaceley had wanted him to investigate the ramifications of her family, no doubt she would have asked him to do so. Yes, when the moon turned to green cheese! What the devil was he *doing*?

He shook his head. 'It does not matter. I met some-one—but it is not important.'

Kenrick's interest was not so readily depressed, how-ever. 'What, you mean you have met a Chaceley? In Sussex?'

'No, in Tunbridge Wells, but—'

'Tunbridge Wells! Lord, Hawk, what in thunder took you to a tumbledown rack of a place like that?'

Denzell grinned. 'I know. Though it is quite a thriving community these days, you must realise—if aged on the whole. My friend Osmond Ruishton lives there.'

'He must be mad!'

'Probably.'

Kenrick slapped his shoulder. 'Tell you what, Hawk. We'll ask my father. Knows the family tree inside out, does my father. Ten to one, though, there ain't no Chaceley in Tunbridge Wells.'

But Bevis Chaceley, when accosted by his son, could not enlighten them. Could not, or would not? Denzell wondered, the urgency returning despite himself. Had there not been even a slight reaction from the fellow?

Kenrick's father was a handsome man of middle

years, running a little to the portly, but still able to cut a fine figure in a suit of green-toned ditto. He was a calm personage, with a pleasant manner and a generally easy temperament. Although Denzell knew Bevis Chaceley for a stern parent, he was not as rigid in his views as old man Chaceley.

'Sussex!' he exclaimed, as if there was meaning in it.

Something leapt in Denzell's chest. He knew something!

But then the gentleman frowned a little, pursing up his lips. 'What part of Sussex?'

'A place called Fittleworth,' Denzell answered, an odd sensation inside him, as of a hunger—for information.

Bevis shook his head. 'I think not. It may be some other family.' He smiled. 'We are not the only Chaceleys to bear the name, my boy.'

Denzell scarcely had time to register the disappointment that attacked him before a new voice interrupted them.

'Ha, young Hawkeridge!'

It was a gruff voice, proceeding from an elderly gentleman, poker stiff, with the figure of a much younger man, but a defiant show of his own grizzled head and well-cut clothing in keeping with the times. Armed with a cane, which he leaned on but slightly, he walked slowly towards them, at his heels two matronly ladies in whom Denzell recognised Mrs Esther Chaceley, wife to Bevis, the heir, and Mrs Camilla Chaceley, the Reverend Hartley's helpmeet.

Recovering his company face, Denzell greeted them all with a mixture of deference and bonhomie, which sat well with the ladies, at least. It did not appear to do him any harm in old Mr Chaceley's eyes, either. The patriarch seemed well pleased, and the reason was soon established.

'Mean to congratulate your mother, boy. She's done excellent well by her girl, excellent well. Rowner, eh? It's a good match. Very good match, indeed. Well done!'

Denzell took the hand held out to him, and found himself the recipient of a hearty, and surprisingly strong, handshake.

'I thank you, sir, and have no hesitation in accepting your words of praise to myself. Lord Rowner is a close friend of mine, and if there has been any matchmaking, I must take all credit, for Teresa met him through me.'

A bark of laughter from the old man rewarded him, and the ladies tittered.

'For shame, Denzell!' scolded Mrs Esther Chaceley, closing her fan and rapping his hand. 'You will not pretend that it is not your mama who has brought him up to scratch.'

'No, I will not, ma'am,' agreed Denzell. 'The truth is that it is Teresa herself who brought poor Freddy up to scratch, without any assistance from anyone else.'

The gentlemen hugely enjoyed what they took to be a joke, while the ladies shrieked and scolded, Mrs Camilla Chaceley going on to tease Denzell that his turn must be next. An idea that, for some reason, instantly clouded Denzell's amusement. He maintained a cool front, however.

'Quite right,' approved old man Chaceley. 'How old are you, boy? More than twenty, I take it.'

'Five and twenty, sir.'

'High time, high time.' He raised a stiff finger. 'But make a good match, boy. Good match. Most important thing in the world. Now, I must kiss the bride, eh?'

With another of his mirthful barks, he went off, accompanied by his acolytes.

'Good match,' muttered Kenrick in Denzell's ear. 'That's all he cares about!'

'Don't most men of property?' Denzell asked mildly, still struggling against the unwelcome resurgence of his earlier sombre mood.

'Precisely,' agreed Bevis, who had not followed his father. He nodded at Denzell. 'I'm glad you spoke up for yourself, my boy. My father likes that in a fellow. He never could stand a show of weakness.'

'Never could stand anything that went against his inclinations,' murmured Kenrick as his father moved away. 'Prideful old... Well, I shall not say what I wish to call him. But I give you my word, old fellow, you would not believe the mean-spirited actions that he has taken on account of this obsession he has with a *good match*.'

'Oh?' queried Denzell, sudden interest driving away his abstraction. 'What sort of thing do you mean?'

But there was to be no answer to this question. Bevis Chaceley had apparently overheard his son, and he stepped back smartly, frowning heavily.

'That will do, Kenrick! It does not become you to speak of your grandfather in such terms.'

Kenrick had the grace to blush, murmuring, 'I beg your pardon, sir.' But he grimaced at Denzell behind his father's back as that worthy turned to him.

'My boy, you spoke of someone you met of the name of Chaceley. I was just wondering, was it a gentleman, or...?'

He ended on a note of interrogation, one eyebrow raised. Denzell's senses came fully alert. Was there something to be discovered here after all?

'No, sir,' he answered readily. 'A lady. A Miss Verena

Chaceley. She was residing with her mother in lodgings in Tunbridge Wells.' He added on a deliberately casual note, 'It is a curious situation.'

'Indeed?'

It was given its usual courteous inflexion, but the question was implicit. He wanted to know more! Like a hound to the scent, Denzell took the plunge. He had nothing to lose, and perhaps—with a lurch of the stomach that he did not even pretend to try to understand—everything to gain.

'Very curious, sir. The mother has remarried, it seems, for she is now called Pateley.'

'Pateley,' repeated Bevis, his tone flat.

Recognition? Denzell did not think so. But there was still interest.

'Yes, sir,' he continued. 'There is a brother on the Pateley side, and the husband is still alive. The conclusion one is forced to is that Mrs Pateley is at the spa for her health, for she is not by any means in plump currant, but—'

He stopped, wondering all at once why he had begun this at all. Bevis Chaceley's expression was blank. There was nothing here to shed any light on Verena's mystery. Oh, deuce take it, Verena! *Still* in his thoughts?

He would have abandoned the matter then. Turned it off, and rushed away to busy himself so hard that the image playing about his inner vision must fade.

But Bevis did not seem to be in a mind to let the matter drop. He raised his brows in a compelling question. 'But?'

Denzell gave an inward sigh, and shrugged. 'Sir, I hardly know how to answer you. Except to say that from my experience of Miss Chaceley—which was not, I grant you, very much—it seems clear that there is some point of contention. I don't know what. But there is in Miss Chaceley. . .' There was a tightening in his chest as it all came back to him.

With a roughening of his tone, he resumed, 'There is both fear and distress. That is all I can tell you, sir.' He paused, and then, as if compelled, he asked again, 'Are you sure she is no relation?'

To his sudden, intense disappointment, Bevis Chaceley laughed in a way that left no room for doubt. He knew nothing! Or at least, that was how he wished it to appear.

'My dear boy,' he said, 'how could I tell? There are innumerable Chaceleys in the world, as I mentioned before.'

Kenrick nodded. 'Hoards of them! I should think even my grandfather does not know them all.'

Denzell eyed them both, wondering if he should pursue it. But to what end? The matter was resolved for him. A servant arrived with precisely the sort of distraction he needed. Teresa had gone to change her dress and his mother wished to speak to him.

By the time he had run the particular errand requested of him by Lady Hawkeridge, the encounter with the Chaceleys had temporarily faded from his mind. It was recalled abruptly at a moment when he was gathered with his cronies as they were taking their leave of the bridegroom, with much ribald comment amid their good wishes for his future.

'Mark my words, Freddy,' warned Osmond, 'your troubles are just beginning. Only wait until the children arrive!'

'This from a man who, by all accounts, dotes on his offspring,' scoffed Aldous Congleton.

'Dotes? He is besotted!' commented Cyril Bedale.

'Exactly,' Denzell put in. 'Pay no attention, Freddy.

You should have heard him eulogising over his new daughter.'

But Freddy was blushing. 'It is early days to be thinking of children. I just want to enjoy—I mean, *we* only wish—'

'Softly, dear boy, softly,' Denzell said gently over the sniggers of the other two. 'We perfectly understand you. Only, as your brother-in-law, I feel compelled to warn you to begin as you mean to go on, and insist on having the mastery in your own home. Otherwise, dear boy, you will assuredly live under the cat's foot.'

'Yes, don't show her you're besotted,' advised Cyril.

'No, no,' protested Freddy loyally. 'What I mean is, Teresa is devoted to me.'

'She may be as devoted as you please,' said Denzell, 'but that will not prevent her from wishing to rule the roost.'

'Lookee, Freddy,' broke in Congleton. 'Take a lesson from Ossie here. Everyone knows he is utterly under his wife's thumb!'

This was so nonsensical an idea that everyone roared, and Freddy himself took heart. Denzell, assuring him that he was only jesting, slapped his brother-in-law on the back and wished him well, and young Lord Rowner was sent on his way with the goodwill of his friends ringing in his ears.

'Now then!' said Cyril Bedale, as soon as the bridegroom was gone. 'I had forgot with all this attention on Freddy, but now is the moment to seize opportunity. You must satisfy our curiosity, Ossie. Tell us all about Hawk's snow maiden.'

Denzell's heart lurched.

'Snow maiden?' repeated Osmond blankly.

'This girl you wrote of,' explained Congleton.

'They mean Verena,' Denzell put in, conscious of a

frenzy in his own pulse. For it had come to him belatedly that Ossie had come up from the very place where Verena Chaceley was living. Or was she? Chaste stars, let her not have removed from there!

But Osmond had turned on the name, seizing his friend's shoulder. 'If I had not forgot! Hawk, I had meant to give you an account of it. You would not believe what a warm heart beats under that icy front. Oh, she is on the highest pedestal in our establishment, I promise you!'

Denzell became aware of a drumming within his chest and his mind blanked. With difficulty, he asked, 'What do you mean, Ossie?'

'I am talking of Verena! She came to us that night, when Unice was brought to bed. At least, I went to fetch her, for she and Unice had become friends. I swear to you, if she had not been there—she and that maid of hers—I don't know what we would have done! She was kindness itself—and her gentleness with Unice, with the boys. . .' He shook his head in wonder.

'Snow maiden, eh?' said Congleton, in a teasing tone. 'Sits well on her, it seems—eh, Hawk?'

But Denzell hardly heard him. The oddest occurrences were taking place inside him. Warmth burgeoned so strongly that he felt it as expanding heat racing through his veins. The vision that had haunted him—that golden, glowing image of vivacity!—was playing in his head. And then, throwing it all out of gear, the picture of her lovely face, the mask shimmering into fragments.

He had known it! All the time he had known it. She was as soft as he believed. It was all a *sham*, a shield erected against the world. To protect herself—poor, sweet, *aching* princess. What a cursed fool he had been! Briefly, he thought again of the Chaceleys. A surge of something unnameable set his chest almost to bursting. It was—ludicrously, for he had no real reason to think it, he knew—as if Bevis had disowned her.

The turmoil inside him had coalesced into a single, driving need. The same intolerable urgency that had made him leave Tunbridge Wells. Only this time, it was having an opposite effect.

He seized his friend's arm. 'Ossie, is she still there?'

'Of course she is. She visits Unice every day.'

A long sigh escaped Denzell, and he rocked back on his heels, smiling at his friend. 'In that case, dear boy, you may expect me for the Season.'

There were shouts of triumph from his cronies, but he did not care. It was as if a mist had lifted, and he knew now what he must do.

Osmond cocked an eyebrow. 'Oh, I may, may I? I suppose I need not ask why.'

Denzell grinned, light of heart all at once. 'That, dear boy, is obvious. I must pay my respects to the new Miss Ruishton!'

Tunbridge Wells in August, at the height of its Season, was a very different matter, Denzell discovered, from the dreary place he had visited at Christmas last.

For one thing, here he was, having barely swallowed his breakfast, already abroad among the brightest of chattering company, having been dragged down to the Pantiles by a determined Unice, eager to thrust her prize into notice. Whose particular notice he did not enquire too closely, but he was conscious of a thrill of anticipation that threatened to swamp him before ever he caught sight of the face that had been haunting him so diligently all this while.

The main venue for most of the Season's events had, in addition, shifted to the Upper Assembly Room, where the heat of summer was the better accommodated in the more spacious edifice, and the brave colours of past fashions—many elderly matrons despising the white muslin now so prevalent among the London belles with their extraordinary high waists—were set off by the superior ornamentation.

Denzell's own town apparel—a dark blue cloth coat over the latest pantaloons of dull yellow with his feet encased in Hussar buskins—felt somewhat odd in this outmoded assembly. But Unice had assured him it would be acceptable; indeed, there were one or two middle-aged smarts similarly attired in this daring new fashion.

Not so the exquisite Sir John Frinton, one of the first people to hail Denzell, suave as always in blue and cream. He came up, grinning broadly, and winked.

'Now here is a sight I hardly thought to see. How do, my young friend? What brings you to our dull delights? Or dare I ask?'

'What but the pleasure of seeing you again, Sir John,' responded Denzell, shaking hands. 'Can you doubt it?'

'With ease, my dear boy, with ease,' returned the aged exquisite, laughing gently. He looked about him. 'I am desolated to disappoint you in your undoubted quest.'

'How do you know what is my quest, sir?' demanded Denzell, grinning.

Sir John twinkled. 'Intuition, Hawkeridge.' He leaned close. 'I will give you a cautionary hint, however.'

Denzell's chest dropped abruptly. What? *What*? A rival, perhaps? There had been, after all, a previous amour and the man was back? Or—deuce take it, don't say she had gone!

He managed a light tone. 'A hint?'

'Look about you,' said Sir John, wafting a well-manicured hand. 'What do you see?'

'A swelling of your numbers, that is all.'

'Ah, yes, but whom? I will tell you. A predominance of aged devotees—as aged as I, alas!—returning with sentimental loyalty to the once fashionable haunt of their own youths.'

He was right, Denzell realised. The place was full of elderly folk, mostly raddled females. He became aware, as his eye passed about them, that a number of them were eyeing him surreptitiously, with that speculative gleam with which he was all too familiar.

'Oh, the deuce!' he muttered. 'Matchmakers in force!'

'Precisely, my dear boy,' laughed Sir John. 'Danger awaits you here! Don't you see the hopefuls about them?'

And, indeed, there were in evidence several young females, flimsily clad in the new muslins, and apparently in attendance on their elders. Denzell had not noticed them. But he did now, seeing at once in one or two eyes as they quickly looked away from his glance, those flickers of interest that would, but a few months back, have piqued him into selecting a potential flirt.

'You see them?' queried Sir John, his amusement plain. 'Indigent relatives, one and all. It is all the fault of one such who came here a year or two since. A delightful girl. She married a local marquis.'

Denzell's glance came back to him, understanding in his eyes. 'I see.'

'I thought you would.'

'Well, they will not catch me. I have other plans.'

'I thought you had.'

Denzell laughed. 'You are far too acute, Sir John.'

Sir John sighed, mock-sentimental. 'The truth is, my

friend, that I am an incurable romantic. Let me advise you to turn your eyes to that archway behind you.'

There was no mistaking the meaning of this. Denzell's heart did a reckless dance, and he looked around quickly. Verena! Warmth flooded him.

CHAPTER SEVEN

SHE had not changed! Verena had not changed in the least. So fresh she looked, in the sprigged muslin gown, honey-gold loose curls spilling on her shoulders from under a chipstraw hat, decorated with knots of tiny artificial blossoms. She was exquisite, like a china doll! That same smiling mask adorning the perfection of her features, dispensing equal attention—and *no* favours, thank God!—to each of the several males inhabiting her orbit. She was standing under an archway, the grace of her figure as elegant as the setting.

Denzell felt decidedly odd, the warmth giving way to a feeling he could not recognise. It was not, however, a feeling he could enjoy, for it was causing him a good deal of discomfort.

Why had he come here? Verena Chaceley was not going to welcome his advent! He must be mad. Where the devil was he to find the gall to approach her? Chaste stars, but he had not thought himself to be such a lily-livered poltroon! He had not been so fainthearted since his green youth, before he had confidence in his ability to secure a lady's interest.

Was it only that, after all? Had Ossie been all along in the right of it? He was piqued, pricked in his pride, and had allowed himself to fall victim to his own vanity. Then what the devil ailed him that he had come chasing down here like a lunatic at the full of the moon, who knew not what he did?

To the devil with it! He would go straight up to her

153

and greet her as if nothing in the world had ever occurred between them to prevent his doing so.

His feet were already moving on the thought, and he had arrived at the knot of persons of which Verena was the centre before he had time to regret or retract. She had her back to him and Richard Cumberland, that unspeakable nuisance of a playwright, was addressing her. He could scarcely wait for the gentleman to arrive at the conclusion of his sentence.

In a voice loud enough—and cheerful enough—to gain him the instant attention of the entire circle, he spoke up.

'Good day to you, Miss Chaceley.'

Shock blanketed out all thought in Verena's head. A jolt seemed to stab in her chest. Out of the fog came only one coherent idea: *hold your countenance*, Verena!

Time seemed to Denzell to be standing still. For a moment, although every other head turned to look at him, Verena did not move. It appeared to Denzell as if she froze. The succeeding silence seemed to go on forever.

But in reality it could only have been an instant before the honeyed hair rippled a little as she turned. The unyielding mask was firmly in place, with that faintest trace of a smile. The exact same level of polite disinterest was in her voice as had been when she first spoke to him.

'How do you do, Mr Hawkeridge?'

The most intense dissatisfaction invaded Denzell's breast. A savage thought sliced through his mind. At least she had remembered his name! Beautiful, serene, and exquisitely polite was she. And not at all the Verena he had expected—nay, longed!—to find.

'I am very well, I thank you,' he said, almost curtly. 'I trust I find you in good heart?'

'Extremely so.'

'And your mama?'

'She is in better—health.'

Was there a stress on the word? It was so hard to tell. How the deuce was anyone to know anything of the woman, when she persisted in this determined shutting off? The devil take you, Verena Chaceley!

Unable to think of anything to say that would not sound churlish and rude, Denzell bowed slightly and moved away. Let others take the field. For himself, he was done with it!

He heard men's voices start up behind him, and found himself wishing for the butt-end of a pistol that he might knock them all on the head, the fools! Wasting their time in such a fashion, with a woman who would take a mile before she gave an inch.

Nevertheless, he could not help but glance back. Startled, he halted and turned, staring at the knot of people he had just left. They were dispersing, but where the deuce was Verena? She had been there but seconds ago.

His eye swept the room—and caught a glimpse of the straw-hatted head. It was bowed a little, and she was hurrying, taking a path close to the walls, passing behind the little groups of persons as if she wished to remain unnoticed. Where was she going? Looking forward, he saw the entrance doors. She was leaving! His eyes went back to her, and he saw now that she had a hand pressed below her bosom. His glance strayed up to her face. She was biting her lip! Deuce take it, Verena, what in the world was amiss?

Thought deserted him. There was no feeling now in his breast but distress for her evident distress, and all he knew of was the need to aid her, if he might.

Without quite knowing how he had got there, Denzell

found himself out on the Pantiles, for the moment thankfully all but deserted. Except for the figure that clung to one of the columns of the colonnade with both hands, breathless and trembling.

'Miss Chaceley!'

Verena jumped violently, her eyes flying open as she looked up. Oh, no! Not he again. Had he not done enough?

'Forgive me, I think I startled you,' said Denzell anxiously. 'I could not help but see—Miss Chaceley, are you ill? May I do anything for you?'

'Ill? No!'

That she was not! Yet what to say—how to explain to him, the author of her confusion, this extreme reaction to *his* sudden appearance? The reverberations of the painful jolt in her breast were not yet ended. How she had kept her countenance she did not know. Thank heaven she'd had her back to him! Otherwise, she could not doubt but that he must have seen it in her face.

And, dear heaven, here he was again! Desperate to retrieve her façade, Verena sought for control, knowing that at any moment he would make one of those outrageous comments—that had done so much to alienate her and yet had set him in her thoughts, as it were, in immovable marble!—that he had made on those previous occasions.

But Denzell, watching the strain in her lovely features as she tried to bring them back under that iron mastery, was beset by so much emotion that he would not have dreamed of adding to her distress by any untoward remark. Moved by the unprecedented desertion of that very control that he had so much deprecated but a few moments before, he searched his mind for some legitimate excuse that might afford her ease. He could not

bear to see her so weakened, no matter the cause. He
would have given much to have swept her up into a safe
embrace—his own. But that was impossible. Spurred by
necessity, he found the key.

'It is insufferably hot in that place, is it not? I confess
I found it so myself.'

A grateful look rewarded him. 'Y-yes, it—it was
airless.'

Denzell glanced up at the cloudless sky. 'I dare say
we may find it increasingly hot outside later on.' He
smiled down at her, noting with satisfaction that she
was recovering her lost control. He offered his arm.
'Meanwhile, do take the air with me for a turn or two,
Miss Chaceley. Is not that what the Pantiles are for?'

A tiny choke of laughter escaped her. 'So I believe.'

The somersaulting sensations in her breast were
quietening, thank heaven! She was so glad of his tact
that she forgot entirely her old resolve to remain aloof
from this dangerous man. Besides, he was waiting so
patiently, his arm ready for her hand. It would be
unkind—even churlish—to refuse him. Her jelly legs
seemed to be firming up, and she tentatively released
her clutch on the column.

To her consternation, she was not as steady as she
had expected. Her knees buckled a trifle. Denzell was
swiftly at her side, grasping her arm—and sending such
a shooting sensation up her body with his touch that
she was obliged to grasp on her other side at the column
again.

'Lord!' she uttered helplessly.

'Don't hurry,' he said smoothly. 'Take your time. It
takes a moment to recover from a near faint, you
know.'

Again he was offering her a fitting excuse. Verena
could have kissed him! She balked on the idea. What

was she thinking of? A flood of warmth caused her to
let go of the column in order to clutch at her cheek to
hide the burning. Faint indeed! True, she had felt close
to swooning, but she was certain her colour belied that
possibility now. If only he knew that all this must be set
down to his own wholly unexpected arrival!

'I am ready now,' she said with a calmness that did
not in any way reflect the tumult of her emotions.

Denzell firmly took her hand and placed it securely
within his own arm. The way she clutched at this
support demonstrated more than anything else the
strain under which she still laboured. His heart seemed
to dissolve.

For a few moments they paced carefully up the tiled
pathway, both concentrating on the effort required. But
as he felt Verena's grasp on his arm loosen, Denzell
looked for some innocuous topic that he might introduce. Searching, he discovered the one thing on which
they might safely embark.

'Is it not an excellent thing that Osmond and Unice
have managed to produce the girl they wanted?'

He could not have found anything better. The most
natural smile creased Verena's countenance, filling her
features with warmth.

'Little Julia! Yes, indeed. I was so delighted for them
both. She is the most beautiful baby, and so *good*.'

'So Osmond keeps boasting. He claims that he has
not once been woken in the night.'

'That,' said Verena sapiently, 'is because, so Unice
tells me, he sleeps like one dead. She says that he would
snore through the lamentations of a dozen babies.'

Denzell burst out laughing. 'By George, how I shall
roast him!'

'Oh, pray don't,' Verena begged. 'Unice wishes him
to believe himself the perfect father.'

He glanced down at her. 'Why, if he is not?'

An unprecedented gleam danced in her eyes as she returned his look. Fascinated, Denzell's steps actually ceased.

'Miss Chaceley, you look the picture of mischief.'

'Do I?'

'Yes. Tell me at once what it is you are thinking!'

Verena bubbled over. 'It—it is just that Betsey—my maid, you know—had warned Unice that girls are much more difficult to bring up than boys, so Unice has vowed she will pass this trouble on to Osmond. Although,' she added as he began to laugh, 'Julia is so angelic that I cannot conceive of there ever being a necessity for her to do so.'

'Really, as a fellow male, I feel I ought to warn Ossie of what is in the wind,' he said, resuming their walk.

'You may safely do so,' Verena agreed, moving with him and smiling. 'Unice has already told him, but she swears he thought she was only jesting.'

He was silent for a moment or two, aware all at once of the extraordinary nature of this interchange. She was so *normal*, so pleasant and amiable. The mask had been dropped! Sudden anxiety attacked him. How long would she remain thus open to him? What might he not suddenly say that could turn her in an instant into the effigy that so depressed him? The fear kept him silent for a space, but it did not appear that Verena felt the absence of talk.

In fact, she was feeling so relaxed that she scarcely noticed how unguarded she was. The companionable nature of this short interlude was so comfortable that she had quite forgotten the dangers. Indeed, she had forgotten everything—all the stresses of her life, the fears, wiped out by the unprecedented materialisation of Mr Denzell Hawkeridge.

'That must be why you have come,' she guessed after a space, still thinking of the new Ruishton baby.

'Why I have come?' repeated Denzell, startled for a moment by the question.

'To Tunbridge Wells, I mean. Have you not come to see the baby? Or, no. Gentlemen have little interest in such matters.'

Denzell pulled himself together. This was dangerous ground. He could scarcely dare to say that he had come because of Verena herself!

'Ah, but Osmond and Unice are very particular friends of mine, and Felix is my godson. I came, if you want the truth, to gratify them with a show of interest.'

'That was well done of you, Mr Hawkeridge!' she exclaimed warmly.

Denzell had the grace to feel ashamed. He grimaced. 'I have scant interest in babies, I admit, but I have been very much amused at Osmond's doting fondness. And I cannot but be delighted to see Unice so radiant—thanks, I believe, in no small measure to your good offices.'

'Nonsense!' Verena said dismissively. 'I was only too glad to be of service. It was—' She paused, remembering those extravagant and wild visions involving this very image that walked beside her now. But it would not do to falter. Drawing a breath, she began again. 'It was an experience I would not have missed for a fortune.'

'I dare say you regretted that your mama was not well enough to have attended with you. I believe all women wish for their elder female relatives on such occasions.'

For a moment he did not realise his own slip. But the silence that greeted this statement grew suddenly oppressive. Glancing down, he saw instantly that the mask had been resumed. Verena barely glanced at him as, disengaging her hand, she took a step away.

'I must thank you for a very pleasant walk, Mr Hawkeridge, but it is time that I was returning to the Rooms.'

With which, she turned on her heel, and walked away.

Desolate, Denzell gazed after her. Her mother! That was what made her turn. Not a lost love. Then what *was* it? In the name of God, what devil's work was it that had created this impregnable shield?

Sitting on her bed, Verena listened with only half an ear to Betsey's long-winded report. There was nothing in it that she did not already know, and besides, she had so much more to think about. Specifically, her encounter with Mr Hawkeridge this morning, and that fatal reference to Mama.

Reality had come flooding back. With it, a cursing sweep of self-abuse.

How could she have been so stupid? How tamely had she fallen to his guile. What had possessed her to allow him under her guard so readily? She had caught herself actually enjoying his company! So much so that she had slipped, almost unknowing, into her natural guise, allowing him to believe—what? What must he believe? What might he not assume, from this, about her possible interest in him?

She was *not* interested. Far from it. It had been shock alone that had given her that painful jolt on hearing the sound of his voice—when she had believed him to be miles away. Small wonder she had felt sick! And then he had spoken to her with almost as great a sense of indifference as that she had herself feigned. She had been glad of that, of course she had. Even though she had been obliged to sneak away, afraid every second that someone might stop her, for she knew that her control was gone.

And *then* he must needs approach her again. Insidiously using some clever tactic that soothed the tumult that he had raised, so that she lowered her barriers all unknowing and gave him heaven knew what advantages. Only then he had mentioned Mama, jerking her back to remembrance, to everything she knew of men, and the disastrous consequences of allowing them the smallest degree of power.

Fool! Unheeding *fool*.

'Miss Verena, are you listening to me?'

With a start, Verena brought Betsey's face back into focus. The maid was eyeing her, grimly suspicious. Verena reached out and clasped her fingers briefly.

'Oh, Betsey, forgive me! I'm afraid I was miles away.'

'No need to tell me that, Miss Verena. I've eyes in my head, you know.'

Verena grimaced. 'Don't scold, pray.'

Betsey looked her over, and then plonked down on the bed beside her. 'What's amiss?' she asked bluntly. 'Apart from the usual, that is.'

'Isn't the usual bad enough?' Verena said bleakly.

'That will do, that will,' said Betsey firmly. 'I've just been giving you an account of the mistress, and you've confessed to having your head in the clouds, Miss Verena. So don't you give me none of that. What's happened to put you all in a pother?'

Verena sighed. 'I am being foolish, that is all.'

Betsey's eyes narrowed. 'You won't fob me off, Miss Verena, so don't think it. He's back, is he?'

Startled, Verena gaped at her. 'Who?'

'Never you mind asking who,' said Betsey severely. 'You know well enough who. You don't reckon there's anything goes on in this town as I don't hear about, do you? Specially as it concerns you or the mistress.'

Verena's heart sank. There could be no doubting what Betsey meant. 'Mrs Quedgeley!'

'The same.'

'What has she said? Why didn't you mention it before? Oh, Betsey, for the love of heaven, say nothing—not a *word*—to Mama, I pray you!'

'Never you fret, Miss Verena,' said the maid soothingly. 'You don't reckon as how I'd open me mouth to the mistress on a matter so delicate.'

But Verena was not impressed. If she had been concerned before, she was now anxious beyond measure. She knew perfectly well that the maid had her interests at heart almost as deeply as did Mama, and she had often enough lamented the self-same thing that Mama was apt to do—the lack in her life of a husband and children.

'Betsey, she must not know! Not that there is anything to know, but if Mama were to hear of this interest, there is no saying what she might not take it into her head to do. You must promise me you will say nothing.'

'I've said so already, Miss Verena. You don't need to tell me! I know the sort of riot and rumpus she'll kick up if she thinks you have a suitor. And with the way she's been carrying on lately. . .'

Suddenly intent, Verena gazed at her. Yes, Betsey had been talking, and she had failed to take it in. She had not listened, because she was herself aware of some progress. Mama was like an convalescent invalid these days. She had improved in physical strength, seeming to need less time at rest. But as that strength grew, so her spirits seemed to gain, not in joy, but in anxiety.

She was restless and fidgety, and much inclined to bemoan their sedentary life here, remembering too often the activities in which she had been engaged at home. It was worrying enough, but what had she missed that Betsey said?

'What are you trying to tell me, Betsey?'

'Well, I didn't want to worrit you, Miss Verena, so I haven't said nothing,' said the maid bodingly. 'But the truth is I don't like it, and that's a fact. What with the mistress getting to remembering what she calls "the good times", though I'm danged—if you'll pardon me, Miss Verena—which times she could call to mind, for I can't. And not that alone, neither.'

'Heavens, but what more, Betsey?' asked Verena, anguished. How could she have been so selfish as to be troubling herself over Mr Hawkeridge when Mama was hovering so dangerously on the brink of just what she so greatly feared?

'Well, you know as how ever since Mr Adam come the first time, the mistress has been sighing over losing her home and her friends—'

'Yes, I know—and Adam has been here again how many times? Three?'

'Four, counting the last. And the worst of it is, Miss Verena, that every time he comes, she's at that bottle as if her life depended on it.'

'The laudanum! Dear heaven, why did you not tell me this before? That is just what I have been afraid of, that she will become dependent upon the stuff. I have heard it said that those who take it too often find themselves obliged to do so more and more. Oh, Betsey, what shall we do?'

'Do? I've done it!' declared the maid. 'Don't you fret, Miss Verena. There ain't no harm going to come to the mistress, no matter if she drinks the whole bottle down in one go.' Betsey grinned widely at the startled question in Verena's face. 'Nothing but sugar water,

Miss Verena. I always sweetened it for her when she was drinking the real thing for she complained of its bitterness, so she don't know the difference.'

Verena found herself laughing and crying at once, seizing the maid's hands and holding them in a clasp that spoke her gratitude more eloquently than any words.

'Oh, Betsey, what *should* we do without you?'

'That's more than I know, Miss Verena. But there. We'll share our little secrets—you with yours and me with mine and the mistress none the wiser, eh?'

A huge sigh escaped Verena. 'You have lifted a load from my mind, Betsey.'

Betsey grunted. 'I'm glad of that, and I only wish I could do the same for meself. The truth is, Miss Verena, I'm that worried that she's thinking of going back!'

Verena patted her hand. 'Let her think of it. I won't let her go back, Betsey. She cannot do so without us, in any event. No, that does not concern me.'

'Well, what then? Something worrits you, don't tell me.'

Verena grimaced. 'It is only that I cannot rid myself of the conviction that Adam is bound to give us away—'

'Now then, Miss Verena—'

'Oh, he does not mean to do it, I know that. But dearly as I value my brother, I *cannot* persuade myself that his tongue can be trusted. You know his temper, Betsey!'

'Aye, I do that. But his care of his Mama is strong, don't doubt it.'

'Yes, I know, only—oh, Betsey, don't you think we should remove from here?'

It would solve everything, Verena felt. Especially if Mama really was considering a return. With the added strain of appearing in a much larger public with the Season in full swing here, she would give much to be otherwhere. Not to mention the new nuisance that had reared its head this day!

But the maid was firm. 'No, I don't, Miss Verena. The mistress *is* better, for all you may not think it.'

'I know she is. Better in body at least.'

'And mind, too. I'd say she enjoys the company. Why, even now she has that there Mrs Felpham come to call.'

Aghast, Verena leapt up from the bed. 'Mrs Felpham! Oh, Betsey, why did you not say so at once? Heaven knows what she might have said to her!'

Her fears were well-founded. Dashing through to the next room, she discovered that Mrs Felpham had but just departed—leaving behind her a creature agonised by what she had been told. Mrs Pateley was half collapsing on the day-bed, agitatedly fingering her gown, her eyes darting aimlessly until the instant that they spied her daughter. She threw out a hand at once.

'Oh, my dearest, I *knew* this must happen! Have I not said over and over again that you must seek your own future?'

'Mama, pray hush!' begged Verena, crossing quickly to the day-bed to take her hand, and sitting down beside her.

'How can I hush, Verena?' uttered the afflicted lady. 'You need not try to hide it from me, for Mrs Felpham has told me all.'

'Mama, there is no "all" to tell,' Verena said, trying for a light note. 'Mrs Felpham is, as you are perfectly aware, the most dreadful gossip.'

But Mrs Pateley would have none of this. 'Do not attempt to hoodwink me, Verena. You do not even ask me what she has said to me, and that in itself shows there is some fire within this smoke. You *know* what she has said, do you not? Do you not, my love?'

Verena managed an indifferent shrug, although she was feeling far from indifferent. Readily could she have murdered Mrs Felpham! But to convince Mama, she *must* maintain the easiest of tongues on the matter. However much it might be that the wretched man had cut up her peace, it would not do for Mama to have the least hint of that.

'There can be little doubt that she has made a song and dance about the arrival here of Mr Hawkeridge.'

Mrs Pateley nodded. 'Yes, and that he instantly sought you out.'

'Yes, for we met at Christmas, remember. It would have been extremely impolite of him not to do so.'

'Impolite? My darling, that is false modesty, when you know very well that a young man of rank and fashion must have a cogent reason for visiting such a place as this.'

This was the fell hand of Mrs Felpham! Such an idea would never have occurred to Mama without it having been suggested to her. But Verena saw how it could be deflected.

'Why, so he has,' she agreed. She managed an amused laugh. 'Mama, have you so quickly forgotten the exciting event in the Ruishtons' life? He has come to greet their new daughter, of course.'

She saw doubt burgeon in her mother's face. It had been his own explanation, and Verena saw no reason to disbelieve him—even had she wanted to, which she did not. If Mama could be brought to believe it, so much the better. She pressed her advantage.

'According to Unice, her husband and Mr Hawkeridge have been inseparable from youth. Though, for my part, it is evident that this "young man of rank and fashion" did not care to miss any part of the Season, and has only come here—belatedly, one might think—at a time when no other amusements offer.'

Mrs Pateley's face fell. 'Oh, Verena. I was in such hopes that he might have taken a fancy to you.'

'Well, hope it no longer, Mama,' Verena advised firmly, thinking how much more for herself it was of fear, than of hope. 'Besides, you know very well that I have no desire to be courted by any man.'

Her mother gripped her fingers tightly. 'You say it only for my sake, Verena. But if chance offers, I *beg* you, my dearest, do not hesitate. Take instant advantage of such an opportunity. Fall in love! Seize what happiness might be open to you.'

Verena commanded herself to produce a scornful laugh at this, but she could not. Why, she was at a loss to imagine. She had not changed her views about 'love'. Certainly not for the sake of Mr Denzell Hawkeridge. As for *happiness*—that was quite beyond her expectations. She was, she hoped, a realist. Life must be taken for what it was, even should that prove to be one's present unaccountable misery. One did not bay for the moon.

'Well, let us not go over all that again, Mama,' she said with an air of calm that she was far from feeling. 'Besides, I have been thinking lately that it may well be in our best interests to remove from here.'

'Remove from Tunbridge Wells?' cried Mrs Pateley, releasing her daughter's hands. 'Oh, Verena, must we?'

Verena eyed her, her attention caught. 'Why, Mama? Are you so fond of the place?'

'No, no, but—'

'But you wish to keep me where I may yet fall victim to some eligible gentleman, is that it?'

Mrs Pateley fidgeted with the petticoats of her gown of French lawn in her favoured lilac shade, looking conscious. 'Not only that, dearest. Adam—'

Verena pressed the hand she still held. 'I know, Mama. But that is precisely my reason. I love Adam dearly, as I know you do, and I don't wish to part you from him. But I am sorry to be obliged to confess that I don't *trust* him.'

'That is a horrid thing to say, Verena!' protested Mrs Pately, snatching her hand away.

'Yes, I know. But it is the truth.'

Angry colour suffused the elder lady's cheeks. 'I don't know how you can be so unkind about your own brother. He would not dream of betraying me.'

'Not when he is sober, no,' agreed Verena deliberately.

Her mother gasped. 'How can you, Verena?'

'Very easily, Mama. In that respect, Adam is proving altogether too much like his father.'

Mrs Pateley burst into tears.

In the midst of an entertainment that should have gladdened even his jaded senses, Denzell was brooding. An impromptu ball replacing the usual Friday night Assembly, on the dry clean grass of Potter's Green, beside Burlington House below the Grove, had been greeted with enthusiasm by the Wellsians.

Flaring torches were placed about the Green, and ringing the area marked out for dancing. Although in the bright summer evening they were hardly needed, they gave a pleasant glow to the scene as dusk began to fall around nine o'clock.

But Denzell, attired for the occasion in the russet coat and embroidered apricot waistcoat on a cream ground that he had acquired for Teresa's wedding, but

worn over satin breeches of his usual black, watched
with a jaundiced eye the gay abandon with which the
dancers executed the various figures. He found himself
unable to enter into the spirit of the event.

'Not dancing, Mr Hawkeridge?' enquired a now
familiar voice.

Stupid woman! Denzell thought irritably. Obviously
he was not dancing. 'Later, perhaps.'

Mrs Felpham sighed. 'So difficult to attach dear Miss
Chaceley for a dance, is it not?'

Touched on the raw, Denzell could have hit her. He
forced a smile to his lips. 'Miss Chaceley is always much
sought after.'

He was rescued by Sir John Frinton, who came up
behind them and surprised Mrs Felpham by slipping his
arm through hers. 'My dear lady, I protest you have
neglected me shamefully this night! Come along and
tell me all the gossip. You will excuse us, Hawkeridge?'

Denzell threw him a grateful look. There was nothing
he wished less at this moment than to discuss his lack
of that particular partner.

Not that it was merely that he had been unable to
secure a dance with Verena that was driving him into
unaccustomed ill-temper, though that was bad enough.
The formality of engaging beforehand for the country
dances which constituted the evening's programme had
been dispensed with, but every time that Denzell
thought to make an approach, he had been forestalled
by others. Whether this was by Verena's design, he
could not tell.

It was all of a piece with the rest of it! Yet why had
she taken against him? She did not dislike him, of that
he was certain. She could not have spoken so easily
with him that first day if that had been the case. Since

then, however, for the best part of the week since his arrival here, she had not allowed him near her!

Every time he had approached her, whether it be in the Upper Rooms, on the Pantiles, or at the theatre where Mrs Baker's company were now to be seen, so Unice had told him, two or three times each week, he had been permitted a bare exchange of greetings and that was all. She would make some excuse—and the devil take his wits if they were not excuses!—and move swiftly away.

She was avoiding him, he could not doubt it. Deuce take it, he could actually feel her poker up on his approach! The mask was always there, but against he himself it positively iced over.

Had she been more normal with him, more as she was with other men, he might have been discouraged. Indifference was an impregnable defence. But she was not indifferent. That he would swear to on his life. What did dishearten him was his growing conviction that she *feared* him. If that was the way of it, he might as well go home this moment! How the devil was he to overcome a fear of which he understood nothing, and which she would not by any means permit him to understand?

This evening there was something more. She looked achingly beautiful, in a gown of lemon tiffany under a short overgown of gold net that shimmered in the torchlight so that she seemed to glow. Yet she was under severe strain. He could see it. Oh, she was making every effort to appear normal. But only look!

There, as she turned away from her partner in the movement of the dance, had not the mask slipped a little? And now—was that a faint tremble in her lip? Watching her still, he saw her eyes close wearily in a

long blink. He could swear it was a wisp of a sigh she
snatched then.

It was as if the cracked veneer was breaking up, as if
he could see beyond it, into the vulnerability that kept
her so resolutely aloof. Chaste stars! He could not take
this any more. She would not keep him at bay! What,
was he a monster to frighten her? He wanted only to
help her, if he could; to brush away the trouble that
haunted her. Oh, he had seen it so clearly—on that now
far-off day when they met on the Common one early
winter morning.

By the veriest good fortune, the next person to attach
Verena for a dance was Osmond himself. Naturally she
had no quarrel with Osmond. He had been admitted to
the ranks of her friends. Not that she had been very
much in evidence at the Ruishton house since Denzell's
arrival. Oh, no. All of a sudden, these 'everyday' visits
to Unice had ceased! He did not have far to seek for
the reason. But she would not fob him off this time.

Moving purposefully, he contrived to intercept his
friend as the couple were threading through the pockets
of the talkative assembly towards the dancing arena.

'My dance, I think, Ossie.'

Without waiting for a reply, he seized Verena's hand,
mittened in gold net to match her overgown.

'Hey!' cried Osmond.

'Hey to you!' retorted Denzell, and was on the move,
regardless of the effect on Verena.

She was too taken aback for a moment to resist, let
alone find anything to say. Besides, the warmth of his
hand about hers was having the effect of rendering her
breathless. He had caught her so much off guard, for in
Osmond's presence she was now apt to be a trifle more
relaxed, that she had been unready for such a determined assault.

Before she had time to recover, she found herself taking up a position in one of the sets then forming. Denzell released her hand as he took his place, and turned to face her, smiling disarmingly.

'Will you forgive me for this piracy? I doubt Ossie will not.'

'I do not think—I mean—'

Verena willed herself to continue, but the effort to control the quivering in her lips was too great. Where was her strength? Thank the lord Mama had elected not to come tonight! For all the work of these few days would be gone in a moment. She had hoped—in vain?— that he had been convinced by her conduct that she did not wish to pursue their acquaintance. She did not indeed. She did not wish even to speak to him, let alone dance with him!

'You don't wish to dance, do you?' he said, as if he had read her mind.

The next instant, just as the music started, he whisked her out of the set, and out of the dancing arena altogether. But not back towards the colourful throng that moved about below the arena. Instead she found herself passing out of the flare from the burning torches, and into the shadows beyond, where the darkness of the Grove beckoned.

'Where are you taking me?' she asked involuntarily.

'Where we may be a little private,' he answered truthfully.

'But—'

'Miss Chaceley, trust me!'

A few steps more and he stopped, right on the edge of the Grove, where sight and sound of the gaiety on the Green was muted, and yet within a few feet of the laughing enjoyment of the crowds therein.

Denzell did not release his hold on her elbow, which

he had used to steer her through, so silently, so rapidly that he doubted whether anyone had observed them depart. Besides, he was ready to wager that theirs was not the first such secret departure. This type of entertainment lent itself precisely to stolen meetings such as this. But for himself, there was no amorous intent.

'This is better,' he said, as he turned to look down into her face, visible quite in the still fading daylight, but sufficiently hidden for the mask to have been dropped. And it was gone! There was a world of confusion in her face. Confusion, and—by George, he had been right!—fear.

'Verena,' he uttered urgently, 'don't look at me so! Why are you afraid of me? God knows I intend you no harm!'

Verena's heart sank. Yes, she did fear him—his effect on her. How had he divined so much? She must not allow him to believe it, for that would weaken her position. Desperately, she fought to regain her control. But that was very difficult when his very touch was causing waves of trembling heat to invade her breast. She shifted away, pulling her elbow out of his grasp.

'Don't run away!' he uttered at once. 'I must talk to you. If you will not allow me to do so in public, then grant me this one opportunity, I beg of you.'

'I h-have no intention of r-running away,' she said on a snap, annoyed with herself for the tremor in her voice. 'And I am *not* afraid of you.'

'Then why are you avoiding me?' he accused. 'Don't try to pretend that you have not been doing so.'

The mask snapped back into place. 'Really, Mr Hawkeridge, I don't know what you mean.'

The coolness of her tone stung him. 'Ah, so you are armed again, are you? Well done, Miss Chaceley!'

His sarcasm distressed her, but it toughened her, too. Even more blandly, she said, 'I am quite at a loss, sir.'

'I am referring,' he said bitingly, 'to this alien creature, who is not you, Miss Verena Chaceley, yet who persists in coming between us.'

'Indeed?'

Exasperated, Denzell echoed, 'Indeed, indeed, indeed, Miss Chaceley! Is that all you can ever say? Of course it is! A crumbling façade before me must put you in grave danger, must it not?'

Verena could not reply. A tremor passed across her features. Why did he taunt her thus? If indeed he knew how hard it was for her to maintain her front, then what devil possessed him to prick at her?

He was glaring at her! All at once the expression in his face was too distressing to be borne. Why, she could not tell. She knew only that she could no longer maintain the façade. That it was indeed crumbling before him. A piercing, inexplicable pain threw her hand up to her breast.

'Why must you be so cruel?'

Her voice cracked. Next moment, she found her hands clasped together between two strong ones, held fast against the male chest before her.

'I'm not! I'm not cruel, Verena. Only I cannot bear it when you shield yourself against me! I know you are deeply troubled. I only want to help you, if I can. I ask nothing more than to be allowed to serve you. You have nothing to fear from me, I promise you. Only don't, I beg of you, Verena, keep me at a distance.'

'I *must*,' she uttered, suddenly anguished. For everything in her yearned to yield to him. To allow him close, to give him access to her deepest thoughts, her deepest feelings.

'But why? Tell me, Verena. Why?'

'I cannot—there is nothing—' she faltered, trying vainly to recover herself, half struggling to free her hands.

'Yes, there is something. Tell me!'

'No, no—you are mistaken.'

'I am not *mistaken*,' he said vehemently. 'Verena, I could not be mistaken where you are concerned. Deuce take it, I have fallen in love with you!'

CHAPTER EIGHT

AGHAST, Verena gazed at him. 'Oh, no,' she uttered faintly.

Denzell stared back, quite as shocked himself by his own words. An odd laugh escaped him. 'My God, I *have* fallen in love with you! Oh, *Verena*.'

Without any warning at all he released her hands, but only so that he might take her in his arms, gently, and in wonderment, oblivious to the stunned expression on her face. Next instant he was kissing her.

Verena's knees instantly gave way. Had Denzell not been holding her so firmly, she would have fallen. Sensation crowded out thought, as the pressure at her mouth sent waves dizzying across her brain. Then a wash of heat engulfed her and she groaned, unaware that her lips were answering his, moving in a hunger that had nothing to do with sense or fear, or even consciousness. Her arms, her hands, all moved seemingly without any volition on her part, snaking up to enfold the hard warmth of his chest closer still.

The pressure on her mouth intensified, and her lips parted at the implicit command, leaving her totally vulnerable to a searing belt of flame that raced through her at the velvet touch that followed.

It was too much! She was burning, suffused with intolerable sensations that threatened to deprive her of her senses. Struggling madly, she fought free and staggered back, panting with effort and hysterical with frantic protest.

'How could you? How *could* you? Never—*never*—dare to do such a thing again!'

Denzell, as charged as she, as much affected, yet realised instantly how wrong, how inconsiderate he had been.

'Verena, forgive me! I did not mean to do it, I swear. I couldn't help it. I promise you, I had no such intention when I brought you here. I had no notion that I had fallen in love with you!'

'Don't say that!' uttered Verena, tremblingly. 'It isn't possible. . .you must not. . .' She drew a ragged breath against the uneven pounding of her pulse. 'You must not—*cannot*—love me.'

'It's too late, Verena. I do love you. Nothing can change that.'

She drew back. 'No. Please, no.'

Denzell reached out and caught her hand. 'Why are you so afraid? What is it that you fear?'

Verena tried to pull her hand away, but his fingers tightened. She was conscious that she was trembling, and could not doubt but that he felt it. He drew her mittened hand up to his mouth, kissed the bare finger-tips, and then let it go. The tenderness of the gesture left her curiously helpless, warmed inside, despite the denial she was trying to hold to. He must not love her, because she could not—*must* not—love him. She did not love him!

'Never speak to me of such m-matters again,' she said shakily. 'I could not love you, Mr Hawkeridge—or anyone.'

'There is someone else!' he uttered, in sudden anguish.

'No one. *No one.*'

'Then—'

'No one!' she reiterated harshly. 'No man shall be

permitted to steal away my heart. I have long determined it. Not you. Not *anyone*. I wear an iron shield and you need not suppose that you have the power to penetrate it. You must go elsewhere with your "love", Mr Hawkeridge, for I will never accept it!'

The look in his face almost caused her to retract. Was he so very much hurt? She was conscious of a rising feeling of guilt, but she thrust it down. Guilt in this instance was a luxury she could not afford. She must remember Mama.

The thought gave her strength. What, had she so readily forgotten Mama's sufferings? Was she so vulnerable, so easily swayed by a kiss, by soft words? No—if only he did not look so devastated!

Involuntarily she put out a hand and her fingers lightly touched his cheek. 'I am sorry, Denzell.'

Then she turned quickly away, and sped rapidly back towards the dancing arena, but skirting it so that she passed around the crowds. She was still overset, her heartbeat irregular, and she did not wish to meet anyone now. All she wanted was to go home. To go home—and to weep.

All the way home in the chair that carried her, she clutched her light cloak about her, beset by an unwelcome image of Denzell Hawkeridge's face. Clearly he had not imagined for a moment that he might meet with such a comprehensive rebuff. She could only trust that he was mistaken in the depth of his feelings, that he would soon recover and 'fall in love' with someone else. It must be that he would, for was he not an accomplished flirt? Perhaps he only fancied himself in love with her because she had not fallen victim to his wiles. He barely knew her, after all.

As she barely knew him. Which had not, a small voice whispered, prevented her from finding him

dangerously attractive, nor from melting with desire at
his kiss.

With a smothered exclamation, she put her hands
over her own ears, as if she might stop herself hearing
such things, even in her own head. He should not have
kissed her! Her face burned at the memory. He had no
right to—to set up a furnace in her body, to throw her
into a state of such unutterable confusion.

She arrived home in a condition almost as bad as that
in which she had run from Denzell, her heart beating
less raggedly, but heavy with a weight of oppression
that threatened every instant to overcome her.

She would have gone directly to her own chamber,
but her footsteps must have been heard, for Betsey's
head popped out of the parlour, a candle in her hand.
The maid both sounded and looked grim enough to
seize Verena's attention from her own dismal thoughts.

'I thought it must be you, Miss Verena. You'd best
come in here straight.'

Still cloaked, Verena moved towards the parlour
door, frowning. 'What is the matter, Betsey?'

The maid was apparently too distracted to notice the
trouble in Verena's face. 'It's Mr Adam.'

'Adam is here?'

'Right enough he is—and with such tidings as you'll
not be wanting to hear neither.'

For a moment the shadows left by the difficult events
of Verena's evening prevented her from understanding.
But as she walked through the door, and saw the instant
apprehension in the faces of her mother and brother
alike, the portent of Betsey's words hit home.

'Oh, dear heaven!' she muttered direfully. 'Don't tell
me, Adam. He is coming after you, isn't he?'

'Dearest, do not be angry,' said Mrs Pateley at once.

Not be angry! Verena was on the point of wild and

hysterical laughter. All that she had been through tonight, and now this. Oh, but the fates were cruel!

Adam was speaking, and she tried to concentrate her attention on his words. '. . .never meant to say a word, you must know that, Verena. But I believe he more than half suspected these visits I have been making.'

'That was the reason, Verena,' pressed Mrs Pateley. 'You cannot blame Adam, dearest. He tried to keep his mouth shut, but Nathaniel drove him to speak, indeed, indeed he did. Cannot you imagine it, Verena? Such taunts at me he made, such dreadful things he said of me. Poor Adam could not abide to hear them.'

'What did you tell him?' Verena asked flatly.

'Why, I threw back at him what he had done to Mama,' explained Adam.

'And lost his temper into the bargain,' put in Betsey shrewdly, for she had followed Verena back into the parlour.

'What did you tell him, Adam?' Verena repeated, her eyes on her brother's face.

Adam shrugged. 'I hardly know. Except that when he taxed me with having seen Mama, I was so angry that I must have let it out that I had done so. Indeed Verena, I did not think I had mentioned Tunbridge Wells, but—'

'But you had,' she finished for him. 'And what does he intend?'

There was silence for a moment. Mrs Pateley came forward, trying to intercept herself between her son and daughter.

'Dearest—'

'Mama, I must know!'

'But there is nothing to be done about it now, Verena,' said her mother pleadingly. 'He will come

here, and we must face him. I can face him, Verena. I
am stronger now.'

Verena was still regarding her brother's tense face.
'Adam, what did he say?'

Her brother drew a heavy breath and sighed it out.
'He has sworn that he will come here and fetch Mama
away. I came as fast as I could—to warn you both.'

'To warn us both,' repeated Verena.

She closed her eyes for an anguished moment. It had
come. The moment she had been dreading for months
and months. It did not seem as if she could take it in.
All she could think was, why *now*? Why at this particular instant, when she was so full of that other matter
that she had no strength left with which to deal with
this one?

She became aware of the quiet surrounding her, and
opened her eyes to find Adam's face—pale in the
candlelight, the look of anxiety so pronounced that she
wondered at the power she must wield. He was afraid
of her, of her anger, of what she might say to him.

Her glance went to her mother's face. Heavens, here
was that look she dreaded most! One of supplication—
of fear and pleading. A look that had so often met
Nathaniel's hideous anger. Yet it was directed at
herself!

Verena's heart contracted. Had she become so hard?
Had she, in her anxiety to protect—whom, dear
heaven? These most beloved creatures or *herself*?—
assumed as forbidding an aspect as the hated spectre
who threatened them all? Into what species of monster
had she herself been turned? Oh, she could see it! They
were almost as much afraid of what she might say as
she herself was afraid of what Nathaniel might do. They
loved her, both of them, yet they knew—expected
almost!—that she could, or would, hurt them.

Unbidden, the image of Denzell's stricken face came into her mind. Stricken! At *her* words. Oh, heavens, did he then indeed love her? And she—brutally unkind—had flung his declaration back in his face! Without so much as a word of compliment, honour or thanks. And all, all of it, out of her own sick terrors.

What had Nathaniel done to her? She was *pitiless*.

Overwhelmingly, the cumulative effects of the night struck at her. She must get away. She could not talk to them now. She must be alone!

She tried to smile and put out a wavering hand. 'We shall—we shall deal with it when the time comes. Pray forgive me. I am tired. . .I must go to bed.'

Turning, she walked quickly out of the room. She did not see Betsey's concerned features watch her pass by. She did not see anything at all, except the blurry outline of the wall and her own bedchamber door. She managed to open this and to stagger within, the cloak dropping from about her to the floor. But it was by feel alone that she found her bed and sank down upon it, her shoulders sagging, the blinding tears wetting her cheeks as she choked on the sobbing breaths that rose up through her tightened throat, and tried with useless fingers to pluck off the mittens from her hands.

She did not notice Betsey enter the room. But when the maid sat down beside her and those firm hands—hands that had so often cradled the forlorn little girl she once had been—took hold of her, firmly removed the mittens, and then drew her against the comforting breasts, she yielded instantly.

'There, my dove,' crooned the maid, rocking her gently. 'There, my little one.'

Verena clutched her, the painful sobs rasping in her throat as she tried to speak. 'Oh—Betsey. What has he—made of me?'

Betsey stroked her hair, held her tight, and patted her. Yet her voice was puzzled. 'Who, my dove? What is it you mean?'

'Nathaniel,' came the choked reply. 'I am *marble*, Betsey—and that is his work!'

The latch clicked quietly behind Denzell's back as he slipped the front door to in the silent house. It was early yet, but the household must already be asleep, except perhaps for the servants waiting to put Osmond and Unice to bed when they returned. For himself, he was glad to think he had given his valet leave for the evening. He did not wish to go to bed just yet. What he wished for was a bottle of his host's brandy!

A candle in a silver holder awaited him on a side table by the parlour door. He took it up and crossed into the little breakfast parlour, where he knew Osmond kept a decanter handy on the dresser for just such an occasion.

The hand with which he poured himself a glass was not quite steady, and he swore softly as a little of the golden liquid ran down the outside of the glass. He wiped the glass with his pocket handkerchief, and was about to replace the stopper on the decanter when he paused.

He might as well go to the devil, might he not? Laying down the stopper, he seized the decanter, dragged a chair out from the table and, stripping off his russet coat and flinging it carelessly aside, slumped into the chair. Then he sat, a silhouette against the candle on the dresser, the glass cradled in his hands, the decanter before him.

But he did not drink. Resting an elbow on the table, he dropped his forehead into one hand, half covering his eyes, and stayed so, helpless against the images that crowded one another through his mind. Images that haunted his heart, that stretched ahead of him unendingly into a future that seemed to promise nothing but defeat.

'Denzell?'

He jumped, dropping his hand. His hostess stood in the doorway, clad in a pretty pink dressing-robe, and holding up a candle. Denzell rose at once.

'I thought you were still at the dance.'

She came further into the room. 'I returned early to feed my little Julia. Is not Osmond with you?'

Denzell shook his head. 'I don't know where he is. I have not seen him since—' He stopped, recalling just when he had last seen his friend, at the moment when he had pirated Verena away from him.

Unice came closer, holding the candle up. There was concern in her features. 'Denzell, you look dreadful! What in the world is the matter?'

A great sigh escaped him, and he sank back down into the chair, looking away from her. But it did not occur to him to prevaricate. He was glad rather to have someone to whom to unburden his soul.

'Oh, Unice, I am sick at heart. I have ruined everything! Though indeed I had no intention—I did not even *know*. . .which was why, I believe. I shocked myself into a too precipitate declaration and—oh, the deuce, I wish I were dead!'

Unice tutted. She retrieved his coat from the floor and laid it on the back of a chair. Then, with an air of determination, she pulled out another chair for herself and sat down, setting down the candle on the table between them. Laying her hand over Denzell's, she squeezed it a little.

'Come now, it cannot be as bad as all that! You have had some sort of disagreement with Verena, I take it?'

'Disagreement!'

'Well, what then?'

'I kissed her.'

Unice sighed in relief. 'Lord, Denzell, is that all?'

He looked round quickly. 'It is not all. And I could have done nothing more prejudicial to my chances.'

'Oh, fiddle! I dare say she may have been angry with you, but—'

'Oh, no, she was not angry. She was—' He stopped, sighing again. 'To tell you the truth, I don't know how to describe it. She responded to me at first. She melted like snow in a thaw! For a moment it was quite as if we *belonged* together, as if she loved me just as intensely as I love her.'

Unice sat up, clasping her hands together. 'Then you do love her. Oh, Denzell, that is splendid!'

'Splendid, ha!' Denzell seized his glass, and tossed off the brandy, putting the vessel down with a snap. 'Do you know what she said? After kissing me back with all the fervour I could wish, mark you! She said that she could never love me, or anyone, and that I should take my love elsewhere for she would never accept it.'

'She said that?'

'That, and a great deal more besides. She even said she was sorry. Sorry!'

'But, Denzell, what is there in that to distress you so?' exclaimed Unice. 'It is obvious that she was denying her own feelings.'

Struck, Denzell gazed at her. Was it possible? 'What makes you say so?'

'Only consider a moment. Here is Verena, whom we know to be sorely troubled by some difficulty that concerns her mama. Has she shown any warmth towards any gentleman? No, she has not. Yet when you kiss her—'

'I only kissed her,' put in Denzell defensively, 'because I had that instant realised that I had fallen in love with her. I told her so, too.'

'Even better. You declare yourself, and kiss her, and she responds favourably. I promise you, she could not have done so had she been indifferent. She must have struggled at once, and probably struck you into the bargain. She didn't, did she?'

'Not with words,' agreed Denzell dejectedly, reliving a little of the painful dismay he had experienced at Verena's wholehearted rejection.

But Unice had not finished. 'Denzell, you must forgive me for speaking so free, but think of this. Verena may be master of her emotions under normal circumstances, but I cannot suppose she can have had an opportunity to learn to control *those* sort of sensations.'

A glow of warmth drove away some of Denzell's gloom. Even the memory of Verena in his arms had the power to move him! What if she, too, had been conscious of an equal strength of passion? Chaste stars, could he doubt but that she had been? That cool, calm, and exquisitely polite Verena had vanished at his touch! A surge of hope rose in his chest.

'You mean her true feelings were in that kiss?'

'Which she afterwards denied,' agreed Unice. 'Out of confusion, in all probability.'

The hope sank a little. Confusion, perhaps. But something more. Something so strong that he doubted he had the power to shift it, just as Verena herself had said. He could hear her voice now. 'I wear an iron shield.'

'Not confusion, Unice,' he said heavily. 'But the bugbear that plagues her life. The thing that threw up this mask she wears. How the devil am I to find my way past that? I don't even know what it may be.'

Unice sighed. 'Would that I could help you, but I cannot. She has not confided in me.'

A thought struck him, and he seized his hostess's hand. 'But she might, Unice. Especially now. If you were to go to her on *my* behalf, pleading my excuses and conveying my regrets—for she cannot realise but that you must be privy to my actions—'

'Yes, but will she then not believe I will pass on anything she says to you?' objected Unice.

'You will, in any event,' Denzell pointed out, 'and I will not have her deceived. It may even be that she will feel safe enough to send a message by you in that manner.'

Unice blinked at him. 'Safe?'

Denzell groaned, leaning back in his chair with a gesture of helplessness. 'There's the rub, Unice. She is afraid of me—I don't know why.'

'If that is so,' Unice mused, 'then it must be because of the way she feels about you.'

If he could but believe that! He shook his head, saying despairingly, 'What's the use of speculating? I feel as though I don't know anything any more.'

Unice patted his hand. 'Leave it to me. I promise you, if I discover nothing else, I will certainly discover what her feelings are towards you.'

A disgusted voice spoke from the doorway. 'Don't tell me you are allowing yourself to become embroiled in Hawk's amours, Unice!'

They both jumped, turning towards the intruder. They had both been too absorbed to hear Osmond come in.

Unice was the first to find her tongue, scolding at once. 'Osmond, what a fright you gave me!'

'Never mind that,' said her husband, strolling into the room. 'A pretty scene, I must say! I ought to call you out, Hawk, drinking alone with my wife in the middle of the night. In shirtsleeves, too. And she in her dressing gown!'

'Oh, be quiet, Ossie!' said Denzell impatiently. 'I am in no mood for your nonsensical gibes tonight.'

'Osmond,' said Unice, imperatively rapping on the table. 'Denzell has had a most upsetting evening. He is in difficulties with Verena.'

'Ha!' triumphed Osmond. 'Let that be a lesson to you not to cut in on a fellow when he is about to dance. Unice, do you know what—'

'Osmond, he is *in love* with Verena.'

Arrested, Osmond gaped at his friend. 'In love? Hawk?'

'What the devil is so fantastic about it?' demanded Denzell. Deuce take it, had his erstwhile conduct been so outrageous that it seemed impossible to his friend that he could have fallen in love?

Not that he had recognised the condition in himself! Now his unprecedented distaste for the Season made sense, as did the avoidance of females of which he had been accused.

'Yes, he is in love,' averred Unice, 'although he has but just discovered it himself. Isn't that so, Denzell?'

A faint laugh escaped him. 'I was so blind, yes. Much good may the discovery do me, however.'

'Don't say that! All will be well. I am determined that it should be. Particularly if I discover that her feelings match your own, as I am certain will be found to be the case.'

'Hey!' called Osmond. 'Not so fast, Unice. If my fool of a friend fancies himself in love, that is one thing. But

I'm dashed if I'll have you involve yourself in the matter.'

Unice stared up at him blankly. 'I cannot believe I am hearing you say such a thing, Osmond! After all that I owe Verena—and Denzell is your best friend.'

'But, dash it, Unice, you know what the fellow's like!' protested her spouse.

'It's true, Ossie,' Denzell cut in, unwontedly meek. 'I *was* a flirt. I did at the start intend precisely what you imagine with Verena. But all that is changed.'

Osmond whistled. 'You don't mean you really are in love with the chit?' Then he drew in a sharp breath. 'Don't tell me you are thinking of marrying her!'

'If I could ever persuade her to have me, yes,' Denzell said simply.

'She *will* have you, Denzell,' Unice urged. 'You have only to be patient.'

'You're mad,' Osmond said flatly. 'You know nothing about the girl. What is her background? Who is she? Dash it, Hawk, how can you even think of marrying her?'

'What do you imagine I care for all of that?'

'You have to care, dash it. You've a title to think of.'

Denzell almost snorted. What nonsense was this? 'Title! Deuce take it, Ossie, I'm only going to be a baron! Do you imagine I am like old man Chaceley, too high in the instep to think of anything but a good match?'

He stopped, aware that both his host and hostess were staring at him in amazement.

'Chaceley!' uttered Osmond blankly.

'Denzell, do you realise what you have just said?' asked Unice, awed. 'Who is "old man Chaceley"?'

'He means that martinet who is his neighbour at

Pittlesthorp,' Osmond explained. 'Dash it, Hawk, why in the world didn't you think of that before?'

'I did,' Denzell replied, shrugging. 'I thought of it at Teresa's wedding. I tackled both Kenrick and his father on the matter, but neither seemed to think there was any relationship.'

'But you do,' Unice said shrewdly, watching him. 'Don't you?'

'Unice, I simply don't know. All I can tell you is that Bevis Chaceley seemed interested, and then. . .just brushed it off. It was rather a feeling I had, than any firm idea.'

'What feeling?' she demanded.

Denzell gave a self-conscious laugh. 'A ridiculous feeling, born I am sure out of my then unrecognised emotions towards Verena. I felt as if they had cast Verena off.'

Osmond moved to the dresser, seized a glass, and poured himself a brandy. Lifting the vessel, he spoke in his most determined voice, just as if, Denzell thought, he had never made any previous objection.

'There is nothing for it, Unice. You will have to go and beard the girl. This matter must be sifted. Ferret out every bit of information you can.'

Verena received her guest in the little parlour. She was wary, and a little sorry that Mama and Adam should have chosen to go down to the Rooms this Saturday morning, for Unice's demeanour indicated that she was going to touch on matters that Verena would prefer not to discuss. It was clearly dangerous to be private with her today. Nor was she mistaken.

'Verena, you look terrible!' Unice began by way of opening. 'So pale and wan.'

Oh, heavens! She knew how haggard she looked, for

the mirror in her bedchamber had told her so, the paleness of her features emphasised by the plain white muslin gown. It was why she had chosen to remain at home. She should have denied herself! Only Unice was too kind a friend to be served so shabbily.

'I have had the headache,' she offered lamely. 'It—it kept me awake the better part of the night.'

'The headache,' repeated Unice in the flattest of tones. She leaned forward and reached across to the other chair, pressing the hand that lay on its wooden arm. 'Dear Verena, you will not fob me off with such a tarradiddle, so do not think it. Headache indeed! You are greatly troubled, are you not? What is the matter, Verena?'

Verena was obliged to force down a rising lump in her throat before she could speak. 'There is—there is nothing the matter, Unice. Beyond the headache, that is.'

But Unice was not to be deflected. 'Oh, Verena, how can you? After you have sat at my bedside all through my toiling with little Julia! We cannot be anything but intimate now. Pray don't reject my friendship.'

Verena swallowed. She managed a faint smile. 'I could not do so, Unice. Indeed, I am grateful for—for your concern. But you mistake—'

'It is Denzell, is it not?' broke in Unice bluntly.

Oh, heavens! Verena closed her eyes painfully, bringing up her fingers to her cheeks, which seemed to burn. She bit at her lips to stop their trembling, and became aware of Unice's fingers grasping her arm tightly.

'Well, he said he had blundered, but I had not thought he had overset you as much as this!' she uttered.

Verena's eyes flew open, and she regarded the other woman in doubt and concern. 'He told you?'

Unice nodded. 'I found him last night, starting on the brandy. He was in such despair, poor Denzell.'

An instant stab of conscience attacked her. 'Don't say that! Pray don't say that, Unice.'

'He loves you, Verena.'

Not that again. Please not that. She shook her head. 'No, he cannot love me. I told him he must not. He does not love me.'

'Well, I have known him a very long time, and I have never seen him behave this way over any girl.'

It was the last thing Verena wanted to hear after last night. Betsey thought she had cried herself to sleep, but she had only lain prone with exhaustion, unable to speak or move as the maid covered her and went away. Sleep had come, fitfully. But mostly she had thought. Thought and thought and *thought* through those long night hours, trying to persuade herself that Denzell had mistaken some other feeling for love.

He did not know her. She had never given him anything but the false picture of herself that she gave to the world. How was it possible that he might love *her*? It must be some image he carried, some creature that he had summoned up in his own mind. But it was not herself! And now, when she was tired and wretched, and on tenterhooks at the expectation of Nathaniel's arrival—though she was trusting that he could not get here for another couple of days—here it was again.

'Unice,' she said in a voice of strict control, 'do not encourage him in this theme, I beg of you. If it was true—if he did indeed entertain such feelings for me, it could only lead to his unhappiness.'

'I don't believe you mean that, Verena,' Unice said quietly. 'If you wish to know what I really think, it is that you care more for Denzell than you dare to say.'

A flare of emotion ripped through Verena. An

emotion she did not recognise. She knew herself to be
trembling, and she could feel a bursting in her chest.
But the little corner of coherent thought that still
remained urged her to refutation of this impossible
idea. She thrust the words up through a throat that
seemed to rasp at every sound.

'You would wish to imply that I am "in love" with
him, is that it?'

'Yes, Verena, yes!' came excitedly from Unice.

A harsh sound—that might have been a laugh—
escaped Verena's lips. 'How little you know, Unice!'

She rose from the chair, pushing herself to the
window and staring out at the green of the trees and
the way the sun dappled through their leaves to fall in
uneven shadows on the ground below. The rough
passage of feeling that had torn through her but a
moment before was subsiding. A hollowness was
descending upon her chest. That emptiness that she
knew she could never fill. Never—because Nathaniel
had forever closed the doors on that possibility.

'I have no heart with which to love,' she said bleakly
into the glass of the window.

'That cannot be true,' cried Unice in a tone of
distress. 'You have such warmth, Verena. You proved
that the night my Julia was born.'

Verena turned slowly, and all the tortured past was
reflected in her countenance for Unice to see.

'Look at me, Unice. Is this an object for devotion? I
have grown too cold, too hard—too *bitter*. I cannot
love—and I cannot bear to *be* loved.'

She saw doubt and concern in Unice's face, and
dredged up a faint smile. 'You would do better to
advise Denzell to forget me, than to try to win me to
his heart.'

There was a moment of bleak silence. Then all at

once, Unice shook her head vehemently, rising to face her. 'No! No, I won't believe it. You speak as if you are past redemption, past all change. That cannot be. You are young, Verena.'

Verena sighed. 'I feel a hundred today.' She moved a little and reached for Unice's hands. 'Pray give it up, Unice. Even were it possible—were I changeable as you insist—there is no power on earth that would persuade me to leave Mama.'

Unice returned the pressure of her hands. 'I understand, my dear. But surely, when your Mama is well again, when she returns home. . .'

Verena dropped her hands sharply, turning away. 'She will never return home!'

'But Verena, you don't mean that you intend—Lord above, you cannot devote your entire life to your mother!'

'But I *will*,' said Verena fiercely, turning on her. 'I had rather lose ten thousand chances of happiness than see Mama endangered yet again!'

'Endangered?' echoed Unice, blinking at her. 'I don't understand.'

'No, you don't understand. Why should you? "Love" in your world, Unice, is all sweetness and light, but I know better.'

Unice shrugged helplessly. 'Verena, what *is* this? You speak of love as of some monstrous thing.'

Verena's eyes filled. It was too much! She could no longer keep silent, not with the danger so close, with Nathaniel practically on the doorstep!

'*Monstrous*, yes.' Her voice grated on the word. Then, instinctively, it softened as she let it out at last. 'Oh, Unice! If you had heard, as I have from a child, the cries of fear and pain, the blows falling, and then seen, when at last you dared to enter where you had no rights, the piteous bruises that disfigured that once lovely face, then—oh, then, Unice, you would not talk to me of "love"!'

'After that,' Unice ended sadly, 'she would say nothing more.'

'Dash it, Unice!' protested her spouse, pushing himself up on his elbow where he lay on the grass under the chestnut tree in the Ruishtons' garden, whither he and Denzell had repaired in the morning heat to await Unice's return and hear her report. They had both discarded their frock-coats, and were lounging in shirtsleeves. 'She can't have left the matter there.'

'Can't she?' said Denzell sceptically, moodily throwing twigs across the lawn. 'You don't know how close she is.'

He was seated with his back against the tree trunk, his legs outstretched and crossed before him, his hat thrown to one side with his coat, and his long fair hair untidily ruffled from its contact with the bark behind him.

He had listened to Unice's account with a heart growing heavier by the minute. He had wanted to know what it was that caused Verena's barriers. There could be no doubting the meaning of the little Verena had told Unice, but its portent did nothing to uplift his spirits.

His first reaction had been one of intense compassion—both for Verena's mama, and for Verena herself to have borne witness to the cruelties of which she spoke. Then followed the inevitable realisation that here was a Herculean task: how to persuade Verena that all men did not beat their wives.

Small wonder she was afraid! Everything she was under that cool veneer had been crushed by a fear so

intense that he doubted his ability to assuage any part
of it. Even would she permit him the smallest opportunity to make the attempt—which of course she would
not.

'I don't know how she did it,' Unice was continuing,
'but she managed to recover that serene face of hers,
and behaved quite as if nothing untoward had
occurred.'

'I can see her doing it!' exclaimed Denzell feelingly.

'But, dash it,' cut in Osmond, 'she could not have
supposed that you would be fooled by it after all that.'

'No, and I said so,' agreed his wife. 'But for all the
good I got by it, I might as well have spared my breath.'

'And she would say nothing about this Chaceley
business?'

'My love, I had not the heart to bring it up after what
she had told me. I tried to express my sympathies at
least, but she would have none of it. She said that I
should not mind it because she should not have said as
much.'

'But she did,' Denzell put in, 'and it is typical of her
that she should clam up just at the point when you had
made a breakthrough. I love her desperately, but I
could willingly shake her when she does that!'

'For shame, Denzell. It is clear enough now why she
cannot confide in anyone.'

'Yes, but I am not "anyone". And as for this absurdity
that she has no heart—I wish I might have her alone
with me for five minutes, and we should see that!'

Osmond grinned at him. 'Rising to the challenge, eh,
Hawk?'

Denzell slumped back, sighing. 'I wish I might. Unice,
did she say nothing else at all?'

Unice shook her head. 'She would only keep repeating that I should not heed her since she was not herself,

and then she invited me to remain to meet with her brother and Mama when they returned from the Rooms.'

A quick frown entered Denzell's eyes. 'So he's back, is he?'

Osmond cocked an eyebrow. 'That sounds grim, Hawk. What's the poor fellow done to you?'

'Nothing,' came the short reply. 'And yet. . .'

'He has been here once or twice since Christmas, Denzell,' Unice said, puzzled. 'What of it?'

'What of it? Do you imagine I am coxcomb enough to believe that these haggard looks you have described are to be set solely to my account?'

'No one believes that, Hawk,' said Osmond soothingly. 'Obviously can't be so, if what Unice tells us is the truth. But why should you think the brother's presence means anything?'

'Because she was agitated by his presence at Christmas. It was the first time I saw her control waver in company. There is something in the wind, I am sure of it.'

This certainty grew upon him when Verena failed to put in an appearance anywhere in company either that evening, or at Sunday service in The King Charles Chapel, even though both her brother and mother were present. When she was again absent on Monday, while the company walked on the Pantiles in the morning, Unice, urged thereto by her house guest, paid her respects to Mrs Pateley and enquired after her daughter.

'The story is,' she reported to Denzell, 'that Verena is feeling a trifle downpin with the gaiety of the season.'

'Fiddle!'

'Why, so I think,' agreed Unice. 'And Mrs Pateley herself is displaying a degree of nervousness.'

'What about the brother?' Denzell asked frowningly.

'Are you at that again?' demanded Osmond. 'Why don't you go and talk to the fellow then?'

'I might just do that.'

'I know!' exclaimed Unice suddenly. 'You can find out from him whether Verena intends to go on this expedition to the High Rocks tomorrow.'

The Master of Ceremonies, Mr Tyson, with his usual enthusiasm, had arranged a picnic to the High Rocks which the majority of Wellsians were anticipating with eagerness.

'Is that tomorrow?'

'According to Mrs Felpham,' put in Osmond. 'Dashed female has never ceased running around asking everyone if they intend to go. You can ask her if Verena is going.'

'I thank you, I had rather Adam Pateley was my informant. And if Verena is going, how will that serve me?'

'It will serve you if she is not,' Unice pointed out. 'You may go and see her and make what peace you can.'

Denzell brightened. 'That is the first sensible suggestion anyone has made to me.'

It was not, however, until very late that evening that he was able to beard Adam Pateley, and then only by accident. In the expectation of the High Rocks expedition, there had been no entertainment arranged beyond the usual gathering for cards or chat in the Upper Rooms, and even that broke up early.

Feeling restless at Verena's continued absence, Denzell did not accompany his hosts when they left for home, but went instead to the Gentlemen's Rooms a few doors down where a number of die-hards were engaged in dicing and wining, or smoking a pipe.

He discovered Adam Pateley slumped over a bottle in a corner. The boy was somewhat the worse for drink, he realised, as he came up to the small table. Adam looked up blearily at his approach. Denzell smiled.

'May I join you?'

A frown descended upon Adam's brow, but he grudgingly moved a little to make room. Denzell pulled up a chair from close by and signed to one of the waiters.

'Bring me burgundy, if you please.' He looked at Adam again. 'I thought you had gone home.'

Adam made an effort. 'Took my mother, thass all. Didn't feel like g-going back to the New Inn.'

'I know what you mean,' Denzell agreed. 'There is little enjoyment in drinking alone.'

'Want to be alone,' said Adam, and then his colour deepened. 'I don't mean—I mean, don't mind you.'

'Thank you,' Denzell said, handing the waiter a coin and pouring himself a glass from the bottle that had been brought.

He looked the lad over. He was only a lad, for all the serious look of his face—faintly dissipated just now, though, which told its own tale, along with the slurring of his words. He must have suffered, too, under such a brutal reign. Was this his way of dealing with it, through a too liberal use of the bottle?

He leaned confidentially towards the boy. 'Adam— may I call you that?'

A faintly scornful laugh came. 'Call me anything you like. Harsh as you like. I deserve it all!'

By George, what an opening! 'Why, Adam? What have you done?'

He shook his head. 'She hasn't blamed me for it. Should've, though. All my fault.'

She? Verena! Had he not known it? But what was

'it'? Really, it was almost as difficult to extract information from the boy in his cups as it was from Verena herself!

'Come, Adam. Your sister must know you meant no harm.'

'Harm! Course I meant no harm. She's my mother. Think I want that devil to hurt her again? Swears he won't. V'rena don't believe him. Not sure I do either.'

Now they were getting somewhere! Denzell tossed off his glass and poured himself another. The boy had a loose tongue all right. It was not difficult to guess the rest. 'You told him where to find them, is that it?'

Adam dropped his head in his hands with a groan. Yes, that must have been it, Denzell decided, nursing his glass in his cupped hands. So that explained the mystery. Verena and her mother were in hiding here, and the boy had given them away. Obviously he had not meant to. But if he was in the habit of drinking, and drink made him garrulous, what price loyalty then?

A thought struck him—stunningly. Was the man Pateley coming here? Oh, chaste stars!

'Adam!' he said imperatively, putting down his glass without sipping at it again. 'Tell me this. Is Verena in any danger? Pateley—your father—will he hurt her?'

The boy dragged himself upright, and tried to shake his head. 'Not V'rena. Too clever.' He threw up a finger and tapped his own nose. 'Used her head. Not like me. Alwaysh flared, me. Got beat for't. Not V'rena. Quiet as a mouse, she was. Docile and ob-obedient, never say boo to a goose. Thass what he thought. He'd look at her, never see anything in her face, never. Give him no reason, she said, no excuse.'

Denzell's heart contracted. Oh, poor darling girl! Was it thus her mask was built? All her warmth, the natural joy of her, pushed under for fear of what this man might do. And he himself, who had fallen in love with what he glimpsed beneath the mask, to be tarred with a like brush? No, Verena! Oh, no, sweet princess.

There and then a new determination was born. If it took him his life long, she would learn to discover him for what he was—not for what she imagined he might be. And he would, whatever it took, release her from that darkness she inhabited, into a world of light and laughter.

'Adam,' he said, on a note of strength brought about by the change in him the boy's revelations had wrought, 'tell me only this. Is Verena intending to go to High Rocks tomorrow?'

The boy shook his head. 'Waiting. Won't come out. Wants me to keep Mama out of the way, much as possible. Thass why we've been gadding about—without V'rena. Hopes to send him packing.'

'Then are you going to High Rocks?'

'Shouldn't think Mama will go. Wants to see him.'

'What? Your mother actually *wishes* to see your father?'

Adam nodded vehemently. 'See if he's changed. Thinks she might go back then. Doesn't want to ruin V'rena's life. But ish no good, 'cos V'rena won't let her go back. Nothing to be done about it.'

Oh, was there not? They would see about that, Denzell promised mentally. He did not know what might be done about it, not yet. But something had to be done. For there was another now who was not prepared to tolerate the ruining of Verena's life!

CHAPTER NINE

VERENA had slept a little better than she had these last few nights. More from exhaustion than anything else. She had felt dreadful on waking, her head thick and heavy, her bones weary. But remembrance of what she was waiting for had soon driven all that away—just as it had every morning since Adam had come with his hideous news.

She had carefully calculated the probabilities, counting days. Nathaniel would come by coach, and he would not have travelled on Sunday. He must have started out a day or two after Adam, and the coach would necessarily make slower progress, for Adam, dependent on speed, had left the gig at home and ridden post. She had waited at home none the less, although she thought she could reckon on two to three days, four at the most. But time was up. He must arrive today!

She was riding on nervous energy, but she was aware only of the necessity to remain alert, to be ready for the moment that must tax every ounce of her strength.

Mama had gone out with Adam, although neither he nor Verena had been able to persuade her to join the expedition to High Rocks. Verena know not whether to be glad of the new determination that showed how Mama had altered, or sorry for it, since she now wished to face Nathaniel herself.

'When all is said and done, Verena, he is still my husband, to whom I am vowed before God,' she had stated with a dignity that greatly became her. 'If you wonder that I am not afraid of him, then I reply that I am afraid. But this respite has given me courage, Verena, and that I owe to you. I am persuaded he will not attempt to do me harm in this place, and therefore I will see him.'

Nothing Verena could do or say served to move her from this standpoint, and it had filled Verena with a dread that swept from her mind everything but this. She had succeeded only in extracting a promise from Adam to keep Mama away from the lodging for as long as possible, that she might make her own warnings to Nathaniel before he could get to Mama.

Pacing the little parlour, attired against the expected visit in a round gown of pale yellow muslin demurely buttoned high over the bosom, with a standing ruff edged with lace and sleeves to the wrist, her hair partly covered by a small mob-cap, she waited, rehearsing in her head all the things she meant to say to Nathaniel. Yet when the door knocker sounded downstairs, her mind froze as still as her body. She stood like a statue, facing the door, in a listening attitude, hearing the clump of Betsey's footsteps going down the stairs.

Her heartbeat began to thud in her own ears as the sound of a male voice smote them, along with Betsey's murmurs. Double thumps now, two sets of feet ascending the stairs.

A plea sang in her head. Heaven give me strength! Her pulse quickened, even more painfully, and she braced herself as the door swung open.

'A visitor, Miss Verena,' said Betsey coolly, and Denzell Hawkeridge walked into the room, easy in buckskins and topboots, and a frock-coat of olive green, a toning waistcoat beneath in a lighter hue.

For an instant, Verena simply stared at him, bewilderment in her brain. Then a wash of relief hit her, dizzyingly, and she took several steps backwards towards the bureau, grasping swiftly at the back of the chair before it.

'Miss Chaceley, are you ill?' came Denzell's concerned tones, as he moved quickly forward.

But Betsey was before him, one hand about her charge's waist in an instant, supporting her drooping form, and clucking her concern.

'There, my dove, now don't you go swooning on me! Here, quick, sit in the chair.'

But Verena was already recovering. She pushed away gently. 'No, no, Betsey, I am all right. It was only—I thought it was *he*.'

'So did I,' agreed the maid grimly, adding in an undervoice, 'I thought you might as well see the gentleman, Miss Verena. It'll take your mind off it for a little.'

Verena looked across at Denzell, standing in the middle of the room and regarding her with a good deal of concern. Without thinking, she smiled at him.

'I beg your pardon, Mr Hawkeridge. I was expecting...'

She petered out as the memory of their last meeting came back to her, the things she had said to him, and subsequently restated to Unice—and given herself away into the bargain! Had he discovered it all from his hostess?

There was no telling any of this from his face. He was returning the smile, a twinkle coming into his eye.

'I am glad to discover that it is not I myself who had such an effect upon you. I should be afraid to walk into any room in which you might be present had that been the case.'

That drew a spurt of laughter from her, and some of her consciousness eased. Betsey, a somewhat grim smile curling her lips, released the hold she still had on Verena's arm, and moved to the door.

'I'll warn you, Miss Verena, when it's the master.'

Verena nodded, watching as Betsey left the room, very properly leaving the door partially ajar behind her. Denzell took a step or two towards her.

'Don't you think you should sit down for a moment?'

'To tell the truth, I am still a trifle shaky,' she agreed, moving to seat herself in the chair.

Denzell came up and perched on the corner of the day-bed, his eyes never leaving her face. He could not doubt but that she was waiting to receive this man Pateley, but he was reluctant to make any further reference to that. He dared not show his own new knowledge. For one thing, it would mean betraying Adam's inadvertent confidences, which could not please his sister. For another, he did not wish to embarrass her by making it obvious that Unice had told him all that had been spoken between them in this very room.

Yet he must refer to their last encounter. He could not begin to make amends unless he first cleared that hurdle.

Verena was no longer looking at him. Her beautiful countenance was calmer, but her fingers were clasped together in her lap, and their nervous movement told its own tale. Only this time, Denzell did not make the mistake of setting it down to his own account! There was clearly a good deal else on her mind today.

'Miss Chaceley—Verena—' he began, and paused as her gaze came up to his again on the use of her given name. Such haunted shadows in her eyes! Involuntarily, he threw out a hand, saying quickly, 'Have no fear! I have not come to distress you with unwanted attentions, nor to plead my cause against your express prohibition. I have come only to apologise for my conduct the other night.'

Verena bit her lip. He had come to apologise! And

what of her conduct? Well she knew that she had given him cause both for anger and confusion. She had treated him so unkindly—and after behaving in a manner that must have encouraged him to believe her willing. Oh, that kiss!

'Denzell—' she began impulsively, and then broke off, recollecting herself. 'I mean, Mr Hawkeridge—'

'Ah, no!' he exclaimed out of the instant warmth that had invaded his breast at her use of his name. 'Let us, I pray you, drop that level of formality.' He leaned forward a little, holding out his hand. 'Can we not at least cry friends, Verena?'

Verena looked at his outstretched hand, then up to his face, and a rush of tenderness engulfed her. Her eyes filled and she put out her fingers towards his, unaware of how her own quivered. Denzell clasped them lightly, bowed his head and kissed the tips of her fingers, and then let them go.

They tingled as Verena returned them to her lap, lacing them into her other hand. She could not look at him, and her voice was low.

'You are—very kind. I am aware that I behaved— that I may have led you to believe—' She stopped, drawing a strengthening breath, and grateful that he did not seek to interrupt her faltering speech. Dredging up from somewhere the remnants of her shielding mask, she composed herself and looked up at him again.

'Denzell, I accept your apology, and I hope that in turn you will accept mine. I did not conduct myself in the manner of a lady in receipt of such a very flattering declaration.'

No, that was too much, Denzell decided. He broke in quickly. 'You did nothing for which you need reproach yourself. Mine is the blame.' He stood up. 'I will not importune you further, but I beg you to believe that,

now and always, if there is some way in which I can
serve you, you may command me in anything.'

Verena rose quickly, holding out her hands. 'Oh, no,
no. You deserve of me better than that. If we are to be
friends, then don't speak of service. Friends are not to
be beholden to one another. They—'

She broke off suddenly, turning her head away, and
dragging out of his grasp the hands which he had so
willingly received into his hold.

'What is it?' he said at once, seeing the warmth in her
face instantly overlaid with fear.

She did not answer, but ran quickly to the window
in the bay and peered down. Denzell followed and saw
below that a travelling carriage was drawing up outside
the front door. Verena seized his arm in a fierce grip.

'Denzell, you must go. Dear heaven, but I knew he
would come this day!'

Still looking down, Denzell saw a middle-aged man
descend, dressed for the road in a light great-coat, his
hat in his hand, and stand looking about him with grim
eyes in a hollow face with an unmistakable resemblance
to the boy Adam. The man moved to the door, and
next instant they could hear the knocking downstairs.

Denzell laid his hand over Verena's which still
clutched his arm. 'This is what you have been home for
these few days, is it not? You have been waiting for this
man. He is the cause of all your fears. Is he not,
Verena?'

'Ask me no questions, Denzell, but go, I beg of you!'
she uttered frenziedly. 'I must meet him alone.'

He plucked her hand from his sleeve and held it fast.
'Verena, I have serious misgivings about leaving you to
face this man on your own.'

She shook her head, moving towards the centre of
the room, so that Denzell, still tightly holding her hand,

came with her willy-nilly. Betsey's face appeared at the door.

'It's him, Miss Verena!' she hissed. 'I saw him from the window.'

'Yes, I know. Go, Betsey! Bring him up.'

The maid disappeared and Verena turned on Denzell, unaware that her fingers clung to his even as she pushed at his chest as if she would dislodge him from her presence.

'Denzell, pray go! I *must* see him alone, for I have much that must be said to him—and I don't know how long I have before Mama gets back.'

'But, Verena—'

'You need have no fear at leaving me with him,' she interrupted quickly. 'He is my stepfather.'

Denzell only just prevented himself from saying that he already knew it. Nor could he say that he feared for Verena's safety at the hands of a man who was a known wife-beater. Adam had stated that Verena never gave her stepfather cause for attacking her, but she looked at this moment as if she might well do so. Frustrated at being unable to speak his real fears, he could say nothing.

Verena was listening for the voices downstairs, and then the footsteps coming up. She dragged her hand out of Denzell's. 'Too late! Promise me you will go the moment he arrives in here.'

What could he do? He had offered his friendship, and his support. If she refused the latter, what more was there to be said? Friendship dictated that he respect her wishes.

'Very well,' he sighed.

Verena only nodded. She could hear the footsteps coming up now, and she had no attention to spare for Denzell. It occurred to her briefly that his presence had been of help, for she was no longer in a state of fear. Her control was back, and she faced the door in the sure knowledge of her own capable strength.

Betsey pushed the door fully open, saying briefly as she entered, 'It's the master, Miss Verena.'

Nathaniel Pateley came in behind her, and paused on the threshold, his hooded eyes passing from Verena to Denzell and back again. His lean features were drawn, etched with deeper carven lines from nose to mouth, and the sunken hollows under his eyes were dark with shadow.

Verena noted these signs of suffering, and could not but rejoice in her heart. The very sight of him filled her with a renewal of that hatred she had nurtured through the years, and she was conscious of an intense satisfaction that he had experienced even a tithe of the torture with which he had broken Mama's spirit. She could not speak, for fear that she might express these thoughts in words.

Nathaniel himself broke the silence, in a voice heavy with suspicion. 'Are you not going to present me, Verena?'

Instinctively, Denzell's glance went to Verena and he almost gasped out. Did she hate the man that much? Her eyes pierced like twin daggers! By George, but there was tension in the air! It must be long since these two had met, but there was evidently to be no exchange of greetings. And Verena, it was clear, had no intention of introducing him.

He bowed slightly. 'My name is Hawkeridge, sir.'

The other eyed him appraisingly, looking again at Verena briefly. He nodded, and began to remove his great-coat. 'I am Pateley. You will excuse us, I trust. I wish to speak with my daughter alone.'

Verena found her tongue. She almost spat the words. 'I am not your daughter!'

Denzell saw the man's eyes flash, and his jaw tighten. A glimpse of possibilities that filled him with instant comprehension. There was a black temper here, a temper unused to be crossed—particularly by this slip of a girl! Yet he was in a delicate position. Everything in him urged him to champion Verena, refuse to leave. But on what grounds? The man had not offered her violence, and Verena herself had already asked him several times to go.

It was Betsey who settled the matter. Having received the great-coat Squire Pateley handed to her, she made frantic signals behind the man's back indicative of her urgent desire that Denzell should absent himself from the scene. He took one more look at Verena's set face, and capitulated.

He turned to Verena. 'I will leave you, Miss Chaceley—unless you feel you would wish me to remain.'

Verena, her sight and mind filled only with the loathed figure before her, scarcely heard him. The concept reached her only as a faint wisp of interruption in the intensity of her concentration. Her eyes never left the man's face, and she uttered only the one word, 'Go.'

Denzell gave an inward sigh, but he bowed briefly and nodded to Pateley as he passed him, noting the careful neatness of his dress, despite a carriage journey. No doubt but the man had come a-courting! Betsey seized his arm and drew him from the room, closing the door behind them both. When Denzell would have spoken, she put a finger to her lips and set her ear to the woodwork. Perforce, Denzell listened also. Pateley it was who spoke first.

'You have practised a fine deceit upon me all this

time, Verena,' he said in a voice that showed clearly his
sense of outrage. 'Through how many years have you
shown that modest and docile exterior, when all the
while you were planning to practise this shameful trick
upon me? Was that done as I deserved? Have I not
ever taken care of you, used you as if you were truly
my own flesh and blood?'

Verena's voice came then, vibrant with scorn. 'I thank
heaven you have not! I pity Adam, that he is obliged to
carry your blood in his veins. But I, sir, am a Chaceley
born, and though I blame my father's family for their
treatment of Mama, I say only, God forgive them. But
if I am to endure to hear you speak of *your* deserts,
Nathaniel Pateley, then I answer you only this: may you
burn in hell!'

There was a silence then. Denzell saw Betsey stand
up straight again, throwing a hand to her capacious
bosom and rolling her eyes. He was not surprised. He
was shocked himself to hear Verena dare so far! Deuce
take it, was she mad? Although it seemed as if Pateley
knew not how to reply to her words. To his relief, he
heard the man actually laugh.

'You amaze me, Verena,' he said. 'I did not think
you had it in you.'

Betsey visibly relaxed. 'All's well,' she whispered,
and shooed at Denzell to move him along the corridor
towards the stairhead, collecting his hat along the way
from the stand in the hallway.

'But can we safely leave her there?' he asked in a low
tone, receiving the beaver from her. 'Is she not in
danger from him if she speaks in such a provocative
way?'

It did not seem as if the maid was surprised to hear
him talk of Verena thus. She shook her head, ushering

him down the stairs. 'Never you fret, sir. It ain't defiance as angers him. He won't touch her.'

'How can you be so sure?' Denzell demanded strongly out of his own deep concern.

'I know him too well. He won't do nothing 'til the mistress has shown her face. It's her as he's come to see. Besides, Mr Adam will be here. Believe me, sir, if I feared for her, I wouldn't be letting you go!'

This was a touch comforting, although Denzell would have preferred to remain within call. But he did not see how he could. He had no rights here, and Verena had made it clear that she did not wish him to intervene.

A thought struck him and he paused at the front door, eyeing the maid in a speculative way. 'You would not care to explain what she meant by her words about her mother's family, the Chaceleys?'

Betsey pursed her lips. 'No, I wouldn't,' she said bluntly. 'If you win the right to it, Mr Hawkeridge, she'll tell you herself.'

He grimaced. 'If I win the right.'

'Go now, if you please, sir,' the maid said firmly, opening the door. 'Family business, this is.' Then she shut him out of the house.

Denzell remained on the doorstep for a moment or two, glancing up at the window above. There was nothing to be heard, and the maid was right. It was family business. Faintly cheered by her words about his possible rights, he moved off, albeit reluctantly, in the direction of the Ruishton home. The travelling carriage had gone, presumably so that the servants might refresh themselves at some inn. Evidently Squire Pateley expected to be here for some time.

He crossed the garden and passed into the open space of ground where Verena had once helped the children to build a snowman. Then he paused and

looked back. It was with some measure of relief that he
saw Adam and Mrs Pateley turning into the drive of the
lodging-house. He wondered what might be the outcome once they discovered the new arrival above stairs.

In the parlour Verena was listening to her stepfather
with a slight cooling of her rage, now that she had
discharged some of it. She had need of her composure,
for the last thing she wished to do was to provoke him
into some precipitate action that might lead to disaster.
Besides, she had to state her unalterable intentions
against his own.

But it was very difficult to maintain even a vestige of
calm in his presence, now that he knew her mask for
what it was. Long habit reasserted itself, however, and
although she could not abate one jot of her defiant
hatred, she did manage to bring her face under control.

'Whatever your personal feelings, Verena,' he was
saying, in a voice of persuasive calm, 'you must surely
see that you have no right to encourage a man's wife to
run away from him.'

'We are not talking of a man's wife,' she responded
coldly. 'We are talking of my mother.'

'There is no tie more binding than the marriage
contract. Not even the blood tie. It is sacred, you see,
and you, Verena, have come between us. You do not
seem to realise the extreme seriousness of what you
have done.'

'Do I not?' Verena asked, and a contemptuous smile
curled her lips. 'You mistake me, sir. You should be
glad of this misdemeanour of mine. For if I had been
obliged to remain at home and watch my Mama suffer,
I would certainly have taken a pistol to your head.'

Nathaniel blenched. '*What*? You cannot know what
you are saying! Shoot your own father?'

'My father,' Verena uttered tightly, 'is already dead.'

'Oh, very well, your stepfather, then. It makes it no better. I think you must be mad indeed!'

'If I am, then lay it at your own door. Whatever I am, sir, your misconduct has made me.'

'Poppycock!' snapped Nathaniel, moving as if he would shift away from her. 'Enough of this! Where is Abigail? I wish to see her at once.'

'You need not take this high-handed tone, sir. You may see her, for she has expressed a desire to meet with you. But mark this! If you harm one hair of her head, if you so much as make a move in that direction—'

'But this is insane!' he interrupted. 'Do you think I have come all this way to—?'

'I know why you have come all this way,' she cut in, 'because Adam told me. You have vowed to take Mama back. If you imagine that I will permit it, however, you are wrong.'

Nathaniel uttered a short laugh. 'And how do you propose to stop me? Come, Verena, you are being extraordinarily foolish.'

'Am I?' Hard and cold.

'Verena,' he began, and stopped, turning as the door opened behind him.

Mrs Pateley stood on the threshold, Adam close at her back. She was almost pretty again in her lilac cambric gown, Verena realised with a start of fear. Her glance flew back to Nathaniel's face, alert for any danger. Into his eyes she saw enter an expression of appreciation, swiftly succeeded by one of intense hurt. Her gorge rose. Dissembler! Worse still, Mama's eyes softened at the sight.

'Oh, Nathaniel,' she sighed, and moved forward.

'Adam!' Verena cried, running to intercept a meeting. 'Don't let him near her!'

Mrs Pateley stopped as her daughter came between

her and her husband. Adam shifted to one side, ready
to intervene. But, to Verena's surprise and acute suspicion, Nathaniel threw up his hands and backed away,
in a gesture of surrender.

'Do you think I have come to bully?' he cried, in a
voice that she could almost believe sincere in its distress. 'No, Abigail—I have come to beg.'

There was a short silence. Verena stared at her
stepfather. What an alteration in his features when he
was confronted with Mama! Yet he had dealt with
Verena herself in a manner that showed all too clearly
how little he had truly changed. She turned urgently to
Mrs Pateley.

'Mama, do not believe him! He is determined on
forcing your return, by whatever means. He will play
upon your conscience, as he has tried to play upon
mine. If he may speak of begging, then let me beg, too!'

'Verena, my darling, don't!' pleaded Mrs Pateley,
tears starting to her eyes.

'I *must*, Mama—' She lowered her voice to a whisper.
'I am so afraid that he will succeed with you, as he so
often has before, and I cannot *bear* to think of it.'

Her mother released her hands and clasped Verena
in her arms, hugging her close. 'My dearest love! You
have been a most diligent guardian, but you must let
me stand on my own feet now.'

Verena drew away, looking down into her mother's
set face. Heaven help her! Was everything to go for
nothing? Mama thought herself strong, but was she
proof against Nathaniel's wiles? Verena did not think
so.

What to do? Where to seek for help? She looked at
Adam, and saw uncertainty in his face. There was
nothing to be got from that quarter. Then it was all
squarely back on her own shoulders. She turned again

to Nathaniel, convinced he was waiting only for the opportunity to get Mama alone.

'Be warned, sir!' she said, her tone hard. 'Mama has too soft a heart, and she will hear you. But do not forget that you have me with whom to deal.'

A sad smile entered his face, and he directed his remarks towards his wife rather than Verena. 'I have come with a humble heart, and if Abigail has compassion enough to soften to my pleas, then shall I be satisfied. You will find me a good deal changed, Abigail.'

Verena's eyes flashed at him. 'Oh, you may offer lies, Nathaniel Pateley, enough to cozen Mama. But you will not take her home again, trust me.'

Nathaniel ignored her. His gaze remained fixed on his wife's face. 'I need you, Abigail. I have had time to learn that I cannot live without you. You know how I love you.'

'Love!' cried Verena frenziedly. 'You call it "love" to batter with your fists until your helpless victim lies almost senseless at your feet?'

'That is in the past!' he uttered vehemently. 'I confess my faults, Abigail. Freely I confess them. I have wronged you, but I will never do so again.'

'No, for you will never have power over her again,' Verena threw at him. 'Not while I am alive to prevent it.'

Suddenly Nathaniel turned on her. 'Oh, leave me be, girl! What in Hades has it to do with you? Haven't you caused enough unhappiness? In any event, you are wasting your breath. I swear to God, I will not leave here without my wife!'

'There, I knew it!' Verena slammed back. She might have laughed if she had not been so angry. *She* had caused unhappiness, he dared to say, himself author of all this!

She turned briefly to her mother. 'You see, Mama? You hear him?' Then she whirled back on Nathaniel. 'Try what you can. Force her, persuade her, *drag* her home. But mark this: I will come to Fittleworth and fetch her away again—at whatever cost.'

Nathaniel's brow grew black, and Adam started forward, seizing Verena's arm. 'Verena, you are distressing Mama.'

Verena wrenched her arm out of his hold. 'Then why do you not say something to support me, instead of standing there like a stock? This is your fault, Adam!'

'I know it,' he answered curtly, 'but I still say it is a matter between my father and our mama. You agreed that Mama might speak to him. Then let be, and do not be stirring the waters so that even discussion becomes impossible.'

His words struck home. Verena hesitated. Yes, she had agreed—perforce. And she had stirred the waters purposely, pushing Nathaniel to reveal his true colours, desperate to deflect Mama's intention to meet him alone.

But she had reckoned without Mrs Pateley's own new strength of mind, until she felt her mother's hand on her arm.

'Adam is right, dearest. Leave us alone for a little.'

Verena stared at her, breathless with dread. 'Alone? You and he?'

'I will be safe enough, Verena,' she said gently. 'Go with your brother, I pray you.'

Mrs Pateley passed her daughter and went to stand behind one of the armchairs, facing her husband and looking him boldly in the face. Watching her, Verena was conscious of a measure of realisation penetrating the blanketing fear. Mama had changed! She was stronger. Perhaps, after all, she might stand up to him. If only Verena could be sure that she would not agree to return with him. She hesitated.

'Nothing will happen, Verena,' Adam said firmly, adding his persuasions to his mother's. 'Mama has a right to this privacy, and you know it.'

'I thank you, Adam,' said his father, nodding in his son's direction. He added on a faint note of sarcasm, 'And if your sister wishes it, do you remain within call to prevent me spiriting your mother away.'

Adam nodded, and taking Verena's arm, pulled her to the door. She turned there, casting one last threatening look at her stepfather.

'If you so much as lay one finger on her. . .'

Mrs Pateley looked across at her. Her tone was both dignified and firm. 'Go, Verena.'

The next moment Verena found herself outside the parlour, her brother moving her off towards her own chamber next door.

'We can wait in your room,' he said.

But Verena was too much on the fidgets to wait anywhere. She paced her bedchamber, while Adam sat on the one chair the room held, regarding her worriedly.

'Verena,' he said quietly, 'be still!'

She continued to pace. 'How can I be still?'

'They must come to an understanding by themselves. We cannot interfere.'

She halted then and turned to him, repeating flatly, 'We cannot interfere. How often have I agonised on that question? Adam, do you know what this feels like?'

He frowned. 'What do you mean?'

'Waiting here in this room,' she uttered, in a tone of anguish, for the memories were crowding in, 'prohibited from going in, knowing that at any moment the shouting may erupt into violence.'

'Verena, there is no shouting,' Adam said, rising and going to her. 'Listen! They are talking—in a civilised manner.'

Verena shook her head, for the visions were too strong. Visions of hateful days, when she had crouched, listening, not daring to move for fear of discovery, for fear of bringing about a worser punishment than that which she could hear—blow after blow, cry after cry, until she must cover her ears and weep those stifled silent sobs into her upraised knees, soiling her gown.

'Civilised?' she uttered in a shaking voice. 'How can it be civilised? He is an *animal*—a brutish animal!'

Adam's arms went round her and he held her close. But the embrace was too stifling and she struggled free.

'I cannot bear this,' she said, crossing quickly to the door.

Adam was before her, holding it fast. 'You will not interrupt them. I won't let you.'

Verena shifted, pushing back and forth. 'Let me go, Adam. I cannot stay in this house.'

He frowned. 'You want to go out?'

'I don't care where I go, but I cannot remain here.'

'Very well,' he said, and cautiously opened the door.

Verena went through it, hesitated an instant or two, looking towards the parlour door. Then she saw Betsey standing guard outside it.

'Oh, thank heaven!' she muttered.

The maid came quickly up to her, whispering. 'All's quiet, Miss Verena. Murmuring voices, that's all.'

'Betsey, I am going out,' Verena said in a hushed tone.

'That's the way, my dove. You can go as you are, it's

warm enough. Don't you fret now. Mr Adam and me will see all's right.'

Verena nodded, and then Adam was ushering her down the stairs, saying, 'Do you want me to come with you?'

'Dear heaven, no, Adam!' she replied, halting in the middle of the flight. 'If you fail me on this occasion—if he removes Mama from this refuge—'

'He won't, trust me,' Adam promised. 'Or trust in Betsey, if you prefer.'

Verena did prefer it. But she knew that Betsey alone could not prevent Nathaniel from taking Mama away. She reached up and touched Adam's hand briefly.

'I trust you.'

Then, before she could change her mind and rush back upstairs to burst in on the conference in the parlour, she hurried down and let herself out of the house.

She walked swiftly, on an automatic course towards the Common, hardly looking where she went, her mind filled with distressing pictures of the past. She did not hear her name called, nor the footsteps running after her, and she was already on the Common, taking a well-worn path, when Denzell caught up with her.

'Verena, wait!' he called, seizing her arm to halt her.

She stopped, hardly able to take in that she was waylaid. She saw the face, and knew it, and spoke its name without thinking, blurting out the confusion of her brain as if she was fully conscious that she might safely do so.

'Oh, Denzell, she is alone with him! He says he will not hurt her, and perhaps he will not. But he will *say* such things. . .and she will believe him! She always did. And it will be nothing but black lies.'

'Verena, calm yourself!' Denzell commanded, taking

her shoulders and holding her fast. 'Come, don't speak yet.' He smiled. 'Where is that famous control that I have had so much reason to deprecate? What, Snow Maiden, have you thrown away your mask?'

An involuntary gurgle of laughter escaped her, bringing her back to the present. The confusion lifted a little. 'My mask has rather deserted me,' she offered shakily.

'Never!' Denzell declared, and putting an arm about her, led her off the path and into the shade of a tree, for the sun was hot. He stripped off the olive-green coat and laid it down, instructing her to sit. Glad to be relieved of the necessity to think for herself, Verena sank down, the pale yellow muslin spreading about her, and watched Denzell settle before her, his attitude relaxed as he sat in shirtsleeves, his hat at one side, the queue of his tied-back fair hair falling over his shoulder to lie upon the subdued green of his waistcoat.

There was an expression of tenderness in the blue eyes as they looked her over with that smoky glow that had the effect of ruffling her breath a little, but her heart and mind were still too full to leave room for what this might mean.

Denzell's own thoughts were all for her distress. He had found himself unable to go all the way home, his concern for Verena's safety causing him to dally in the square of open ground. When he saw her leaving the house, he was glad of his own irresolution, and had hurried after her at once, for it was obvious from her demeanour that she was greatly overset.

When he stopped her, the distraught look in her face and the trembling outburst of that hurried speech had gone straight to his heart. He wanted only to comfort her, to alleviate her distress by any means in his power.

She was looking at him with more openness than she

ever had before. Expectantly almost, as if she trusted in him to deliver her. He smiled warmly.

'Now, my princess, tell me the whole.'

Verena noticed nothing amiss in this form of address, nor in his assumption that she would confide in him. She fetched a sigh, and shrugged.

'What am I to tell? I am in dread that he will succeed with Mama. He will cozen her with his pleas and promises, for she is in no condition to resist him.'

'You mean your stepfather?'

'Nathaniel, yes.' She sighed again. 'I have been persuaded to let them alone—that is why I came out. I could not abide the waiting. It was too reminiscent of earlier times.' She threw her hands up to her face, pressing them to her cheeks, closing her eyes. 'Oh, if you knew the dreadful, unkind things he said of her! All to give himself reason to inflict upon her the vicious punishment of his heavy fists.'

Despite the fact that he had understood that this must be the meaning behind the little she had told Unice, Denzell found himself shocked and distressed by the picture these words painted.

Almost he shied away from asking further, from hearing any more, for, to himself—and he was persuaded, to those of his intimates whom he knew almost as well as he knew his own mind—such a shameful use of a man's strength was not to be tolerated. No gentleman would strike a lady, never mind administer this kind of beating. Deuce take it, but that was for prizefighters! Were such a thing known in his circles, the perpetrator would be shunned by society—and rightly.

But here was Verena, whom he loved, and who had memories that she must long to eliminate from her heart. He had no mind to hear them, but he would share them, for her sake.

'What sort of things, Verena?' he asked quietly. 'What would he say?'

Verena's shoulders shifted, as if the burden of the memory was too great to bear. But she answered, her hands dropping down to pluck aimlessly at her muslin petticoats.

'Oh, that Mama did not love him. That she had an eye to some other man. That she was his alone, despite her desires for others—despicable lies! Mama never *looked* at another man. She would not have dared to do so, for fear of such consequences as must ensue.'

'And then?' Denzell urged.

Verena shivered. 'And then, when she denied it all, when he had driven her to a quarrelsome frenzy, he would hit her. When she cried out, he would do so again. He would say that he must demonstrate his mastery this way, if she would not permit him to do so—the other way.'

Denzell went cold. Had Verena's mama refused her husband his rights? By George, that was foolhardy! Any man must be frustrated by that, but such a man as this would be angered beyond bearing. And Verena *knew* of this? Chaste stars!

But Verena was still speaking, her eyes unseeing, her mind far away, receding into the memories that haunted her.

'When he was satisfied—when he had punished her enough for his temper to begin to cool, he would leave her, slamming himself from the room.' Verena drew a shuddering breath. 'That was the moment when I used to find the courage to creep in. I had to, for Mama was incapable of tending to her own hurts. Either myself or Betsey had to do it.'

She did not notice the tears that slipped down her cheeks, tears that rent Denzell in pieces as he forced himself to remain still, and to listen while she talked on, moving into the present tense as if the events she related were happening this moment.

'She lies there, swollen and bleeding at the mouth. Her eye half closed—you can see the bruise beginning there already. I take the basin and bring some water, and gently—very gently, for she is hurting so—I clean away the blood, and press the cold flannel to her bruises.'

One hand came up and her fingers dashed automatically at the wetness on her cheeks, and she sniffed, shaking her head. 'So many, sometimes, that I could not do them all in time. She suffered them on her back and her neck, for she must have turned from him to save her face. Then I had to hurry, for you see he would always come back—in due time.'

'Come back!' uttered Denzell, out of the dreadful confusion of compassion and revulsion warring in his breast. 'How could he dare to come back?'

Without thinking, he automatically plunged his hand into the pocket of his buckskin breeches and brought forth a handkerchief. He thrust it into her restless fingers, and Verena held it, her eyes focusing on his face as the tears gave way to the stirrings of that rage he had seen in her countenance when she met Nathaniel earlier in his presence.

'Oh, yes, he dared. He would come back all right, with a mouthful of apologies, a heart—so he claimed—full of remorse, speaking of his great "love" for her.' Her face twisted as she repeated with an inflection of sickening disgust, '*Love*—oh, how often have I heard him use that word and wished I might cut it on his skin with a blunted knife!'

Denzell heard the vicious wish with a surge of emotion. If he had only known with what a legacy he had to deal when he spoke to Verena of 'love'! Small wonder she reacted as she had. He watched her dab at her eyes with his handkerchief, and his chest tightened. But his heart stilled as she spoke on, for there was worse to come.

'I should not have heard these things,' she said, and her voice was hard again. 'Only there were occasions when I was not quick enough to escape before he would re-enter the room. I used to hide under the bed, and be forced to listen to him begging forgiveness, saying he had not meant a word of it, mingling his false tears with her own. And then. . .and then he would. . .'

She could not go on, her fingers wrestling his handkerchief into a ball. Denzell, quite appalled by the implication, reached out a hand and seized her fingers, handkerchief and all, almost crushing them in his anxiety to relieve her mind.

'Say no more! I understand.'

What a hideous fate! That a child should have been obliged to witness such scenes and learn of lovemaking in this crude manner. The thought crossed his mind that he had taken on an impossible task, but it was overborne by the need to give Verena what comfort he might. To let her begin to know that what she had been so unfortunate as to experience was the exception rather than the rule.

He relieved her of the maltreated handkerchief and took her other hand, holding both together in a strong clasp between his own. 'Verena, this is not "love" as most men know it, my poor girl. Only look at Unice and Osmond. You surely cannot imagine that anything of the kind might occur between them. They are the fondest couple I know.'

Verena made no attempt to remove her hands, but they lay limply in his grasp, and her voice was bleak.

'Those that saw Nathaniel and Mama together would never have imagined it of them either. They hid it well between them. Even I did not know until I was eight. Mama was thought to be sickly, that is all, for she was indisposed for days at a time. That is why I chose Tunbridge Wells, so that it might be given out, when it became known that we had gone, that Mama was here for her health.'

'Verena, you delude yourself!' he said urgently. 'One does not live on an island. Such things as you have spoken of are the stuff of servants' gossip. Can you truly believe that the matter was unknown in your circles? I frankly doubt it.'

She nodded. 'Yes, so do I. But that does not mean that people were able to observe it in their public conduct.' A tiny smile came and went. 'Only look at me. I am a past master at my company mask, as you call it. Mama was almost as good. It is only since she has been here that she has given way to her misery.'

There was silence for a while. Denzell would have given anything to show her how mistaken were her views, how narrow. How, he knew not. But this was not the time. She was calmer now, and he must keep her so, not risk distressing her anew.

'How was it you were able to come here at all?' he asked, for he had long pondered the question of how mother and daughter could be supporting themselves.

'Grandpapa Whicham—my mother's father—left me money in trust,' she answered readily. 'I had only to wait for my majority, by which time I had resolved how I would use it.'

The answer threw the whole matter of the Chaceleys back into his mind. Tentatively, in a casual tone, he tried a subtle probe. 'What of your father's family?'

A shadow flitted across her face, and a slight reserve

entered her voice. 'I know nothing of them. Mama married above her station, and they did not wish to recognise her.'

Deuce take it, this was too painful! Poor princess. Abandoned by one family, only to be crushed by another. But life had not always to be so. *Love* had not always to be so. How could he show her that? Unless she could be brought to see for herself—by his own conduct towards her. Or did she already know it?

He eyed her. 'Why have you allowed me under your shield, Verena? Why, if not that you trust me?'

His grasp had slackened a little, and Verena removed her hands from his, looking away. 'I trust you as a friend.' A smile flickered again. 'Besides, I was over-wrought, and you were by.'

'Is that all?' he uttered, and knew the disappointment sounded in his voice.

Her pulse quickened, but she turned and met his eyes. 'Denzell, can't you see? Have you heard me say all this, and not recognised the impossibility of what you seek of me?'

She saw in his face that he had, and her chest tightened. But he reached out again, and firmly took her hand, drawing it into his lap.

'I recognise your fear, Verena, and I see upon what premise it is based. But it is a false premise. Your experience is one in a million. I could cite you story after story to refute your fears.' He smiled. 'But I will not waste my time. You cannot know it, Verena, but there exists a purer love than this—a love that has nothing to do with pain and brutality.'

Verena's fingers shifted within his grasp. 'If I could only believe that!'

His hand tightened. 'If I could only convince you!'

CHAPTER TEN

VERENA'S pulse quickened. Oh, but this was too dangerous! She snatched her hand away, and got up swiftly. He rose too, and she faced him, her barriers up, although she felt as if her mask could not anywhere be found. Not in this man's presence. Not any more.

'The risk is too great, Denzell,' she uttered roughly. 'Besides, even were it possible, were you to find some way to change me, I could not leave Mama. She needs me.'

'That I appreciate,' he conceded.

'Then don't speak of this again,' she pleaded. 'I must go back now.' She hesitated, and managed a slight smile. 'I do thank you.'

Denzell shook his head. 'Don't. And you are premature. I will escort you home.'

From this determination he would not be moved, and Verena accepted his arm with gratitude. The remembrance that she could not leave Mama had brought back the present problem to her mind. Yet she was eased in having told her tale, and she found herself much less agitated, although still nervous of the outcome of the enforced private conference.

Denzell left her at the front door, and she knocked in some trepidation. It was opened almost immediately by Mrs Quedgeley, the landlady. The woman was looking quite agog, Verena noted, but she refrained from asking any questions. The reason for this was not far to seek, for as Verena started up the stairs she discovered Betsey waiting for her above, in full sight of Mrs Quedgeley.

'A rare day's entertainment for her!' whispered Betsey, seizing her young mistress's arm.

'Betsey, what has happened?' Verena asked quickly.

'He's gone,' said the maid reassuringly. 'And Mr Adam with him.'

Verena fixed eyes of painful enquiry upon Betsey's face. 'Mama?'

'In the parlour, waiting for you.'

'Oh, thank heaven!'

She hurried along the passage and threw open the door. Mrs Pateley, who was seated in the armchair that half faced the door, looked up at her entrance. She smiled, and stretched out a hand.

'My dearest girl!'

Verena ran to her, dropping to her knees beside the armchair, and seizing her hand. 'Dear heaven, Mama! I was so afraid you might have gone!'

Mrs Pateley stroked her face. 'As if I would have done so without your knowing.' She smiled again, with an effort, Verena thought, and gestured to the other chair. 'Sit down, dearest. I want to talk to you.'

Rising from her knees, Verena was conscious of an instant drop in her chest. This boded ill! What did Mama wish to talk *about*? She was not distressed, but she seemed subdued, and thoughtful. On what had she determined?

'What had he to say for himself?' she asked, seating herself in the other chair.

Mrs Pateley gave a tiny sigh. 'He assures me he has changed.'

'I thought he would say so.'

Her mother shook her head. 'Do not speak so harshly, Verena. I believe he was speaking the truth.

There can be no doubt that he is—different. He does realise his wrongs to me, and he has had a lesson, which he will not forget.'

'Until the next time,' cut in Verena bitterly.

'No,' said Mrs Pateley firmly. 'He is truly repentant.'

'I cannot imagine why you should think so! He always claimed to be repentant, and yet he always did it again.' A note of desperation entered Verena's voice, for she was beginning to fear the worst. 'Why should you think him changed? Why should you suppose it will be any different?'

'Because it is as I said,' stated Mrs Pateley calmly. '*He* is different. He knows that he may lose me entirely, and that is new for him.'

Verena looked at her, acute suspicion writ large across her countenance. 'Mama, do you tell me you are contemplating a return? In your sane mind, can you even think of it?'

Her mother chose not to answer this directly. She met her daughter's eyes. 'What of your future, Verena?'

'We have been through all that,' said Verena impatiently, brushing it aside.

'But it is another case now, is it not?' insisted Mrs Pateley. She smiled. 'I am not blind, Verena. And I could not mistake Betsey's veiled hints.'

A trembling began inside Verena. This was precisely what she had feared all along. Now what was she to do? Before she could think what to say to dismiss this wholly unwanted subject, her mother threw her into even more confusion.

'Does he love you, Verena?'

It was out before she could stop it. 'He says so.'

'And do you love him?'

'No!' She knew her hands were shaking, and she bunched them into her lap. 'No, Mama. I don't. . .I

can't. There is no possibility of—I *told* him so. I cannot
love *anyone*. Heavens above, Mama, you must know
how it is with me!'

Mrs Pateley sat up, and leaning across to the other
chair, reached her fingers out to close briefly over those
unquiet hands. 'Because you have set your face against
it, that does not mean that it cannot happen, my
dearest.'

'Mama, don't speak of it, pray,' begged Verena
shakily. '*You* loved, and look how little good it has
done you.'

Mrs Pateley nodded and sat back again. 'That is true,
but only because there was so little time.'

The trembling abated slightly, for this did not make
sense. Verena stared. 'What in the world can you mean,
Mama? You must have loved Nathaniel once, I quite
see that.'

Mrs Pateley looked full in her face, a note of finality
in her voice. 'You are wrong, Verena. I never loved
Nathaniel.'

'What?'

'I never loved him,' she repeated. 'Which is the
reason he used me so shockingly. He knew from the
beginning, for I never pretended. I tried to love him,
God knows. Perhaps if he had not taken to abusing me,
I might have succeeded. When that began, I tried even
harder. But it is difficult to love someone who mistreats
one so badly.'

Impossible, Verena would have said, could she have
said anything at all. She was astounded. Could it be
true? It did not make sense!

'Why did you not leave him years ago?' she asked,
finding her tongue in a rush. 'How could you stay, allow
him to use you thus, if you did not love him? And how

can you speak of having loved, Mama—and try to tell me that I should love?'

At that, Mrs Pateley's features softened into a smile of such tenderness that Verena was startled. 'I do not mean Nathaniel when I speak of having loved, dearest. I am talking of your own father.' Her eyes glowed. 'Lambert and I were so much in love that we neither of us cared for the consequences.'

Verena was feeling more and more bewildered. 'But Grandpapa Whicham told me that the Chaceleys treated you shockingly, refusing to assist you when you were widowed. You have yourself told me that Nathaniel rescued you from an unenviable situation.'

'He offered me the chance of respectability, of security,' corrected Mrs Pateley. 'Come, Verena, you know very well that my station in life was not what I am raised to now. Papa was a lawyer.'

'I know, and therefore the Chaceleys cast you off.'

'Not me, Verena. They cast off poor Lambert for making a misalliance. At least his father did.'

Verena knew the story. Mama had been sent to the seaside under the care of a cousin to convalesce after a bout of fever. There she had met with Lieutenant Lambert Chaceley, on his way to rejoin his vessel at Chichester. After they were married, Lambert had returned to sea, and was drowned in a skirmish in which his ship had been engaged.

Verena had been born fatherless. It was Nathaniel whom she had known in that capacity from her earliest years, but him she had repudiated once she knew what he was doing to her mother. She had never again called him 'Papa' from the day she found out, preferring to be fatherless once more, and forever. This possible aspect of Mama's feelings for her real father had never entered Verena's head.

'But if you loved my father—' she began.

'We fell in love at first sight,' recounted Mrs Pateley, a long-forgotten dream in her countenance. 'It was on the beach at Little Hampton.'

'Little Hampton!' echoed Verena. Then that was why her stepfather had chosen to search in that place. But Mrs Pateley was still lost in memories.

'Nothing would do for him but my promise to marry him on his very next leave. We would not have waited as long, but that there was no time to arrange a marriage and I was under age. His papa refused his consent, but we were married in spite of it, and my own papa swore he should house us both.' She sighed. 'I do not know how it would have gone had Lambert lived. Perhaps his father might have relented in time.' She looked at Verena again. 'But this I do know. Our love was strong enough to have withstood any amount of trouble, and Lambert would have died before he raised a hand to me!'

'How can you be sure?' Verena uttered, out of those deep-seated fears that would not allow her to feel— what she knew she *could* feel. 'How can you possibly know?'

'I know, Verena, because Lambert had my heart. You see, my dearest, Nathaniel knew me before my marriage to Lambert. He had always an eye to me. Papa persuaded me to accept his proposals in the end, for I had you to think of, and Papa was ill, and he feared for my future if I was left alone with a young child to bring up, and already you were two years old. So I married Nathaniel.'

'To your cost,' Verena said tightly.

'And his, Verena,' said Mrs Pateley quietly. 'I married him without love, for advantage only. He was jealous, you see, dearest. He *did* love me, and he never

could forgive me for loving Lambert instead of him.'
She gave a rather wan smile. 'Sometimes I think it was
a judgement on me for marrying above my station.'

'Oh, Mama!' Verena protested. 'God is not so cruel.'

'No, no, dearest. The judgement was that I should
have lost Lambert, not that I should have been punished by Nathaniel.' She sat forward again and leaned
across to take one of Verena's hands. 'I am only telling
you this, Verena, to show you that love can be a very
different thing from my experience with Nathaniel. So,
if you do care for this young man—'

'That will do, Mama!' said Verena firmly, rising
swiftly to her feet. 'There is no question of that. I know
what you are thinking. That you must make it possible
for me to be free to marry. Well, I tell you now, I will
not hear of such a thing. You must not think of it!
Where is Nathaniel now?'

'He has gone back to the New Inn with Adam,' her
mother told her, getting up. 'He is waiting for my
decision.'

Verena turned a face of horror upon her. 'You mean
you have allowed him to hope? No, no, Mama. You
should have sent him packing. Lord in heaven, he will
come back and coerce you, I know he will!'

Mrs Pateley came to her and patted her arm. 'Verena,
don't fret yourself to flinders! He has promised that he
will not create any scenes, but will wait quietly for my
decision, and respect it.'

'And you believed him? Heavens, Mama, what does
it take to convince you? He has broken so many
promises! I have lost count of the times he promised
never to hurt you again, yet he did so—I know not how
often.'

'Yes, that is true, dearest,' Mrs Pateley conceded.
'But you and I, Verena, cannot continue in this way

forever, of that I am certain. Don't you see? I must seriously consider this opportunity.'

Verena thought she was going mad. Opportunity! Had Mama taken leave of her senses? Desperately, she clutched her mother's arms.

'Mama, you are out of your mind! Believe me, I will *kill* Nathaniel before I allow you to return to him. Do you imagine I could enjoy an instant's happiness with Denzell, knowing what you must be suffering?'

Mrs Pateley reached her hands up to her daughter's shoulders, an odd look in her face. 'Verena, do you realise what you have just said?'

Verena's heart stilled. What had she said? She had talked of Denzell—and enjoying *happiness* with him. Oh, sweet heaven, she *was* going mad! This could not be. She wrenched herself away.

'You have confused me, Mama—all this talk of love and my father. Don't you know that *you* are more important to me than anything in the world?'

With that, she turned and rushed out of the parlour, almost running into Betsey as the maid came towards her.

'Now what's amiss?' demanded Betsey, catching at her young mistress and holding her. 'Steady now, Miss Verena. What's to do?'

'Oh, Betsey, help me!' Verena cried. 'We must leave here at once. Go far away—abroad. Yes, abroad! Anywhere—only so that we get away from *here*.'

She glanced back to the parlour door, but Mama was still within. Hustling Betsey, she pushed her into her own bedchamber and shut the door.

'Betsey, give me an answer!'

'I would, my dove, if you would but tell me the question!' uttered the maid in a bewildered tone. 'Now simmer down, do, and talk sense.'

Verena drew a steadying breath. 'Betsey, how am I to persuade Mama that I have no interest in Denzell? You must help me to disabuse her mind. We must convince her that I am not in love with him.'

'And what about you, Miss Verena?' demanded the maid shrewdly. 'Are you convinced?'

'Oh, Betsey, don't you begin! In any event, he has not *asked* me to marry him. He has promised, besides, that he will not speak of the matter again.'

'Has he now?' said Betsey sceptically.

'Betsey! Don't tease me, pray. Whatever I felt, you cannot possibly conceive that I would allow Mama to sacrifice herself for me.'

'No,' agreed Betsey, adding sapiently, 'but I'm certain sure she'll try if she thinks there's a fair chance of you being settled.'

'Exactly.' If Betsey agreed with her, then the fear was very real. Verena was calmer now. She knew precisely what she must do. Mama might believe what she liked of her daughter's emotions, but she did not know Denzell. Therein lay salvation. She drew a determined breath.

'There is nothing for it, then. She must be made to believe otherwise.'

The High Rocks revellers were in fine fettle, attending the Friday night dance at the Rooms with renewed energy. Even Sir John Frinton claimed to have enjoyed it.

Despite his abstraction, Denzell laughed. 'Are you trying to convince me, Sir John, that you spent the day clambering among those huge boulders?'

Sir John twinkled. 'In this heat? Come, come, my dear boy. Though I have done so in my day.'

'Your "day", sir, seems to have consisted of enough

mayhem to tire out the hardiest spirit,' Denzell said tartly.

The old man laughed. 'But you see, my dear young friend, with your attention elsewhere, I am able to flirt outrageously with all the other pretty females. That is why I enjoyed myself that day.'

'I can readily believe it.'

But his attention was not fully on the conversation, and Sir John, apparently recognising the fact, wandered away in search of other amusement. Denzell's attention was indeed otherwhere. He had only one end in view in repairing to this local haunt.

Would she come? He had not felt himself to have earned the right to intrude upon the family gathering—albeit a gathering from which its members expected to derive little pleasure—by returning to the lodging to discover the outcome that was of such vital concern to Verena. But to hear nothing for two days! To see nothing of any member of the family, let alone Verena herself.

He could only possess his soul in what patience he might, passing the time at the Ruishtons' in relating to Unice all the new evidences that had come to light, and hope that his love would put in a public appearance this Friday night.

He was obliged to parry a number of claims to his attention, but at length his patience was rewarded. Verena entered with her mother. They were alone! All must be well, Verena's worst fears unrealised. Relief flooded him, and the now familiar sensation of warmth at sight of her burgeoned in his breast. She was once again the fairy princess, in cobweb lawn that seemed to float about her as she moved, her honey-warm tresses unbound and free.

He wanted to fly across the room and drag her into

his embrace. A procedure that was, unfortunately, quite ineligible. Neither here in public, nor—to his intense frustration—in private. Not yet, in any event. For after those intimate confidences, in spite of all evidence to the contrary, he could not suppress a growing feeling of hope. He was himself in the apricot and cream wedding garb tonight, the russet coat on his back—an unacknowledged omen perhaps.

Verena might have reassumed that serene look of hers that gave nothing away, but Mrs Pateley's demeanour was encouraging. She was clearly in spirits, pretty in lavender silk—now he could see where Verena had her looks!—dispensing smiles and laughter to the crowd of gentlemen that instantly gathered about the little group. She could not possibly have decided to return to her husband!

By and by, Denzell found an opportunity to move towards the usual court surrounding Verena, without appearing to particularise his interest. Rather to his surprise, Mrs Pateley herself singled him out.

'Mr Hawkeridge, how do you do?'

Her hand was held out to him, and he clasped it. Did he imagine it, or was she pressing his fingers rather more strongly than tradition dictated? He eyed her with some little puzzlement as he politely responded.

'I hope I find you well, Mrs Pateley?'

'You find me excellent well, Mr Hawkeridge,' she said in a tone that seemed to wish to encourage him in some way. 'I believe I may safely say that I am on the road to full recovery. I cannot think but that Verena will soon be able to cease worrying over me.'

Denzell blinked. He could not possibly mistake the significance of this! It was lightly done, but he had heard that note in the tongues of too many matchmaking mamas in the past not to recognise it. She knew of his interest, and she was trying to tell him that she approved of it.

Instinctively, he glanced at Verena—and suffered a severe shock. She was fully armed, and *icy*.

His heart dropped. What had been said? What in the world had occurred since he had seen her two days since, to cause her mother to make a play for him while the object of this intention showed herself to be plainly against it?

No, no, this was not to be tolerated. He must immediately express to Verena that he was at the mercy of her own desires, not those of her mama. She surely could not believe that he would enlist Mrs Pateley's support when Verena herself had so clearly forbidden him to speak of his love. Yes, he wanted to win her. But *win* her, not entrap her!

'I am relieved to hear you say so,' he replied to Mrs Pateley, in a certain tone—one that he had long ago mastered—which was a nice blend of deference and politeness, but which in no way admitted that he had taken the hint.

He saw a question come into her face, and smiled. 'I am sure all your friends must be delighted and encouraged by this improvement in your health and spirits.'

'Thank you,' she responded, and he was glad of the faint disappointment in her face. Capital! Now she could no longer be certain of his supposed interest in Verena.

Denzell stepped aside to make way for another gentleman, and discovered that Verena had managed to free herself, shifting slightly away from the crowd. He moved towards her, a quick word of reassurance forming on his tongue.

But Verena was too strung up to be capable of noticing his carefully structured response to her mother.

She had seen Denzell instantly when she entered the room, and was thankful that she had herself so well in hand. Deliberately—and desperately!—she had tried to keep her attention off him. And then Mama must needs attempt to force the issue by that embarrassing display.

Verena neither knew nor heard how Denzell answered. Her whole concentration was on maintaining her control, so that she might carry out her intended design of keeping away from her unwanted suitor—and of driving him instantly from her side when he chose to claim her attention.

As he came up, she showed him her blandest face, complete with that faint smile of total disinterest. She nodded dismissively, and murmured politely, 'Mr Hawkeridge.'

Denzell stopped dead, a frown forming between his brows. His voice was hard. 'Good evening, *Miss Chaceley.*'

Verena took in the tone. Dear heaven, but he had taken it amiss! He must not speak to her. Not in that mood. Not in *any* mood. From panic at what he might say, she jerked out under her breath, 'Go away from me, for the love of heaven!'

Instant hurt registered in his eyes. Verena's heart gave an involuntary twist. Oh, heavens! But she could not afford the tiniest degree of sympathy. Turning away, she moved towards a knot of people by one of the graceful pillars and engaged herself in their conversation.

Denzell gazed after her. There was an actual physical pain inside him. He'd had no notion one could be subject to such a sensation. It dulled after a moment, leaving him with a sense of bleak disillusionment. He had not deserved that! Had his conduct been so alien to her that she could not give him credit for any degree of thoughtfulness? Did she not know that as far as she was concerned, he must ever be endlessly considerate? Oh, Verena!

Turning away from the distressing sight of her icy mask, he recollected all at once that he was in company, and must behave accordingly. Only—he could not!

Making as swift a passage through the throng as he might, without drawing attention to himself, he left the Assembly Rooms and made his way out onto the Pantiles. There were a few couples taking the air—or engaging in light dalliance—but Denzell was too pre-occupied to notice them.

Darkness had not yet fallen, although the shadows were gathering, hollowing out caverns within the spaces between the slim pillars of the colonnade. Unknowing where his feet led him, Denzell wandered up the paved walkway, and down again, dallying foolishly between a desire to make away with himself or to shake Verena until the teeth rattled in her head. The realisation that he was even contemplating such a violent act towards the woman who held his heart captive so much disgusted him against himself that he turned again, and paced restlessly back up the Pantiles once more.

'Denzell!'

The whisper came at him out of one of those dusky holes in the colonnade. He halted, turning to peer into the blackness there. A shadow moved in a gap between two of the houses that made up the sequence of little shops running the length of the Pantiles.

His heart thrilled, for although he could see only the ghostlike wisp of a gauzy outline, he knew instantly that it was she. He moved swiftly in that direction.

'Verena!'

'Hush!' she begged, and he saw the whiteness of her hands reach out. He took them in his, and they pulled to draw him into the shadows with her so that they stood together in the narrow gap, barely silhouetted in the fading light.

'What are you doing here?' he asked, low-toned.

Heaven only knew! she thought. Except that she did know. She had seen him—with that peripheral vision that betrayed her into watching him when everything dictated that she must not—moving steadily out of the big room towards the entrance. Without even thinking, she had sought some excuse and sneaked forth to waylay him thus clandestinely.

'I slipped out unseen,' she answered. 'I could not bear you to think me so ungrateful.'

'If that is what you believed me to think,' he uttered in a rough tone, 'then you are vastly mistaken. Besides, I have no use for your gratitude!'

Her fingers tightened involuntarily on his, for both tone and words were poison to her. 'Don't be angry, Denzell, pray! There is—there is a reason for the way I acted.'

'So I should imagine,' he retorted. 'Only I was not aware that you thought so little of me.'

'Think little of you? But that is not *true*.'

'Is it not?' He released her hands. 'I do not know why your mama should suddenly take it into her head to encourage me. But could you not trust me to obey your wishes rather than hers? Could you not, Verena?'

His eyes were adjusting to the lack of light, and he thought he discerned a tear glistening on her pale cheek. It had the effect of turning his anger against himself, but it did not assuage the hurt. Such hurt as even her rejection of his initial declaration had not dealt him.

'You need not weep,' he said in a dead voice. 'I have brought all this upon myself. You owe me no vestige of trust, nor loyalty. It is my own misfortune that I should have crossed your path. I am not the first man to be disappointed in his hopes of marrying the woman he loves.'

Verena blenched, her distress deepening. But so attuned was she to him at this moment that she recognised the underlying pain beneath his words.

Quietly she asked, 'Is that designed to repay the hurt I have inflicted upon you?'

Denzell's tone hardened. 'I am not trying to make you feel guilt, if that is what you mean. I have no secret desire to hurt you, Verena.'

'No more had I, Denzell, when I spoke to you so harshly in the Rooms. I was in no case to be thinking of what you might or might not do, not with any rational consideration. You see, Mama has conceived the notion that I—' She faltered on the words hovering on her tongue. That was not an admission she wished to make, not even to herself!

But Denzell had caught it. 'That you?' he prompted, a faintly eager note in his voice.

She was silent. The sudden spurt of hope died again in Denzell's breast. Yet her words had lifted him. She had not intended to repulse him. She had been victim of her own emotions—would they might be what he so ardently desired!

'Forgive me,' he offered more gently, 'if I have misjudged you.'

No, that was more than she could bear! 'You have not misjudged me. I am so little mistress of my own heart, Denzell, that I cannot answer for myself. Yet I *must* distance you. If Mama thinks that there is any slight possibility of my finding a future with you, she will return to Nathaniel. He is even at this moment waiting for her answer! Now do you understand?'

'Deuce take it, yes!' he said at once.

In some dim recess he treasured those hasty words she had uttered about her own heart, but the purport of this speech hit him all too strongly.

'Even were it possible, Denzell, that I could think of—of loving you, or of marriage, I could never seek my happiness at the cost of Mama's renewed sufferings.'

'No, nor ever forgive me for making it happen.'

'You do understand!' she exclaimed.

'Understand? What do you take me for?' He caught at her shoulders, unheeding that he crushed the delicate fabric of her gown. 'Verena, why did you not send to me, and tell me this? You must know I would not dream of putting you to the risk of such a thing.'

'I should have known. Had I not been set so much into a frenzy, had I been able to think rationally—'

'Never mind it! Rest assured that I will not approach you or show by the flicker of an eye that I have any serious intent towards you. I can dissemble almost as well as you when necessity arises, you know.'

A choke of laughter escaped her. 'I had not noticed it.'

He grinned at her in the darkness. 'No, because all my effort with you has been in the direction of proving my sincerity.'

'There is no need of that,' she said, so warmly that he reacted without thought, jerking her towards him, his arms slipping about her. She stiffened against him. 'No, Denzell!'

He did not release her, but held her so, looking down into the pale oval of her face, her features barely discernible except as a silhouette—the mere shape of her lips all too enticing.

'Verena,' he breathed. 'Am I to hold aloof forever? Is this all there will ever be?'

His closeness sent her senses soaring, and her stiffness melted away. She felt too weak to resist, even to protest. Her eyes closed without volition as the shadow moved above her. Then a gentle pressure, soft and yielding, caressed her lips. A kiss so tender that she all but lost her senses.

It could only have been an instant or two later, although it felt to Verena like an age, and he drew back, his hands dropping from about her. Intensely she felt it. So intensely that she almost cried out. She was *bereft*.

'You had better return to the Rooms.'

His tone was roughened by the strength of the passion he was resolutely keeping in check. To Verena it seemed harshly alien, a painful distancing that threw her on the defensive. But she answered with a calm born of her instant resumption of the control that had ever come in against pain.

'Yes, I shall be missed.'

She began to move away, but Denzell's hand on her arm stopped her.

'One moment! How long, truly, do you wish me to keep up a pretence of uninterest?'

'Only until Nathaniel has gone. After—' She hesitated, for she knew that her next words must wound him.

'After? When then?'

Had he guessed what she would say? There was suspicion in his voice. She drew on her remaining strength.

'After he has gone, we will find another refuge.'

There was a silence. Then Denzell rapped out, 'Where?'

'I don't know. I only know that we must remove from here. I cannot trust Nathaniel to accept Mama's rejection.'

Denzell gave a soft laugh. 'I see I must prepare myself to search the length and breadth of England's watering places to find you again.'

'No!'

'What do you mean, no? Dare I imagine that you will tell me where you decide to go? No, that is asking too much!'

Verena came a step closer and reached out to place a hand on his chest. 'Denzell, it will be kinder—to both of us—if you let me go.'

His hand closed over hers. 'Then I fear I must be unkind.'

She did not withdraw her hand, but a distinct plea entered her voice. 'You said this morning that I might command you in anything.'

'I didn't mean I would be willing to commit suicide!'

'Don't jest!'

'I'm not jesting.'

'Denzell, you will do me the greatest service imaginable if you will only—*leave* me.'

His breath was ragged, but she could see even in the dim light that he was shaking his head.

'I cannot do that, Verena. I would die for you, but leave you I cannot!'

Her hand slipped out of his clasp. 'Then you will force me to vanish in secret.'

He was silent, a heaviness settling about his heart. From the depths of his being, he asked, 'Do you know what you are asking me to do?'

There was a cry in her own heart, but she forced it down. 'I know.'

He felt dead. It did not seem as if his voice belonged
to him. But he said the words nevertheless.

'Then so be it.'

It was eleven of the clock before Denzell left his room
next morning. Even then he was moving with some
care, for fear that the dreadful symptoms that had
attacked him might start up again. The headache had
reduced to a bearable level, but any sudden noise or
movement made him start and wince.

His hosts, he was informed by the manservant
Mayberry, had repaired to the garden, whither Denzell
followed them, having rejected with loathing an offer of
breakfast and requesting only that some hot coffee
might be sent outside.

He paused on the threshold of the rear door that led
from a small back parlour to the neat patch of lawn
behind the house, lifting one hand to shut out the glare
and frowning under it towards the chestnut tree. Unice,
looking decidedly cool in her muslin, was seated in one
of the iron garden chairs dotted about the tree, the
infant Julia in her arms, while Osmond, in his shirtsleeves, lay at his length on the grass, his two boys
gambolling about him.

The sight of this contented domestic bliss did nothing
to lighten Denzell's grey mood, belied somewhat by his
having allowed his valet to help him into his olive-green
coat and waistcoat. Moreover, the shrieking welcome
of Felix and Miles served only to make him close his
eyes in anguish.

Osmond laughed out. 'That'll teach you to roll in
drunk as a wheelbarrow at three o'clock in the morning,
Hawk!'

Denzell held up a hand. 'I thank you, the lesson has
already made its mark.'

But Unice was eyeing him with a grave look in her face. 'It is not in your style, Denzell.'

His shoulders shifted, as if a full shrug demanded too much of him. 'Much that I do these days is not in my style.'

He carefully sat himself down under the chestnut tree, thankfully leaning his back against the trunk and closing his eyes again to the persistent and unwelcome memory of last night's events. He had been as good as his word. Returning to the Rooms, he had conducted himself in a manner that had drawn down even Sir John Frinton's censure upon his head.

During a brief lull in his flirtatious perambulations among a selection of young females whose faces he had not even seen clearly, having been performed in a travesty of his erstwhile game and over a sensation of blankness that had dulled all feeling, the old roué had approached him with the faintest of disapproving frowns between his brows.

'To what, my dear young sir, do we owe this sudden excursion into your old tricks?'

Denzell had been unable to summon the vestige of a smile. 'To circumstance, Sir John.'

'It would be well,' the old man had returned tartly, 'if your circumstance did not inconvenience a series of vulnerable young females with hopes raised unnecessarily.'

Denzell's jaw had tightened. 'I cannot help that. There is more at stake here than you know.'

The light of compassion had entered the other's eyes. 'Matters go against you, do they? Is there anything I can do, my boy?'

'Nothing, I thank you.' He had grimaced. 'Unless you care to ensure that my remains are suitably interred in a hackney cab later tonight?'

Sir John's brows had risen. 'You are not, I trust, contemplating a violent end?'

'I am contemplating a violent inebriation!'

The aged exquisite had laughed gently. 'You may rely on me, dear boy.'

He had been as good as his word. Better, in fact. For not only had he accompanied Denzell to the Gentleman's Rooms, matching him glass for glass — deuce take it, the man had a head like a rock! — but he had seen him escorted into his own coach and personally deposited the body into the hands of Osmond Ruishton himself.

Denzell came out of his reverie to discover his hosts calling for Dinah and the infant's new nurse, both of whom were within earshot. His eyes flicked open, to find that the boys were being led off to the larger ground beyond the garden to play, while the baby was lowered into a basket crib and removed to a position just outside the house.

'Now then,' said Osmond on a determined note.

Denzell glanced from one to the other of them. Unice was still watching him with that solemn look in her face, while Osmond was frowning.

'What?' he demanded.

'Yes, that's just what we want to know,' said his friend. 'Not like you to be secretive with us, Hawk. And just because we didn't accompany you to the Rooms last night, does not mean we haven't heard of your doings.'

'Doubtless Sir John told you,' groaned Denzell.

'Dash it, Hawk,' said Osmond for answer, 'what should take you to get into a sudden burst of flirtation with every pretty girl in the room —'

'Except Verena,' put in Unice.

'— and then, just as though you'd exhausted the

supply of eligibles, go off to drink yourself to death in the Gentleman's Rooms?'

Denzell put up his fingers to knead at his aching brow. 'What would you have me do? I was obliged to demonstrate to Mrs Pateley that she was mistaken in supposing me to be interested in Verena.'

'I should think you did that all right!'

'But, Denzell, why?' asked Unice. 'Why were you so obliged?'

He dropped his hands and looked up at her. His voice was bleak. 'Because Verena wished it. And, if you must have the full sum of it, I steeped myself in liquor because I could not otherwise bear the command she has laid upon me.'

It took Unice and Osmond some little time to drag the whole story out of him. But it was told at last, to the accompaniment of a cup of hot strong coffee which his hostess pressed upon him, poured from the pot that the butler sent out by the hand of one of the maids, and a good deal of critical comment from Osmond at least, who was inclined to think Denzell should count himself well out of it.

'I mean to say, Hawk, if you have been unable to win the girl out of her indifference—'

'She is not indifferent!' Denzell interrupted roughly, and winced at the discomfort his own raised voice cost him. 'She is—I will not say "in love" because the very thought of love is anathema to her—but she *does* care for me. She very nearly said as much.'

'Did she indeed, Denzell?' asked Unice eagerly. 'I must say, that is very much the impression I had myself—if only she will allow herself to feel it.'

Denzell nodded, and his features dropped, drawing down into despair. 'There's the rub.' He laid down his empty cup. 'And as long as her mama is in question, I don't believe she will allow herself to feel it.'

Osmond snorted suddenly. 'Dash it, Hawk, this ain't like you! Never known you to be so defeatist.'

'Circumstances alter cases,' Denzell said glumly.

Unice was looking thoughtful. 'Is there not some way in which her mama might be accommodated—within your future with Verena, I mean?'

'What future? According to Verena, we have no future.'

'Yes, but that is surely because she is unable to think beyond the present necessity. There are always other solutions. Why should not Mrs Pateley live with you both at Tuttingham, for example?'

Denzell's features lightened for a moment. He stared at Unice. 'I had not thought of that.'

'Think of it now then,' Unice urged.

But Osmond was shaking his head. 'That's no use. You don't suppose Verena will agree to have the whole story let out to Lord and Lady Hawkeridge, do you? Dash it, the woman has left her husband! It ain't a thing you bruit about lightly, Unice.'

'But no one could blame her for leaving such a husband,' Unice protested. 'Why, I should suppose Lady Hawkeridge must be the first to condemn such brutal practices.'

'She would, of course,' Denzell agreed, but he sighed too. 'Yet I believe Osmond is in the right of it. Besides which, Verena will not wish to have her mother sue to strangers for an asylum.'

Unice was daunted for a moment, but she rallied quickly. 'Not strangers, Denzell. They would be her parents-in-law.'

'You are forgetting, Unice,' Denzell said heavily, 'that I have first to overcome Verena's reluctance even to consider the question of marriage—let alone allowing her mother to become the pensioner of myself or my parents. She has a great deal of pride.'

'Yes, false pride. I declare, I am very much of a mind to talk to her myself.'

'I doubt it would do any good.'

'I agree with Hawk,' chimed in Osmond. 'If he can't persuade her—given that she does care for him—then I don't see her paying any mind to you, my love.'

'And before that, I must persuade her also that there are men who do not demonstrate their love by beating their wives.'

'Well, if she won't accept even that, then there's nothing for it, Hawk. You'll have to do as she asks.'

'I have already given my word that I will.'

'There you are then. Forget the girl, dash it!'

'That,' said Denzell flatly, 'is impossible.'

'Pooh! It is only because you can't have her that you want her so badly. Mark my words! Within a month or two, you'll be mooning over some other wench.'

'Osmond Ruishton!' exclaimed Unice crossly. 'I don't know how you can be so blind to your best friend's deepest feelings.'

'Well, but—'

A commotion at the rear door interrupted them. There was a hubbub of raised voices within the room behind. Mayberry came through the open door, and was rudely shoved aside. Verena herself pushed past him, and stood glancing frantically about the garden. Hatless, out of breath, and plainly distraught, she cast about until she spied the trio around the chestnut tree.

'*Denzell*!' she cried, and, lifting her muslin skirts, began to run towards him.

Denzell, for a moment blank with surprise, no sooner took in her distressed condition, than he leapt to his

feet, disregarding the instant twinge to his head the
sudden movement caused him. He took two strides
before she reached him, and had only time to seize the
hands she was holding out before words started tumbling from her mouth.

'Denzell, help me! Oh, pray help me! What am I to
do? He has prevailed and it is all in vain. Mama
has *gone*.'

CHAPTER ELEVEN

SHOCK held all three silent for a moment, staring blankly at the newcomer. For both Unice and Osmond had also risen, flanking Denzell. Not a trace of the mask remained in the lovely face, for Verena was looking up at the countenance above her as if her life depended upon his ability to handle this hideous turn of events.

Nor did Denzell fail her. His ailments were shrugged aside.

'Of course I will help you,' he said instantly, collecting his wits and drawing her firmly towards the chair lately vacated by Unice. 'Sit down a moment.'

Verena held back. 'No, no, I cannot! There is no time. I must—'

'You must be calm, Verena!' he instructed firmly. 'Nothing will be resolved with panic.'

'Denzell is right, Verena,' said Unice. 'We will all help you, never fear.'

'Come, sit,' Denzell urged.

He fairly pushed her into the chair, and made to release her and turn to the others hovering behind him. But Verena's hand clung to his fingers.

'Don't leave me!'

'I won't,' he assured her. His head turned to Osmond nevertheless. 'Fetch some brandy, Ossie.'

'No, no, I want nothing.'

'You are in shock, Verena,' said Unice, leaning over her on the other side and laying a comforting hand on her shoulder. She called out to her husband, who was already on the move. 'Hartshorn, Osmond! I think hartshorn would be better, Denzell.'

'Brandy,' Denzell said firmly, and reached out to pull one of the other chairs closer that he might sit beside Verena. When he turned back to her, he saw not only that her bosom under the wrap-over bodice of the all-white gown palpitated with her uneven breath, but her lips were quivering and he could feel the trembling of her fingers within his grasp. Unable to help himself, he lifted the hand to his lips and kissed it.

Verena stared at him. She was unable to think beyond what had happened, but she felt a little of her panic dying away, and wondered at the power he seemed to have to calm her.

'How do you do it?' she asked involuntarily.

'Do what?'

'Make me believe that all is not as bad as it seemed only moments ago.'

He smiled. 'It's no special magic, Verena.'

'Yes, it is,' chimed in Unice unexpectedly. She patted Verena's shoulder. 'It is the magic of love.'

Verena did not look round at her, but continued to stare at Denzell's face. Her fingers moved within his grasp, turning so that, without meaning to, they laced with his.

'Is it?' she asked of the smoky blue eyes.

'Yes,' he responded simply.

For a moment longer the look held between them. Then a sound, half-sob, half-sigh, broke from Verena, and she blinked as her trouble came back to her.

'Mama,' she murmured, and her gaze moved away from him.

But by this time Osmond was returning, a glass of brandy in his hand. Denzell took it from him, curled Verena's fingers about it, and made her drink.

Verena sipped at the liquid, and choked on the fiery sensation as it caught in her throat. She tried to push the glass away. 'No more.'

'Yes—another sip or two,' Denzell insisted, obliging her to put the glass to her lips again.

She was in no condition to resist him. This time the liquid ran down more easily, and she felt a burning in her chest. And indeed, she thought wonderingly, it was having a calming effect. The sensation of panic began to subside.

'That's better,' Denzell said, removing the glass. He tossed off what remained himself and handed the empty vessel back to Osmond. His head was the clearer for it, and he felt ready to deal with this emergency.

'Now, Verena, tell us the whole. From the beginning.'

Verena shivered, and without knowing that she did so, groped for his hand again. She was aware only of the gathering despair in her breast as the events of the morning crowded into her memory. But they did not have quite the same power to overset her, for the burden of settling the business no longer seemed to lie wholly on her own shoulders.

She spoke only when she felt again the comfort of Denzell's hand closing about her own. At first she addressed herself almost exclusively to him.

'I thought all was well after last night. When Mama saw how you conducted yourself, she appeared to be convinced that she had been mistaken in your sentiments—as we agreed she should be made to believe.'

'She said something then?' Denzell asked.

A faint smile flitted across Verena's face. 'She said that if there is one thing worse than abuse, it is the pain caused by philandering husbands. And Mrs Felpham was quick to come up and gloat that you had fallen into your old ways—'

'She would,' cut in Osmond.

'Hush!' Unice uttered. She had herself taken a seat on one of the other chairs, seeing how easily Denzell seemed able to attend to Verena's immediate needs without any help from his hostess. 'Let Verena tell her tale.'

'Go on, Verena,' Denzell said, faintly grinning. 'I take it you did not disabuse Mrs Felpham, any more than your mama.'

'No—' casting him a slightly deprecating glance '—I was too busy trying to disabuse myself.'

The picture leapt back into her mind. So carefree he had seemed, laughing and casting sheep's eyes all over the room. Oh, the pain of watching it! And despite the fact that she had wanted him—had, indeed, demanded of him—to create that impression of uninterest in herself, she had actually begun to believe that it was true!

She saw him start to speak, and quickly shook her head. 'Don't scold! I know—oh, I know. But to see you flirting with other females. . .'

'Ha!' came from Osmond under his breath. Unice frowned him down, but she need not have worried. Verena had eyes and ears only for Denzell as he murmured his reassurance.

'You would not have concerned yourself for an instant had you seen me at a later time. I have even now been suffering the most devilish head!'

The tiniest of laughs lightened her features for an instant. 'So that is why you finished my brandy for me. Are you well again?'

He grinned. 'No, but let that pass. I am the more troubled for you.'

Her features clouded again. 'Oh, but she fooled me very successfully. Mama, I mean. We were discussing the matter at some length, and when I saw that she had abandoned the notion of my marrying you, I begged her also to abandon any thought of this foolish determination to return with Nathaniel.'

'Did you agree that she would abandon it?'

'She said so, but adding the proviso that she might tell him she would ever be ready to go home should I fall in love.'

'To which you replied—what?' Denzell asked, with a brief resurgence of his headache as the heaviness that had so beset him earlier returned in some small measure.

'That I never would!' Verena uttered vehemently. She looked away, muttering in a low voice, 'I did not add my thoughts.'

'What thoughts?'

She shook her head. There could be no admission of that! She could not tell him how she had tried to push away such thoughts—as could never be pushed away. How could she fall in love at some future date, when her heart was already given?

'Suffice to say,' she said quickly, 'that Mama believed me, as I thought. But this morning—' drawing a breath against a renewed rise of the panic in her breast '—I was obliged to go out, leaving Mama alone with Betsey. Had I had the slightest inkling of what she intended, I should never have gone. But it is no use in saying that. I went only to make a purchase at Mr Sprange's shop. I was gone some while, but I never dreamt. . .'

'Verena,' Unice put in earnestly, 'you cannot blame yourself. How could you have expected that your mother would deceive you?'

'Never mind that, Unice. Go on with your story, Verena,' Denzell said firmly.

She drew a breath, and continued. 'When I arrived

home, I discovered that Mama had gone. Betsey said that a note arrived, and the next thing she knew, Mama had quietly put on her cloak and bonnet and walked out of the house. It had not even occurred to Betsey to try to stop her!'

'Perhaps she thought she was going for a walk,' suggested Unice.

Verena shrugged. 'I don't know what she thought. She does not have my imagination, and she must have supposed—as I had—that there was nothing to be concerned about as regards Nathaniel.'

'What did you do then?' Denzell asked, keeping her to the point.

'I ran straight to the New Inn, of course. Adam was putting up there, and I knew that he had taken Nathaniel with him to secure a room there also.' She pressed her free hand to her cheek. 'You m-may imagine my feelings when I discovered that both he and Adam had packed up and gone that very morning!'

Suddenly she wrenched her fingers out of Denzell's hold, and threw both hands over her face, shaking her head in a frenzy of distress. Her words came muffled, but the despairing anger could be heard within them.

'I will never forgive him, never! He knew—he *knew* how I felt.' The agitated hands returned to her lap, gripped together, as she glanced at the surrounding faces, disbelief in both feature and voice. 'How could he do it? How could he *connive* against me, knowing to what Mama must be subjected?'

Osmond and Unice looked at each other in some puzzlement, but Denzell understood.

'You are speaking of Adam. But you do not know for certain, Verena, that he has done any such thing. Did you make any enquiries at the New Inn? Had your mama come there, someone must have seen her.'

The once more ravaged features turned back in his direction, but it was obvious that she was too lost in the dread of the meaning of these events to take his meaning.

'I did ask,' she uttered in a frustrated tone, 'but do you suppose those fools in that place could tell me anything? One ostler had seen Nathaniel leave. But he could not say whether he had seen anyone with him, and no one observed a woman come to him.' She struck her hands together. 'But it *must* be so. What else could have occurred? They planned this behind my back, and they have all gone together!'

'But you do not know that, Verena,' objected Osmond sensibly.

'Ossie is in the right of it,' said Denzell firmly. 'You can be certain of nothing at this present.'

Verena gazed at him in dumb wretchedness for a moment. Then, in a helpless, pathetic sort of way, she said, 'What shall I do? I don't know what to *do*.'

Unice got up and came over to her. 'Poor Verena. You need do nothing, I am sure. Osmond and Denzell will take over this investigation. You will stay here with me.'

But Denzell was frowning in thought. 'Wait a moment! Verena, has your mama taken all her things?'

Verena gazed at him blankly. 'I—don't know.'

'You said she left the house in her bonnet and cloak, but carrying nothing else.'

'It did not occur to me to look!'

Denzell smiled. 'You jumped to a very natural conclusion, but perhaps there is some simpler explanation.'

Her hands went up to her temples again. 'What other explanation could there be?'

'I don't know that,' he admitted, 'and to tell the truth my head is none too clear just now. But it does occur to me that if she had intended to go home, she must have taken her clothes. And in all conscience, do you believe that your Mama would use you in such a way after all you have done for her?'

Verena blinked at him dazedly. That aspect had not even crossed her mind. Something came back to her. Had not Mama said that she would not leave without letting Verena know of it? Yes, she had. Was she allowing her own dread fears to overcome her common sense? She no longer knew. She looked from one enquiring face to another, and came back to Denzell's concerned features.

'You make me seem foolish.'

'Not in the least,' he said decidedly. 'You have every reason to be troubled by this matter, and it is no surprise to me that you should have allowed yourself to become panic-stricken at such an unprecedented absence.'

Verena sighed. 'Well—thank you for that. But now. . .I don't know what to think any more.'

Unice had reseated herself, but she leaned forward. 'Verena, do you indeed think—should it be the case that your mama has gone back—do you indeed think that your stepfather will misuse her again? Will not your brother prevent it?'

'He would if he were by,' Verena answered, her face clouding over again. 'But you see, he is unlikely to be present on these occasions. Besides—' twisting her fingers in her lap and looking down '—we have been neither of us in the habit of interfering.'

The bitter inflection twisted Denzell's heart, and he reached out to cover her unquiet hands. It was Osmond who answered her, surprisingly indignant.

'Dash it, you were only children! How could you interfere?'

A trifle shamefaced, Verena glanced up at him. 'It was not childhood that prevented it, Osmond. It was fear.'

'I knew it!' Denzell uttered, gripping her hands. 'He had hurt you, too, hadn't he?'

Verena's eyes came round to his face. 'Only on the one occasion. I should have been warned, for Adam had attempted it now and then and suffered Nathaniel's vengeance.'

Denzell's blood was up at the very thought of what she might say. Yet he persisted, for he felt her need to relate the tale, to relieve her heart. 'What happened to you?'

Her fingers tightened in his grasp. 'I think I was about twelve. I could not endure it all at once, and I ran into the room and tried to stop him. I remember I hit at his chest. Mama shrieked at me to stop, but Nathaniel snatched up his whip—he had but a few moments before come in from riding and thrown it down on the bed—'

'Don't tell me he used his whip on you?' uttered Unice, aghast.

Verena nodded. 'But I received only two or three blows, I think. For Mama threw me down and lay on top of me and—and took the blows herself.'

Her voice shook, and her eyes pricked at the memory. The others were silent, but the movement of Denzell's fingers on hers eloquently spoke his feelings. Her glance, as she looked at him, was luminous with unshed tears, pleading for understanding in a matter for which she had suffered years of pointless guilt.

'Mama made me promise—afterwards—that I would never do so again. She said she had rather suffer ten times the torture than see me hurt.'

'Which is why you are willing to sacrifice your own life on her behalf,' Denzell opined quietly.

'More than that.' She gritted her teeth. 'I would have taken *his* life, if I could.'

'Surely not!' protested Unice.

'Pooh!' scoffed Osmond. 'You delude yourself.'

'No, she does not,' Denzell cut in. He remembered her words of the previous day, that she had wished to scar his wicked 'love' upon Nathaniel's person, and he knew she was speaking nothing but the truth. He picked up her hand and held it between both his own, asking gently, 'Did you try?' Verena nodded, and the hatred gleamed in her eyes. 'Once. I took his pistol. I loaded and primed it—Adam had taught me how. I did it with the utmost deliberation, and then hid it under my pillow. In the night, I went into his room and held the pistol to his head where he was sleeping.'

'And?' Denzell prompted.

'I cocked it.' She let out a short, despairing sigh. 'But I had not the courage to pull the trigger.'

Denzell lifted her hand and held it to his cheek a moment. 'You are a woman of infinite courage, and I love you deeply.'

Her eyes filled, and Denzell quickly leaned towards her. But before he could speak, there was another flurry of activity at the rear door to the house. This time Mayberry was pipped at the post and Betsey lumbered out onto the lawn.

Verena saw her, and quickly rose, Denzell beside her. 'Betsey, what news?'

'You're to come home, Miss Verena,' announced the maid tersely. 'The mistress is there, and—'

'Mama is at home? Oh, thank heaven!'

Verena sank in relief, falling against Denzell as of instinct. He caught her, steadying her with one arm about her shoulders. But his attention was quickly back on the maid.

'She had not gone away then?' he asked.

'No, sir. She's all in pother, howsomever, and I'm to take Miss Verena back straight.'

'But where had she gone?' demanded Verena, recovering again and taking in the suppressed air of excitement that hung about her trusty maidservant. 'What's to do, Betsey?'

Betsey threw her eyes to heaven. 'Oh, deary me! I was told off to keep my mouth shut, but I'm danged if I can, Miss Verena. The mistress has a gentleman with her.'

Both Ruishtons cried out at this, and Denzell frowned as Verena's countenance blanched. 'Not Pateley?' he rapped out.

'Not he,' said Betsey, on a note of scorn. 'Two of 'em, there are, in fact.'

'But who is it, Betsey?' Verena demanded, catching a little of the maid's mood. 'For the love of heaven, tell me!'

'Come, Miss Betsey,' added Denzell persuasively, 'has she not borne enough suspense already this day?'

Betsey looked her young mistress up and down, and made up her mind. She nodded in a determined way. 'That's right enough, sir. Well then, my dove, I'd not add to your troubles, but you'd best brace yourself.'

Unable to stand any more, Verena seized her wrist. 'Who, Betsey? Who is it?'

'The mistress says as how it's him as was papa to your own father, Miss Verena. It's your grandfather Chaceley.'

The two visitors seemed to dwarf the little parlour. As of right, old Mr Chaceley occupied the prominent position before the fireplace, his stiff figure, immaculately suited in plum-coloured cloth, fronting his granddaughter in an attitude of defiant pride that was mirrored in Verena's own pose.

To one side, a kindlier look in the features that ran appraisingly over his niece, stood Bevis Chaceley, discreet in a dark blue frock-coat and buff breeches. He was taller than his sire, larger in every aspect, but the dominating charisma of the old man cast the son into the shade.

A somewhat flustered Mrs Pateley had performed the introductions, seizing on Verena the instant she entered the room, Denzell hard on her heels, and drawing her forward.

'My daughter, Verena. She has a great look of Lambert, don't you find? My love, this is your grandfather.'

Verena stood mute, staring blankly at the old man, taking in the prideful arrogance that emanated from his very posture, and the hard eyes that raked her from her head to her heels.

'Make your curtsy, Verena,' hissed Mrs Pateley.

But Verena barely heard her. So this was the man who had cast off his son for marrying Mama. Oh, she could readily believe it! A surge of resentment flooded her breast, and flashed in her eyes.

Old man Chaceley's brows rose. 'Looking daggers, eh? Don't think I'll answer to a chit of a girl for my actions, for I won't!'

Old habits died hard. Suddenly aware of her own reaction, Verena swiftly donned her mask. She dropped a curtsy, demurely lowering her eyes.

'How do you do, sir?' she murmured politely.

Her grandfather looked somewhat taken aback, and Denzell, an interested observer, was obliged to suppress a grin. Chaceley had a deal to learn of his granddaughter!

Bevis Chaceley instantly stepped into the breech, coming forward and holding out a hand, reassurance and kindness in both smile and voice.

'We are delighted to meet you at last, my dear child. I am your uncle Bevis, and I am bound to agree that your mother is in the right of it. You are very like my poor young brother, as I remember him.' He had covered the hand she gave him with both his own, and he pressed it gently. 'He must have been more or less your own age, you know, when I saw him last. I can vouch for it that he would have been enchanted with you.'

Verena softened, smiling in genuine gratitude. 'You are very kind, sir, and I thank you.'

Bevis shook his head, releasing her hand. 'No, no, no, my dear child. If you must thank anyone, let it be young Denzell here.'

'Denzell!' exclaimed Verena, turning to look at him as Bevis Chaceley moved to shake hands with him.

'Glad to see you, my boy,' said the elder man, smiling. 'And we certainly thank you for bringing the matter to our attention.'

'I am only glad it has resulted in your presence here, sir,' Denzell said, 'although that was scarcely my intention at the time.'

'But I don't understand,' Verena said.

'You see, dearest,' explained Mrs Pateley, coming up to her daughter and putting an arm about her waist, 'it seems that Mr Hawkeridge mentioned our presence here, and your uncle, believing that perhaps you might be related—'

'Stuff and nonsense!' broke in the old man. 'No perhaps about it. Knew it at once, the instant the boy

mentioned your name, ma'am.' He addressed himself
to Verena. 'Think I haven't been aware all these years
of your situation, girl?'

Verena released herself from her mother's grasp and
turned back to him. She could not control the rough
hostility in her voice, for the speed and turn of events
had ripped her erstwhile mastery to shreds.

'How should I know, sir? I have certainly been
unaware of yours!'

'Don't be pert with me, girl!' he barked.

Verena faced him, her figure as stiffly erect as his
own. 'By what right, sir, do you censure my conduct?
You did not choose to own me these many years, yet
you expect to assume all those rights of obedience you
have abrogated.'

'Verena!' gasped her mother.

'I expect common courtesy, young lady, if nothing
else,' snapped the old man, his eyes narrowed and
glaring.

That pulled Verena up. She could not abate one jot
of the pent-up emotion within her, but she bit down on
another retort, and tried for a milder note, which only
partially succeeded.

'Every stranger has a right to that, sir.'

Mrs Pateley seized her arm, uttering almost tearfully,
'Verena, that is not at all a proper way to speak to your
grandfather. Pray beg his pardon, do!'

There did not look to be very much expectation of
Verena doing any such thing, Denzell decided. He
waited, almost breathlessly, for the outcome. If he'd
had any doubts about Verena's identity, this encounter
must have laid them all to rest. She was all too plainly
old man Chaceley's granddaughter!

He was glad he had insisted on accompanying Verena
back to the lodgings, although it had not been entirely

for her sake. If the Chaceleys were indeed in Tunbridge Wells—assuming they were the Chaceleys he knew so well—there could be no doubt that those casual words of his to Bevis had been instrumental in bringing them here.

The two protagonists were still glaring. Verena knew she was manifestly in the wrong. She ought to apologise. But the words refused to be uttered.

'Verena!' pleaded Mrs Pateley again.

But quite suddenly, the old man threw back his head and uttered a shout of laughter. 'By God, you're a plucky little piece! Here's my hand, girl. I'm proud to call you granddaughter!'

Verena sighed out her resentment, and accepted the proferred hand, her stiffness melting away. She smiled. 'Indeed I do beg your pardon, sir.'

'Well, don't spoil it, girl,' protested her grandfather. 'Only female in the family who ever dared stand up to me.'

'It seems,' put in Bevis, his amusement plain to see, 'that your granddaughter is practised in standing up to authority.'

'I have had to fend for myself, perhaps,' Verena said, wondering how much he knew. 'But I should not have spoken so. Let my excuse be that I have endured a morning of dreadful anxiety.'

'Oh, my poor love!' exclaimed Mrs Pateley.

'I thought you had gone away with Nathaniel and Adam,' Verena uttered, with a resurgence of her earlier fears. 'He has gone, you know.'

Mrs Pateley took her hands. 'Yes, Betsey told me. My dearest, I knew he would, for I sent to him last night after we talked.'

Verena blinked dazedly. 'You wrote to him?'

Her mother nodded. 'I told him that I would not

come home, not for fear of what he might do, but
because I could no longer bear to distress you with the
thought of my going.'

Tears started to Verena's eyes and her mother
embraced her tightly. Denzell, watching the two visitors, thought Bevis Chaceley looked to be quite as
affected as he was himself. But the old man looked on,
apparently unmoved, yet with a look of interest as if he
was still summing up his granddaughter.

'If only I had known!' Verena said huskily, when they
separated again. 'I went to the New Inn to find you.'

'I should have left you a message by Betsey. I am so
sorry, dearest, but you see, when your grandfather's
note arrived, asking me to go and visit him at the
Angel—that is where your grandfather is putting up,
you must know—I was so shocked that I could not
think straight.'

'You see, my dear,' explained Bevis, 'if it transpired
that you were my brother's daughter, it seemed incumbent upon us to discover under what circumstances you
had found yourselves obliged to come to Tunbridge
Wells thus alone.'

Verena looked towards Denzell, frowning. 'What did
you tell them?'

'That you and your mother were living in lodgings
together,' he answered readily. 'Also that there was
some mystery attached to your presence, and that you,
my princess, were quite clearly in some fear and distress—upon what account, of course, I was unable to
say.'

Mrs Pateley's ears pricked up at his use of this
suggestive form of address, and she looked across at
Denzell with an expression that seemed to indicate that
she had only just taken in his presence, and was
beginning to realise its implications. A gleam of amuse-

ment lit his eyes, but his attention was claimed by Verena.

'But why did you say anything at all?' she demanded, unsure as yet if she was glad or sorry that he had done so.

He met the uncertainty in her gaze, and admitted frankly, 'Because I was intrigued—or so I believed then. Yet only at my sister's wedding did I recall that I had neighbours who bore the same name as you.'

'Neighbours!'

'My father's estates are within a few miles of Mr Chaceley's. I know almost all your relatives, I believe.' He grinned. 'You don't know it, but you have numerous uncles and aunts and cousins.'

Verena blinked dazedly. 'Have I?'

'Indeed you have, my dear,' broke in Bevis Chaceley, 'and you shall meet them all.'

A frown came into her face. 'I don't know that, sir.' She turned to her grandfather. 'Why have you come?'

Mrs Pateley bustled in again, seizing her daughter's hands. 'That is just what I have been dying to tell you, my love! Come, why do we not all make ourselves comfortable? Betsey will bring wine, and—'

It was some moments before the company had settled themselves, turning the armchairs inwards so that they might all face each other. Mrs Pateley, whispering in her daughter's ear her satisfaction that she should luckily have chosen to don her lilac chemise gown today, settled with Verena at her side on the day-bed.

The two older gentlemen occupied the armchairs, and Denzell, having first gone as he was requested to ask the maid for refreshments, took up a position on a straight-backed chair opposite the day-bed at the other side of the fireplace, from where he could watch Verena's wondering features as the tale unfolded.

It seemed that Mr Whicham, Verena's maternal grandfather, had written to inform old man Chaceley of the existence of his new granddaughter after Verena's birth.

'He had the audacity to add—all the same, these lawyers!—the exact terms of his will, with the purpose of letting me understand, I don't doubt, that he would provide for the chit without any assistance from me. It was a stiff letter your father wrote me,' he said, turning his fierce gaze upon Mrs Pateley, 'and stiffly proud. Don't mind telling you I was infuriated by it. Pleased, too, at the same time. Relieved me of the necessity of worrying about the girl.'

'Naturally you need not have concerned yourself, sir,' put in Mrs Pateley, 'once my papa had informed you that I was remarried, for he told me he had done so.'

'He had, and damned impertinent I thought him! What the deuce had it to do with me?'

'It was, however, another matter,' put in Bevis, quickly taking up the tale, 'when we discovered that you, my dear Verena, were no longer sheltered under your stepfather's roof.'

'Sheltered!' uttered Verena involuntarily.

Reassurance entered Bevis Chaceley's handsome countenance. 'We know all about it, my dear. Your mama has been very frank.'

'You need not look reproachful,' barked her grandfather. 'Your mother had no choice, for I demanded to know why she had left the protection of her husband.'

Mrs Pateley had averted her gaze, looking shamefaced. Verena put an arm about her, and she groped for her daughter's free hand, holding it rather tightly. Denzell saw Bevis nod approvingly.

'That's the way,' he said encouragingly. 'Your poor mama has given us the full sum of it. How you helped her to escape, and brought her here in secret, using your own means to do so. I've never heard of such selflessness. Dashed if you aren't a little heroine, Verena!'

'I am nothing of the kind,' Verena said quickly. 'I have been all too long a coward. I should have killed him long ago!'

There was an outcry at this from both Bevis and Mrs Pateley. But Denzell, watching old man Chaceley, saw a light in the aged eyes that he had never thought to see. He belonged to a bloodier age than this, when a man might have been called to account for such doings as Nathaniel Pateley had been engaged in. It was plain that to Chaceley, Verena's words evoked a spirit that spoke to his depths. Perhaps it even reminded him of his dead son, for Denzell could swear there was a shade of grief lurking in the iron gaze.

Here was the source of Verena's strength of will! That incredible iron control that had upheld her through the years of pain and dread. Iron that had so very nearly shielded her heart from the penetration of his own deep feelings. For it was pierced! He could not doubt it now. Only, would Verena admit it?

The remembrance of the barrier that kept her from him made him glance quickly from the Chaceley men to Mrs Pateley and back again. By George, was this deliverance? Had they come with something more than good intentions—intentions dictated by old man Chaceley's conscience, that was clear.

As if she read his mind, Mrs Pateley answered the question at that precise moment.

'Never mind all that now, my dearest,' she was saying, a flush of excitement entering her cheeks. 'We have not yet told you the best. Your grandfather has offered us a refuge!'

Verena stared at her. 'What?' she uttered faintly.

'Yes, my dear child,' said Bevis Chaceley, leaning towards her. 'You must not believe your grandfather to be all stone, you know. As soon as I told him what I had heard, he immediately resolved to bring you home to Pittlesthorp—and your mama, too—should circumstances turn out in such a way that this might be desirable.'

'Is it not wonderful, dearest?' uttered her mother, radiance in her face.

Verena blinked. It was the answer to a prayer! And yet—how was it that the prospect did not fill her with the bubbling enthusiasm that Mama evidently felt?

'You may rest easy, for I will be safe, and we need not hide away,' she was saying, such a note of hope and joy in her voice as warmed Verena's heart. 'Adam may visit us at any time he wishes, for Mr Chaceley has said so, and also that he will not permit Nathaniel to bring me away. We will have a new family, dearest, for as your uncle Bevis has pointed out, these were once my relatives-in-law. But best of all, Verena, you will be *free*. You may seek the future you deserve, and that will make me the happiest creature in the world!'

Verena knew that it was incumbent upon her to reciprocate Mama's delight. But she could not. All at once the concept of 'freedom' seemed altogether unreal and—empty. Yet she must say something!

'Mama, you must be—why, that is—' She faltered to a stop, unable to think of anything beyond the dreadful notion that all she would be left with was the most appalling sense of loss.

Her glance flicked from her uncle's face to that of her grandfather. Then, as she turned to bring her gaze back to her mother, she caught sight of Denzell's countenance and her eyes became riveted there, as of their own volition.

There was a slight question in his face, as if he sought to know what was passing in her mind. Quite suddenly, it was as if they were alone in the room, and it seemed the most urgent thing in the world that he should be consulted.

'Denzell, what do you think?'

He regarded her gravely. 'I think your mama should accept.'

'Mama! But—'

Denzell smiled at her, and the world suddenly seemed brighter. 'I have no desire to see you living with your grandfather. I want you to live with me.'

A slow pulse began to beat in her veins. It was as if she was hearing the idea for the very first time. She was, in one sense. For the first time, it had become a *possibility*.

She hardly noticed the stunned silence of the others in the room, for she was scarcely aware of their presence, until old man Chaceley erupted, pushing himself to his feet.

'What in thunder do you mean, sir? I'll thank you to keep your disrespectful suggestions to yourself, you impertinent puppy! Do you dare to offer my granddaughter a *carte blanche*?'

Denzell rose quickly, but there was a twinkle in his eye as he answered. 'You misunderstand me, sir. It is— and has been for some days—my most ardent desire to *marry* your granddaughter.'

'You young dog, Denzell!' came from a laughing Bevis, who had also got up. 'Do you wish to give my father an apoplexy?'

'I had no intention of expressing myself so maladroitly,' Denzell said apologetically. 'I was speaking to Verena, and she is already very well aware of my suit.'

The old gentleman glared at him. 'I ought to give you the thrashing of your life, boy!'

'Pray don't, sir,' begged Denzell. He added seriously, 'I think Verena has had her fill of violent proceedings.'

He looked round as he spoke, and discovered that Verena was looking at him extremely oddly. There was both bewilderment and distress in her face, and—surprise, was it? She looked as if she did not even know that Mrs Pateley, beside her, was clutching her arm in obvious delight. He crossed quickly to the day-bed. Reaching down, he took her hands and drew her to her feet.

'Don't look so troubled, my princess.'

But Verena was not ready for this. She withdrew her hands, her head in a whirl, and her heart now beating like a drum. 'This is all too fast! You speak as if everything were in a way to be settled already.'

'On the contrary,' he said calmly. 'I am all too aware that I have a long way to go. But it would be most improper for me to continue wooing you now, without the consent of your guardians.'

'You mean my grandfather?' Verena asked in a flurried sort of way. 'But what has it to do with him? He has offered us a home, yes, but he does not control my life. Besides, I am of age.'

'Mr Hawkeridge,' interrupted Mrs Pateley firmly, rising herself and reaching out her hands to Denzell, 'be sure you have my consent at least.'

'Mama! No, no, this is not possible!'

'But it is perfectly possible, Verena.'

'I thank you, Mrs Pateley,' Denzell said, taking her hands and kissing them one by one. 'I hope you will forgive the deceit I practised upon you. Verena would not have me show my real intentions, for fear of what you might do.'

She nodded, pressing his hands before releasing them. 'I quite understand.' Then she turned to Verena. 'But now, my dearest girl, you need no longer fear for me, and you may follow your own inclinations.'

'Inclinations!' burst from old man Chaceley suddenly. 'Do you tell me, girl, that you hesitate over this match? Good God, child, the boy is going to be a baron!'

'Oh, the deuce!' muttered Denzell under his breath. This was no help at all! As if Verena gave a fig for his status. Any more than he had given for hers when he knew nothing of her background. He must get Verena out of here—and quickly.

To his intense surprise, it was Mrs Pateley who intervened. She left Verena's side, and moved to confront her erstwhile father-in-law. Quite in the manner of a tigress protecting her young from the hunter!

'Mr Chaceley,' she said, bravely bold, 'I will not have my daughter influenced by any such consideration, for I know its cost. I do not forget my darling Lambert's unhappiness in being estranged from his family. By God's grace, it did not last long, for I lost him all too soon.'

'What in thunder—?' began the old man.

She ignored him, continuing as if he had not spoken, 'I shall be ever grateful to you for what you are doing for me—and it *is* for me, for my Verena would willingly have sacrificed herself on my behalf and it is from that alone that you have saved her. But believe me, sir, I had rather lose this chance of a refuge with you than see my daughter marry for anything other than love!'

'Bravo, Mrs Pateley!' Denzell said. 'I am in complete agreement with you. And—' turning to seize Verena's hand and drag her forcibly towards the door '—since that is precisely the question that I wish to thrash out with Verena, I must beg you all to excuse us for the moment.'

Verena, uttering a half-hearted protest, found herself suddenly on the other side of the parlour door, with the latter firmly shut. She opened her mouth to speak as Denzell turned to her.

'Don't say a word!' he warned, and his lips came down on hers so hard that she groaned a faint protest.

But the warmth of his mouth sent a wash of intense heat flooding through her body, and her knees weakened so that she sagged against him. She was barely permitted to recover from this sudden assault, when he pulled away.

'Come!' he cried, and dragged her after him towards the stairhead.

Verena, all her concentration on remaining on her feet as she was rushed down the stairs, did not notice that this little episode had been overlooked. Betsey, coming down from above with a tray containing a decanter and glasses, had paused as the door opened. She smiled with grim satisfaction as she watched her young charge disappearing in the wake of her determined suitor.

Once outside, however, Verena dug in her heels and pulled hard to stop the onrush of these too speedy events.

'Denzell, *wait*. Oh, pray, wait for a moment!'

He paused and turned to look at her, so much tenderness in his face that her heart somersaulted painfully. 'What is it, dearest Snow Maiden?'

'What are you doing?' she asked breathlessly. 'Where are you taking me?'

He uttered a short laugh. 'To tell you the truth, I don't know. I had to get you alone.' Taking hold of her arms, he drew her towards him. Gently, he asked, 'Am I rushing you?'

'Yes!'

Denzell sighed. 'Forgive me! I am so elated, I cannot help myself.'

Verena looked up at him with trouble in her eyes. 'But I am *afraid*, Denzell.'

He stilled, his hands running up to her shoulders. His gaze roved over her features, caressing the curves that made up that perfect oval, the sculptured bow of a mouth, the eyes set wide apart. Lightly, like a warm breeze, he spoke.

'There's no need.'

Verena's breath caught in a half-sob. 'You make it sound so easy.'

A smile entered his eyes. 'It is, to me.'

He released her then, and slipping one hand about her fingers, he said in the most normal of tones, 'I want to show you something.'

He led her across the driveway, and into the patch of ground that separated her lodging from the Ruishtons' house. They walked in silence, Verena a touch mysti-fied, until they were more or less in the centre of the ground. There, Denzell released her and stepped back to look at her.

'We talked here once, but that is not what makes it dear to me.' He drew a breath of deepest satisfaction. 'This, Verena, is where I first saw you. You were building that snowman, and your guard was down. I caught sight of your beauty, and I was dumbfounded. Then you laughed—I have the image of it imprinted on my memory! And you know what I think? The real Verena floated there and then, right into my heart. You see, I never truly believed in the existence of that other beauty—serene, and exquisitely polite.'

Verena stared at him in mute fascination. Could it be true? Was it possible that she also, despite her instant damping down of the betraying sensations, had lost her heart to him the very first time they met? No, it could not be so!

She shifted her gaze, plucking aimlessly at her white muslin petticoats. 'I do not know how this has happened. I have been fighting for so long—not to feel.'

'But you do feel,' Denzell said quietly. 'Can you deny it?'

Verena shook her head, still not looking at him. 'I have tried to deny it. It would be—it would be a lie to say I don't love you.'

He moved a step closer. 'Then say that you do. It isn't so hard, Verena.'

Slowly she brought her eyes up to meet his. His heart sank at the confusion in them still. She did not speak, but her lips quivered, and it was all he could do not to snatch her into his embrace, overbearing her resistance, forcibly suppressing her doubts. A wisdom born of his knowledge of her held him back. If he wanted her whole heart, free of doubt, she must come to him of her own will. His voice was tender.

'What is it that troubles you, dear love?'

Verena caught her breath. 'If I say it—if I make the admission, then I give my life into your hands *forever*. My life—my happiness—everything! It is so. . .final.'

Denzell reached out and with one finger caressed her cheek lightly. 'Nothing in this world is final. The only certain thing we have is our intentions, and even they may change. We cannot see into the future, my darling. Life itself is a gamble.'

'Then you can offer no better refuge than my grandfather!'

A gleam of mischief lit his eyes. 'Oh, I think I can

safely promise you that it will be far more amusing to marry me than to live with old man Chaceley.'

A choke of laughter escaped her, lightening her features a little. 'I can readily believe that.' Then she frowned. 'I only hope Mama can be happy there.'

'If she is not, at least you have the satisfaction of knowing that her misery is not bought at the expense of any bodily hurts,' he said seriously. 'But, Verena, I think she will be happy. And I am sorry if I should offend you by this, but I believe she will be far happier than she could ever have been living alone with you.'

Verena sighed. 'You do not offend me. I know it only too well. This past year has been—unimaginably hard. For both of us. But while we had no alternative. . .'

'You need no longer fear for her, my princess.'

She glanced up at his face, a puzzled look in her eyes. 'Why do you call me that?'

He grinned. 'Because that was how you first struck me. A fairy princess, catching at snowflakes.' He took her face between his hands. 'So beautiful, so enchantingly vivacious, so *warm*—and nothing like the Ice Maiden who depressed my pretensions in no uncertain manner the very first time we properly met!'

Verena gurgled with mirth. 'If you only knew how hard it became for me to maintain that front in your presence.'

'I do know,' he told her, and bent his head to kiss her, very gently.

Verena sighed under the touch of his lips, and her hands came up, involuntarily, to clasp lightly about his back. She felt her face released, and his strong arms go about her, and the kiss intensified. That now familiar warmth invaded her breast. Remembering the fears to which this gave rise, she struggled a little, dropping her arms from about him and pushing at his chest. He released her mouth at once, pulling back slightly, although his arms still encircled her.

'I will wait, Verena,' he uttered low-voiced. 'If you wish it, I will wait. You will, after all, be living well within my reach at Pittlesthorp. But I warn you that I will lose no opportunity to press my suit—beyond the time when you are able to withstand me.'

She bit her lip, her eyes questioning. 'Do you think that waiting will change me?'

He grimaced. 'How can I tell? It may allow you to grow in confidence. In trust, perhaps.'

'And if you do not wait, what then?'

'Then I will marry you here in Tunbridge Wells and take you home as my wife.' He fetched a sigh. 'I need scarcely say that the second option would be my preference, but I can understand that you find it frightening.'

Yes, it was frightening, she thought. But to go among strangers, to resume her mask, to be obliged to pretend to a happiness she could not feel—*without* him? Oh, no. Unendurable!

She could not have stopped the smile breaking. 'Less so than the first, if you want the truth.'

The sudden brightness in his face rewarded her. Denzell's arms tightened. 'Verena! Do you mean that?'

'I would not otherwise say it.' Her fingers reached up to his cheek, and he quickly turned his lips to kiss them.

'Verena, I swear to you, you will not regret it!'

She put her fingers over his mouth. 'Oh, Denzell, don't say that! There is only one thing I ask of you. Make me no promises that you cannot keep.'

His arms dropped from about her so that he could catch her hands in his. 'You are right to ask it of me, and although I would at this moment give my right arm before I hurt you, I cannot promise that I will never do

so. Yet if I did, it could only be with words, and never—
never, on my life!—will I lift one finger against you.
And on that you may depend, if nothing else.'

Tears pricked at Verena's eyes, and her voice was
husky. 'You had no need to promise that. You see,
Mama taught me something about love. She said that if
Nathaniel had had her heart, he would not have beaten
her. I did not believe it—until I watched you flirting last
night. Denzell, I wanted to *kill* you.'

Denzell gazed down into her face for a moment.
Then he let go her hands and swept her into his
embrace, kissing her with the full strength of his
passion.

Verena felt as if she was drowning, helpless with the
heat that raced through her veins, pulsing in secret
places of whose existence she had hardly been aware. If
she remained standing, it was only by virtue of the grip
of Denzell's arms about her back. She sank into him, a
soft moan sounding in her throat.

When at last his lips released hers, it was only to
mouth his way across her cheek, bury his lips into the
hollows of her neck, and then return, hungrily to caress
her mouth again, pressing his way into the innocent
velvet touch within.

Verena groaned deeply, but her hands grasped
harder at his back, her brain dizzily clouding out of all
capacity to think. There was no reality but this envel-
oping sensation, and truth, erupting into life, gave her
all the certainty she would ever want or need.

Against the touch of his lips on hers, she whispered
it. 'I do love you—oh, I *do*.'

And then she could not speak at all, for Denzell's
mouth claimed hers ever more strongly, and it was some
little time before any coherent thought penetrated into
her mind.

Just out of sight beyond a certain garden gate, Osmond and Unice Ruishton peeked at the couple so amorously entwined. They looked at each other. Osmond grinned down at his wife.

'If you knew how smug you look!'

'I have every right to look smug,' retorted Unice. 'I have assisted in making a most delightful match.'

'You think she will make him happy, then?'

His wife's eyes softened into tenderness. 'She loves him, Osmond.'

'In that case, my darling,' he said, slipping his arm about her, 'his happiness is assured.'

'And hers.'

Verena, resting in Denzell's close embrace, her head on his shoulder, was aware of a feeling of ease within her breast and the gentle touch of Denzell's fingers stroking in her hair. She sighed contentedly, and felt him raise her head so that she had to look up at him. The misted eyes of blue roved her face in mute question.

A smile wavered on her lips. 'I rather think you have prevailed, Mr Hawkeridge.'

Denzell grinned. 'I rather think you have succumbed, Miss Chaceley.'

A little laugh escaped her. 'Yes, I have. I cannot say that all my fears are laid to rest, not yet. But what can I do, Denzell? My shield has gone beyond my reach. If there is a risk, I have no choice but to take it—with you.'

His fingers cradled her cheek as he scanned her eyes. They were smiling, free of shadows, and Denzell's heart soared.

'No more mask then, Snow Maiden?'

Verena's hand reached up, and their fingers met, and laced. 'What mask, sir, is that?'

Historical Romance

Coming next month

AN UNWILLING CONQUEST
Stephanie Laurens
REGENCY ENGLAND

Having seen his sister Lenore and brother Jack caught in
Parson's mousetrap, albeit willingly, Harry Lester had *no*
intention of following their example. Now the news was
out that the Lester family fortunes had been repaired,
Harry knew the matchmaking mamas would be in pursuit,
so he promptly left London for Newmarket, only to find
himself acting as the rescuer of Mrs Lucinda Babbacombe,
a beautiful *managing* widow, who refused to accept his
advice! No matter that he desired her—marriage was out!

THE COMTE AND THE COURTESAN
Truda Taylor
FRANCE 1789

After ten years in Paris under the protection of the elderly
Marquis Philippe de Maupilier, Madeleine Vaubonne was
well aware that she was mistakenly thought to be his
mistress. Even so, it was a nasty surprise when Lucian de
Valori, the Comte de Regnay, offered to replace Philippe
in her bed! She forcefully refused his proposition, but
when Philippe died Lucian was the only one to offer help.
Reluctantly she agreed to his escort to her home in
Brittany, the start of a journey neither had expected to
make…

Delicious Dishes

Would you like to win a year's supply of simply irresistible romances? Well, you can and they're FREE! Simply match the dish to its country of origin and send your answers to us by 31st December 1996. The first 5 correct entries picked after the closing date will win a year's supply of Temptation novels (four books every month—worth over £100). What could be easier?

A	LASAGNE		GERMANY
B	KORMA		GREECE
C	SUSHI		FRANCE
D	BACLAVA		ENGLAND
E	PAELLA		MEXICO
F	HAGGIS		INDIA
G	SHEPHERD'S PIE		SPAIN
H	COQ AU VIN		SCOTLAND
I	SAUERKRAUT		JAPAN
J	TACOS		ITALY

Please turn over for details of how to enter ☞

How to enter

Listed in the left hand column overleaf are the names of ten delicious dishes and in the right hand column the country of origin of each dish. All you have to do is match each dish to the correct country and place the corresponding letter in the box provided.

When you have matched all the dishes to the countries, don't forget to fill in your name and address in the space provided and pop this page into an envelope (you don't need a stamp) and post it today! Hurry—competition ends 31st December 1996.

Mills & Boon Delicious Dishes
FREEPOST
Croydon
Surrey
CR9 3WZ

Are you a Reader Service Subscriber? Yes ❑   No ❑

Ms/Mrs/Miss/Mr _____

Address _____

_____

_____ Postcode _____

One application per household.

You may be mailed with other offers from other reputable companies as a result of this application. If you would prefer not to receive such offers, please tick box.   ❑

C396
F